Praise for *Murder in Lascaux,*
the first Nora Barnes and Toby Sandler Mystery:

"If you like a murder mystery you can get your teeth into, give this one a try. Bon appétit!"—*Mystery Scene*

"This . . . marvelously detailed excursion through the Dordogne will leave you dreaming of castles, chateaus, and caves. . . . This multifaceted read will hold great appeal for art, food, travel, and oh yes, mystery readers."—*Library Journal* (starred review, Mystery Debut of the Month)

"A whodunit that nicely balances a breezily light travelogue with urgency and suspense. . . . The first of a series."—*Publishers Weekly*

"That the book feels like the seamless work of a single author is no coincidence; readers of Draine and Hinden's first mystery will be both entertained and educated by what is clearly a shared passion for the Dordogne and its considerable charms."—*Capital Times*

"A strong first mystery that tells a traditional amateur detective story in a fascinating setting."—*Chicago Tribune*

"Some fascinating French history—and prehistory—is layered into the plot. . . . The cooking classes evoke the delicious tastes and aromas of the Dordogne—magret de canard, foie gras, and walnut cake, to say nothing of the wines. . . . Skillfully blends travelogue with an intriguing mystery."—*France Today*

"Into the intricate plot the authors were able to weave Cro-Magnon art, a medieval religious sect, and Nazi intrigue, not to mention cooking lessons." —*Ellery Queen Mystery Magazine*

Praise for *The Body in Bodega Bay,* the second Nora Barnes and Toby Sandler Mystery:

"If you're a fan of Alfred Hitchcock's *The Birds*, you will thoroughly enjoy this murder mystery." —*Mystery Scene*

"*The Body in Bodega Bay* is set on the northern California coast and involves a mysterious death, Alfred Hitchcock artifacts, angels, and a husband-and-wife team set on solving the crime." —*Madison Magazine*

"[This] writing duo have now done for California's North Coast what their earlier *Murder in Lascaux* did for France's Perigord: brought it wonderfully—and eerily—to life. A winner." —**Aaron Elkins, Edgar-winning author of the Gideon Oliver mysteries**

"This crime's solution takes us into the world of Russian icons, the Russian past in Sonoma County, and even into the realm of communications from guardian angels. This novel delivers. Grab it and enjoy."
—**Richard Schwartz, author of *The Last Voice You Hear***

"Nails the vibe and history of . . . the Sonoma County coast. Antiques dealer Toby Sandler teams with his art historian wife, Nora Barnes, to help solve a murder and art theft." —*Sacramento Bee*

"Betsy Draine and Michael Hinden must be having a wonderful time researching and writing their mystery series. It certainly is a lot of fun reading their books." —*Capital Times*

Death on a Starry Night

A Nora Barnes and
Toby Sandler Mystery

Betsy Draine and Michael Hinden

The University of Wisconsin Press

The University of Wisconsin Press
1930 Monroe Street, 3rd Floor
Madison, Wisconsin 53711-2059
uwpress.wisc.edu

3 Henrietta Street, Covent Garden
London WC2E 8LU, United Kingdom
eurospanbookstore.com

Printed in the United States of America
This book may be available in a digital edition.

Library of Congress Cataloging-in-Publication Data

Names: Draine, Betsy, 1945– author. | Hinden, Michael, author.
Title: Death on a starry night / Betsy Draine and Michael Hinden.
Description: Madison, Wisconsin: The University of Wisconsin Press, [2016] | ©2016 |
Series: A Nora Barnes and Toby
Sandler mystery | Includes bibliographical references.
Identifiers: LCCN 2015036321 | ISBN 9780299307301 (cloth: alk. paper)
Subjects: LCSH: Gogh, Vincent van, 1853–1890—Fiction. |
Murder—France—Saint-Paul (Alpes-Maritimes)—Fiction. | Saint-Paul
(Alpes-Maritimes, France)—Fiction. | Art teachers—Fiction. |
Americans—France—Fiction.
Classification: LCC PS3604.R343 D43 2016 | DDC 813/.6—dc23
LC record available at http://lccn.loc.gov/2015036321

This is a work of fiction. All names, characters, places, and incidents are either products of the authors' imagination
or are used fictitiously. No reference to any real person is intended or should be inferred.

For the cousins

Death on a Starry Night

I didn't mean to shoot him. I can still see him clutching his side and looking at me like a wounded animal. He kicked over his easel and stumbled to his knees. The painting he was working on fell to the ground. Later they said he shot himself, but that isn't true. I did it. I wanted to help him but instead I killed him, and I've been sorry for it all my life.

1

A STARRY NIGHT—it seemed made to order for the opening of a Van Gogh conference. And what location could be more idyllic? Not far from the beaches of the French Riviera, the village of Saint-Paul-de-Vence is stacked upon a dramatic hilltop, its stone houses encircled by medieval walls. In summer, the town is a beehive swarming with tourists. Tonight, in mid-December, all was quiet as we climbed the steep cobblestone street into the village. It was the dinner hour, clear and cold. I could see my breath. The shops that lined the pedestrian street looked closed for the season, and many of the houses were shuttered.

We reached the crest of the hill and stopped to admire an old stone fountain shaped like a Grecian urn. Spigots dripped water into a basin with a rim high enough to sit on. Toward the top of the urn a decorative fringe suggested a laurel wreath. I think of it now as a funeral urn, for an image of death clings to that lovely stonework fountain. But that evening all was serene.

Behind the fountain, two arches housed low pools, which in the old days must have been used for washing clothes. These same arches served as supports for the terrace of a restaurant overlooking the square. That was our destination. We circled the fountain and climbed another cobbled street toward the restaurant's entrance. Overhead, stars sparkled against the black sky.

Despite the chilly evening, I was thinking how lucky I was to be here, on what my sister called a paid vacation. I called it "professional development." As a professor in the art history department of a small liberal arts college, I'm eligible to apply for support to present a paper at an international conference once every five years. This one was sponsored by the Society for Vincent van Gogh Studies and was hosted by the Maeght Foundation, a mecca for modern art located just outside the ramparts of Saint-Paul. Off-season rates pared the cost of travel and accommodations, and because the dates overlapped with my winter break, I didn't have to miss a class. I'm not an expert on Van Gogh, but I do teach a course on nineteenth-century painting, and I was counting on learning a lot at the conference.

You might not associate the Riviera with art, but artists have been coming here for a long time. The trend began with the Impressionists. Once painters started working outdoors, it was inevitable that they would migrate south, following the footsteps of Van Gogh, to take advantage of the climate and the light. Many stayed. Picasso settled in Vallauris, Bonnard near Cannes, Matisse in Nice, Renoir in Cagnes-sur-Mer, and Chagall right here; he's buried in the little cemetery behind the village. That's why the Maeght was an inspired choice for the conference site. With morning sessions devoted to papers, the afternoons would be free for excursions. Our program for the week included side trips to Vence to see a chapel decorated by Matisse, to Cagnes-sur-Mer to visit Renoir's studio, and to Saint-Rémy-de-Provence to tour the asylum where Van Gogh spent almost a year.

It didn't take much to convince Toby to join me. We'd been to France before and can manage the language well enough to keep up our end in a conversation. Our last trip, to the Dordogne, found us embroiled in a murder investigation, which gave our French a needed workout but upended our vacation. This time, I hoped, we were set for a carefree visit. That wasn't to be.

Another reason I'd been looking forward to this trip was that my sister, Angie, was coming with us. Angie is six feet tall, but I still think of her as my little sister. We're close, but I hadn't seen her for several months, during which time she'd gone into a convent. Her decision came as a shock, and I was having trouble accepting it. Angie's not your typical postulant. Young and restless, sexy and fun-loving, she nonetheless has a searching soul. Frankly, I had my doubts that she would stay to take her vows. She was wise enough to realize that her spiritual longings might not translate into a lifelong commitment, so she signed up for a trial run as a "sojourner" at Grace Quarry, near Rockport, Massachusetts, where we both were raised.

Angie's traveling companion and chaperone was Sister Glenda, who was an invited speaker at the conference. Sister Glenda is an authority on "The Spirit of Art through the Ages." That's the name of her textbook, used in introductory art history courses in a number of universities and colleges, especially those with religious affiliations. "The Spirit of Art" is also the name of her weekly show on public television. Rockport's "art nun" is syndicated in thirty-five states and Canada. When I learned that Glenda and Angie were coming to the conference, I immediately sat down and wrote my proposal.

I was still getting used to Sister Glenda. She bears a passing resemblance to Julia Child, not physically perhaps, but in manner. Julia was tall and straight-backed. Sister Glenda is short and rubbery, but she has Julia's gobbling voice. It goes up and down in a reedy register, yet carries the mark of conviction. Her order permits the wearing of street clothes, and today she had on a baggy wool sweater over wash-and-wear slacks. The only nunlike element in her outfit was a bare cross on a necklace made of cheap cord. But for her TV appearances, she dons a habit and wimple. It's what her audience expects. "It's a costume," she once explained. "Just like Stephen Colbert. He wears a suit on TV. At home I bet he doesn't." From under her wimple she likes to squint at the camera as though she's lost her wire-rimmed glasses, even when she has them on. Her baffled look belies the fact that when it comes to art she absolutely knows her stuff.

One reason for Sister Glenda's popularity is her cavalier attitude toward convention. As we reached the restaurant, she flashed a gap-toothed smile and said, "I hope they have a sit-down bathroom and not another hole in the floor like the place we stopped at for lunch. I need to pee." She often did, I soon discovered. Sister Glenda likes her liquids. Once inside, Angie and I hustled Glenda to *les toilettes* up two flights of stairs. She would be the first to discover whether "the little corner," as the French call it, provided a hole flanked by footrests or a modern convenience. Angie volunteered to wait for Glenda while she was using the facilities, such as they were.

My colleagues were milling around the bar. This was to be a small conference, with only eleven speakers. The sessions were open to the public, but the audience was expected to be mainly the scholars and their guests. Ray Montoni, the organizer, had dubbed the event "Van Gogh: Enduring Mysteries." The title was meant to draw the interest of granting agencies and private funders, and it did. Although modest in number, our group was international. Montoni was American, as were two other speakers besides me: Sister Glenda and Benjamin Bennett. There were three participants from France, one from the Netherlands, one from England, and another from Ireland. A late addition was a French woman whom none of us had met but whose inclusion had excited tremendous interest. Her name was Isabelle La Font. The word was that as a boy, her grandfather had known Van Gogh around the time of his suicide. It was said that Madame La Font had startling information to reveal about the circumstances of Vincent's death.

That would be a hot topic. A new biography of Van Gogh had caused a sensation with its suggestion that, contrary to popular belief, the artist had been murdered. The claim ignited critical fireworks. If Madame La Font could settle the question of Van Gogh's death, our conference would change art history. Her talk was slated to open the proceedings in the morning.

Scanning the room, I noticed a striking woman sitting on a barstool, smoking and talking to a man who looked about her age. His expression was sour. Professor Montoni, after checking that all his charges were accounted for, elbowed his way to the bar and inserted himself between the pair. Montoni planted kisses on the woman's cheeks and offered his hand to her companion. It wasn't taken. She spoke to both men, as if making introductions. After submitting to the social niceties, the frowning man shifted his weight on the barstool and turned his head. Not one to be easily affronted, Montoni took the opportunity to swoop the woman into the room. She hardly had time to put out her cigarette.

That must be Isabelle La Font, I thought. She carried herself with the grace of royalty. Her skin was lined, but its alabaster tone set off emerald eyes. The regal effect was heightened by sandy-white hair pulled back into a silver band that suggested a crown. A gray brocade jacket formalized a simple black turtleneck and slacks. One shoulder supported the chain of an enormous red leather bag.

It's a Chanel, gasped my inner fashionista.

I guessed she was close to seventy. She may have been "of a certain age," but she was vibrant, beautiful, and impeccably turned out. Next to her, Montoni appeared slovenly. He was a large man with too much dark hair—on his hands, neck, head, and face. He looked a bit like the aging Pavarotti, but without the bounding confidence or resounding voice. His long black cardigan covered a black T-shirt, the better to camouflage a belly.

He held his guest close with one arm and propelled her awkwardly around the room. As they reached me, she managed to shake her elbow out of his grasp. He put his hand on my shoulder and pulled me toward her. "Madame La Font, permit me to present Professor Nora Barnes, our art historian from California." Montoni's accent in French was noticeably more polished than his social skills.

She extended her hand. In my slow and deliberate French, I said, "I'm delighted to make your acquaintance, madame."

She made a polite reply and looked inquiringly at Toby and Angie, who had come up behind me. Montoni hemmed, not having memorized the names of the speakers' dependents. So I continued. "And may I present my husband, Toby Sandler, and my sister, Angela Barnes."

Sister Glenda stepped forward before Montoni could retake the initiative and introduced herself in French, though it didn't sound like it.

"Well!" Montoni said, rubbing his hands briskly. "Let me get you something from the bar."

"I'll take care of that," said Toby. "You have a lot to do." There were people behind us waiting to meet Madame La Font, so we moved out of the way. Toby turned to Glenda. "What are you drinking?" he asked.

"Scotch, thank you."

"A glass of white wine for me," I said.

"Just sparkling water," said Angie.

Toby, who's naturally more gregarious than I am, wended his way to the bar, greeting people he'd met at our hotel or on the walk up the hill. Some were waiting to order a drink. The only person sitting on a barstool was the man I had noticed earlier talking to Madame La Font. While she was moving around the room, he remained alone, concentrating on his glass and scowling at the mirror behind the bar. He was following her with his eyes. Was he her husband? If so, Montoni had been derelict in his hosting responsibilities, but Madame La Font made no gesture to include him, either. Slouching over the rim of the bar, he looked slight, but he had a rugged face, taken up mainly by an imposing Charles de Gaulle nose. Toby stood next to him and said "*Bonsoir*," to which he received a grudging reply. The man tapped his cigarette and let ashes fall to the floor. Toby ordered our drinks and returned with them.

Rather than circulate, we stood in place, sipping and chatting. It was a little tight standing in the space between the bar and the tables. The members of our group were still at the first stage of social acquaintance when conversation is stilted. I could tell by Angie's darting eyes that she felt uncomfortable. Toby seemed amused and curious, which is often the case when he's brought to an academic event. He was enjoying his kir, a delightful mélange of white wine and crème de cassis. That's what I should have ordered. My white wine, the anonymous house offering, needed a little help.

A middle-aged couple standing next to us introduced themselves. Dr. Hans de Groot, a big bear of a man, taught art history at the University of Utrecht. He shook our hands vigorously and presented his business card, which was printed on one side in English and on the other side in Dutch. A gold sun surrounded by Latin lettering, the emblem of his university, was embossed next to his name. His wife's card was equally impressive. Klara de Groot, as tall as an Amazon warrior, had a crushing grip. The card she proffered told us she was a research chemist and worked in a lab for the human genome project. Having no card of my own to present, I felt outclassed, but Toby dug out his, which advertises the antiques gallery he owns in Duncans Mills, California. We live in Bodega Bay, a few miles from there.

"They left out the apostrophe," observed Klara, after studying the card. She knew her English. This woman demands perfection, I thought. It wouldn't be easy to work under her disapproving gaze.

"It's not a misprint," Toby explained. "That's how the town is spelled. Don't ask me why, but there's no apostrophe in Duncans Mills."

"Where in California is this wayward town?" Hans asked.

"On the coast above San Francisco," Toby answered, but Hans didn't have much to say to that, and the conversation petered out. Soon enough, Montoni announced that it was time for dinner.

The Hostellerie de la Fontaine was a rustic bistro with exposed stone walls and simple furnishings. The wooden chairs had straw seats and the tables had no tablecloths. "Sit where you like," Montoni told us.

"We won't be formal here." However, he conducted Isabelle La Font to a table set for six that had a card on it saying *Réservé*. They were joined there by Benjamin Bennett and his wife, Shelley, and by an older British professor named Bruce Curry with his wife, Jane.

Two other tables were also set for six. Angie, who wanted us to stay together, stood behind a chair at one of them and waved us to seats surrounding her. Those speaking French gathered at a third table, and the Dutch couple joined them. They must be as capable in French as in English, I thought. That left only one person to be seated. I patted the chair next to mine to invite Maggie McBride to join us. We'd met earlier at the hotel. She was red-headed, nicely rounded, and full of fun.

"Maggie, come sit with us."

"With pleasure, if you don't mind Emmet." That's when we noticed the blue-gray pup, standing steady and silent, at her heel. "He's a desperate pest when other dogs are around. Other than that, he's strictly trained. So will you have us?"

"Of course," I replied, again patting the chair next to mine. The dog leaped right onto it and firmly planted his rear.

"You'll see. He won't move again till I tell him. Or he wants to." Maggie gave a gravelly laugh and parked her own rear on the next empty chair.

"I love the name Emmet," Angie said. "How did you come up with it?"

"Have you not heard of the Irish rebel Robert Emmet? He was hanged by the British, bad cess to them."

Hearing his name, the canine version of the martyred hero thumped his tail on the chair. "Good lad," said Maggie, and she popped a piece of bread into his mouth. He chomped once and gulped but didn't otherwise move.

Over kirs (I got mine after all, when a tray of them was delivered to each table), Maggie told us she was in France for a year, on research leave from University College Dublin, and naturally she had brought her best friend. In France, as Maggie knew, well-behaved dogs are welcome in restaurants. It's common to see them sitting under the table or even occasionally curled up nose to tail, dozing on a chair. Emmet was on the alert, and when the waiter brought an appetizer tray with prosciutto on it, he rose to four paws, gazing expectantly at his mistress.

"Sit!" Maggie hissed, looking away from her dog, as if to shun him. Emmet licked his chops and sat.

"I'm famished," said Angie, unfolding her napkin and spreading it on her lap. "What's for dinner?" She handed me the menu for translation. We were offered a set menu of typical bistro fare. A vegetable terrine as first course, followed by coq au vin, a selection of cheeses, and profiteroles for dessert.

"Sounds good!" Angie said. And so it was. The wine was plentiful, served in pitchers that were replenished as soon as they were empty. The bread was warm and crusty. The chicken was succulent in its red wine sauce, thick with mushrooms, pearl onions, and bacon. Simple boiled carrots were served alongside.

When conversation lagged, I glanced over to the bar and saw that the sullen man remained on his stool. Obviously, he had not been invited to the dinner, nor did he belong to our group. Then how did Isabelle La Font know him? And since she did, why hadn't she asked him to join us? After all, Toby and Angie and Emmet were eating with us, and they weren't giving talks this week. Some of the other diners glanced in his direction as well. For her part, Madame La Font occasionally looked his way with a strained expression. But Ray Montoni made a point of paying him no attention. As the meal progressed, the man at the bar kept his back to the diners, nursing his drink.

I reminded myself that he was none of my business and turned my attention to making Maggie comfortable. "Angie and I have Irish grandparents on our father's side," I told her.

"And where are your people from?"

Angie's the family historian. "Our grandmother was from Headford, outside Galway," she said.

"I know it well. My father used to take us there when he went salmon fishing. And your grandfather's people?" Maggie looked to Angie for the answer.

"County Tyrone. The town is Bally-something."

"Naturally. There's a batch of Bally-somethings in the North. Protestant towns mainly. But your people are Catholic, like mine, I take it," she said, with a nod toward Sister Glenda.

Angie replied. "That's right. These days, I guess I'm more serious about it than some in my family."

"That would be me," I admitted. "I hardly ever go to church, and then it's only to make my father happy. After Mass, he likes to show us off to the priest."

Maggie plonked down her wine glass. "A fine lot they are, chasing after boys' bums."

With a nun and a half at the table, how was that going to go down?

Sister Glenda sniffed and then let the air out in a puff. "May those that do it rot in hell," she said. She downed her wine and poured another glass. Was that her third? Her fourth, maybe? "They're not all like that, not at all, but the ones who do it are a scandal to the Church."

At my right side, Emmet whimpered softly. He didn't take well to the tone of conflict. Maggie scratched his forehead.

Toby took the opening and changed the subject. "Tell us about your dog. Is he an Irish breed?"

"That he is, a Wicklow Terrier. Now, his people were Irish on *all* sides. Dog-people, of course." She laughed, and that restored the banter.

We were then occupied with choosing from the cheese cart. I knew what I wanted—the goat cheese I'd picked up a taste for in the Dordogne. While waiting for the others to make their choices, I glanced around the room and saw Isabelle La Font rise and walk over to the French-speaking table. She greeted the table in general and then kissed one of the two Frenchmen on both cheeks, twice over. I guessed that meant something warmer than hello. He remained seated but tilted his cheek for the busses and looked up at Isabelle with an opaque expression. She stayed bent toward him, putting her hand on his shoulder and casting her head at an angle, giving him what looked to me like an affectionate smile. He shifted slightly, away from her. She removed her hand from his shoulder, turned, and walked back toward her seat. As she passed me, she looked hurt.

It was soon time for dessert. Each of us had a profiterole the size of a baseball, filled with berry ice cream and covered by a hard caramel glaze. My kind of dessert, especially when accompanied by the queen of sweet wines, Muscat de Baumes-de-Venise. Pure golden nectar.

Over at Ray Montoni's table, the discussion was heating up. Benjamin Bennett, the American professor, was doing most of the talking, and I could guess why. The issue was surely the current dispute over Van Gogh's death. Bennett was working on his own biography of the artist, and his conference paper was billed as a rebuttal of the controversial theory suggesting the possibility of the artist's murder. Bennett had the most at stake if Madame La Font supported the conclusion of his rivals, so my guess was he was pressing for a preview of her talk. She kept her eyes on her plate, looking up only to shake her head no. "Tomorrow," I heard her say twice. Ray Montoni appeared uneasy. Bennett persisted. Finally, his wife glared at him, and he sat back in his chair.

Then there were raised voices at the bar. I gathered that the solitary customer was demanding another drink, while the bartender was coaxing him to go home. Heads turned. Madame La Font spoke to those near her, got up, and carried her glass over to the bar. She stood next to the belligerent man and talked to him, with her head close to his. I couldn't make out what they said, but the hostility in his voice carried throughout the room. She touched his wrist and lowered her voice to a whisper. That seemed to help. They continued in this manner for a few minutes but then his voice became loud again. Abruptly he slammed his hand on the bar, slid off his stool, and strutted cock-like out of the restaurant. She lowered her head for a moment, then raised it and drained her glass.

Returning to the table, she flagged the waiter. Her companions seemed to be questioning her about the man who had just walked out. She shook her head a few times, not speaking. Gradually the sound level in the room returned to normal as people picked up the threads of interrupted conversations. The waiter brought her another glass of Baumes-de-Venise. She lit a cigarette.

My attention turned back to our table, where Toby was explaining to Maggie his non-role at the conference. "I'm just along for the ride. I'll take any excuse for a trip to France. The food is great and the scenery's fantastic. I even like the French. I don't know why they get such a bad rap."

"It's the waiters," Sister Glenda said with authority. "They can be rude."

"So what?" Toby continued, undeterred. "I mean, we're talking about the people who gave us the cancan, foie gras, and Edith Piaf, not to mention the bidet."

"Or the Declaration of the Rights of Man," Maggie added.

"Or Chartres Cathedral, if it comes to that," noted Glenda.

"There you go," said Toby. "It's churlish not to like the French."

I've heard Toby on this riff before, so I tuned out and turned my attention to the head table. It's not that I meant to eavesdrop, but my hearing tends to be sharp enough to follow conversations from a distance. I think that's true of most women. We're more interested in strangers than men are. And we tend to get away with it. Nobody minds if a woman glances their way occasionally, whereas any man who tries that looks like he's on the prowl. I could see Madame La Font was growing uncomfortable. Her face was flushed, and she was rocking back and forth in her chair. After some minutes, she reached a hand to her chest. She pushed back her chair and stood up, unsteady on her feet.

I dropped my napkin and went over to her table. "Are you all right, madame?"

"Yes, please don't trouble yourself. I've had too much wine, that's all. I'll be fine." Her host, Montoni, rose in concern. "No, no," she demurred, waving her hand. "Please sit down. Finish your dessert. I'm just going to step outside to get some fresh air."

"Let me come with you," I said.

"That won't be necessary," said Montoni. "I'll go."

"No, I insist," she said. She was keeping her balance by pushing down hard on the table. Her command was firm. "Please, everyone. It's nothing. I need a breath of air, that's all. I won't even take my coat. I'll be back in two minutes." She shouldered her bag and made for the door.

Emmet bounded from his perch and trotted after her, yipping excitedly.

"He wants to be let out," said his mistress.

"*Bon!*" said Isabelle. "He can keep me company."

"That's fine," said Maggie. Raising her voice a pitch, she called, "Go ahead, boy. Go with the nice lady."

Emmet barked happily as Isabelle let him through. He scampered outside, and she followed him.

Reluctantly, I returned to my seat.

"Will she be all right?' asked Angie.

"She says she will," I replied.

"She didn't look all right to me," said Sister Glenda. "Dessert wine will do that to you. You can't drink too much of it. It fools you, never mind how easy it goes down." Sister Glenda had switched to cognac.

At Isabelle's table, Bennett and Curry leaned toward each other, talking intently. Ray Montoni seemed to be napping. His elbows were planted on the table, with palms raised to support his drooping head. Bennett's wife, Shelley, kept turning toward the door, anticipating Isabelle's return, or perhaps trying to decide whether to go after her.

I kept an eye on the door too while I did justice to my dessert, finishing it slowly, with a sip of Baumes-de-Venise between each bite. When my dessert plate was spooned clean, I still had a half glass of the fortified wine in front of me. I was determined not to waste a drop. Even so, when the waiter came to clear the glasses, I gave mine up with at least an ounce of liquid gold still in it.

Coffee was served, espresso. It came black, of course. In France, it's never offered with milk or cream after dinner. Angie, though, wanted milk with hers. "You can ask for it, but you won't get it," I warned her.

"That's ridiculous," said Angie. "Why can't I ask the waiter for milk?"

"Try it," I said. "Say, '*Du lait, s'il vous plaît.*'"

"Doo-lay, siv-oo-play," Angie said to the waiter when he went by. He looked at her quizzically. "*Comment?*"

I tried to help. "*Du lait, pour mademoiselle, s'il vous plaît.*"

He nodded. It never arrived.

Angie was pouting over her espresso when Emmet sounded the alarm. First we heard him barking outside the door. The waiter opened it, and the blue-haired terrier ran in, his nails clicking on the tile floor. Maggie got up. "Something's not right. He never barks like that unless there's something wrong." Emmet circled back to the door and stood with a foreleg raised. He looked back at his mistress. "He wants me to go see," she said. She hurried out, as several others stood up, including Toby and me. Toby was out the door at a racer's pace.

Maggie and I caught up with him in the square, beside the fountain with its sculpted urn. Isabelle La Font was hanging over the rim of the basin, her head and right arm submerged in water, her feet no longer touching the ground.

Toby sprang to the fountain, grabbed Isabelle under the arms, and raised her out of the basin. "Call an ambulance!" he shouted to the waiter, who stood outside the entrance to the restaurant in a cone of light. The waiter had been clearing tables and still held a plate in his hands. "*Vite!*"—Quickly!—Toby urged.

"Tell him to call the police too," I said to Toby. The red leather bag that Isabelle had been carrying was gone.

The dog's eerie howling prompted a neighbor to open her shutters to see what the commotion was. I looked up as the shutters squealed on their rusty hinges. Stars still shimmered against the deep black sky.

It wasn't his mangled ear you noticed first. No, it was those piercing eyes and the way he stared straight at you, straight ahead no matter what. If something caught his interest off to one side, he would swivel his entire head rather than follow the movement with his pupils like anyone else. His eyes seemed fixed in place like a doll's. And when he painted, he would step back, squint, and squeeze his eyelashes almost shut, and then he would paint like that. How could he even see what he was doing? As for that ear, it was hideous. The others teased him about it. But I refused to look at it, which is why, after all this time, it's the eyes that I remember, those piercing, watery blue eyes.

2

TOBY HAD, on instinct, lifted the body from the fountain and laid it on the ground. Someone needed to take charge. I looked around for Ray Montoni. He was retching onto the cobblestones.

"Have you checked her pulse?" I asked. Toby put his finger to Isabelle's neck and waited. He looked up at me and shook his head.

"Help me straighten her out," I said. We had to try artificial respiration. You couldn't know if a drowning victim was really gone, in spite of outward signs of death. Girl Scout training. I tried for a long time, but it didn't work. I lifted my head up, exhausted. Maggie took me by the arms and helped me into a sitting position on the rim of the basin beside the unresponsive body. Sister Glenda crossed herself as she stood over Isabelle's inert form.

"I'll be all right," I said.

"That's what *she* said," Maggie humphed.

Glenda's murmured prayer rose into the winter air. Then there was silence.

The restaurant owner came out to tell us the police were on the way. Their instructions were to have someone stay with the body. Meanwhile, the rest of us were to return to the restaurant and wait.

"I'll stay with her," Toby volunteered. Professor Montoni, as head of the conference, was the appropriate candidate for that duty, but he was already heading back to the restaurant. I followed and saw that he was hurrying to "the little corner." I stopped to ask the bartender to bring Toby his coat and then joined the others in the dining room. The English speakers were gathered around one table and, either seated or standing, were asking each other what might have happened. The French speakers seemed to be doing the same in a huddle on the other side of the room.

"She was all right until dessert," said Bennett. "Ray was right next to her during dinner. Maybe she said something to him that the rest of us didn't hear." He looked around for Montoni.

"You can check *les toilettes*," I suggested. Bennett went off on that errand.

Professor Curry turned to me. "You were watching that fellow at the bar. What do you think he was up to—moping at the edge of our party?"

"Does anyone know who he was?" I asked. Heads shook and shoulders hunched.

Bennett reappeared with Montoni in tow, and Curry rose to give Montoni his chair. Our leader looked wretched. "Nausea," he explained.

"Here, have some water, Ray," said Shelley Bennett. I noticed they were on a first-name basis. Then I remembered that the Bennetts and Montonis knew each other from Philadelphia. Ray Montoni taught at an art college in South Philadelphia. Ben Bennett was an associate professor at Drexel.

Montoni swallowed some water but he still looked bad.

"How well did you know the La Font woman?" Curry asked him.

"Not well. She got in touch with me a few weeks ago when she learned that our conference was coming to the Maeght. She lives close to here. She said she discovered something about Van Gogh's death while going through her grandfather's papers. She thought we would want to know about it." He stopped for air.

"Well, what was it?" demanded Bennett.

Montoni said, "I don't know."

"Didn't she tell you?"

"I'm afraid not." He took a deep breath.

"You haven't read her paper?"

Montoni looked at Bennett with annoyance. "It was just a proposal. She wanted to keep the information to herself until the conference. She may have had the paper with her tonight. It was probably in her briefcase." He was sweating. He took out a handkerchief and mopped his brow.

"You mean that red leather bag?" I asked.

"I guess so."

"Well, it's missing," I informed him. "She took it out with her, but it's gone."

"Gone? Are you sure? Could it have fallen into the fountain?"

"I looked," I said. "It's not there. Someone must have taken it."

Shelley Bennett had a different explanation. "She was sick. Maybe she wandered around the square and lost her bag and then collapsed when she was trying to splash water on her face. Like this." She stood at the table's edge and hinged herself over it, waving her hands as if to scoop up water. She was starting to demonstrate a collapse when her husband grasped her by both elbows and forced her into a seat. She shook her shoulders, silently protesting.

"When did she first look sick?" I asked.

Jane Curry said, "Not until after dessert. Then quite suddenly she seemed distressed."

I turned to Montoni. "That was after she went back to the bar to talk with that man she knew. They seemed to be having an argument. Do you know who he was?"

Montoni cleared his throat and said hoarsely, "I do, but let's wait for the police. Otherwise, I'll have to go over all of this twice. I don't feel up to it. They'll be here soon." He sighed heavily, then closed his eyes. People shifted slightly, to form a circle that excluded him. Bennett was opening his mouth to speak when I heard Jane Curry whispering behind me, "It's all right, dear. It will be all right." She was speaking to Angie, who was standing stiffly, visibly upset. Her face was pink from the effort to control herself. My sister feels things keenly, often with the immediacy of a child. I felt a tinge of shame at how rationally I'd just been analyzing the situation. No one spoke again till we heard voices at the door.

First over the threshold was a slim woman in civilian dress: tight black jeans and a snappy leather jacket that let her curves show in the back as well as the front. In France, even the cops are sexily dressed. Her brunette hair was swept back into a bun at the nape of her neck. A sharp-featured man following behind her was also casually dressed. They were detectives. Then came two gendarmes in peaked caps and short blue jackets with a big white stripe, which made them look like soccer players, except for the handguns hanging from their belts. The gendarmes were from Vence, the next town. The tall one was young and fresh-faced; the short one was lined and weathered. Toby came in behind the officers, with the collar of his coat turned up. It had been a cold vigil, watching over the corpse of Isabelle La Font.

The woman in the leather jacket introduced herself. She was Lieutenant Monique Auclair, head of the investigative unit of the Police Judiciaire of the Gendarmerie of Grasse. Her French was clear and easily understood. For those whose French was rudimentary, or in Angie's case nonexistent, the lieutenant tasked the young gendarme to translate. She introduced him as Maréchal des logis-chef Robert Navré. He began by translating his own title: "You may call me Sergeant Navré." (I love French, but it's a language that goes in for elaboration. All those verbal sashes and epaulettes for the equivalent of sergeant.)

"It's late in the evening," the lieutenant continued, "so let me pose a few questions while you are together. Later, if necessary, we'll follow up with individuals. From what we know at this point, it's possible that the victim died of natural causes. We'll know more after the medical examination; but since it's been reported that her purse is missing, I'm treating this as a suspicious death. You all spent the evening with the deceased. I understand you had drinks at the bar, followed by dinner in the dining room. Let's start with the bar. Who spoke first with Madame La Font?"

Montoni stepped forward. "I did. Raymond Montoni. We met before the conference opened. I'm the organizer. It's an international gathering of the leading scholars on Vincent van Gogh." In asserting his prominence, he seemed to regain his energy.

"Is everyone in this room a participant in your conference?"

"Yes. A few are guests related to the speakers."

"Go on. You were the first to address Madame La Font?" The lieutenant glanced toward her plainclothes assistant to check that he was taking notes. I was impressed by her brisk, professional manner.

"Yes," answered Montoni. "I came up to her to say hello and to introduce her to the others at our conference. But she was talking with someone at the bar when I reached her."

"And who was that?" asked the lieutenant.

"Her brother. His name is Yves La Font."

"Was he here as a participant or as a family member?"

"Neither. I didn't invite him to the conference, and the restaurant was reserved for our group after six this evening. He seems to have been at the bar for a while. I think he was here to cause trouble."

"Oh? And why was that?"

"He and his sister were not in accord about her intention to address the conference. Madame La Font told me he didn't want her to discuss matters that were private to the family."

"Such as?"

"Their grandfather claimed to know Vincent van Gogh when he—the grandfather—was a young boy. Madame La Font wrote to me that she had new information about Van Gogh's death based on her grandfather's recollections. She had discovered some letters or papers, I don't know which. What this important information was I don't know either, but she seemed believable. Naturally, I was interested, so I invited her to the conference. We were all waiting to hear her presentation. Her brother didn't want her to speak. That's what she told me."

"To protect the reputation of the family?"

"I couldn't say. I don't know the details."

"You say they were arguing here tonight?"

"It seems so, yes."

"Then what happened?"

"She became ill during dinner and went outside."

The lieutenant walked to the door and looked out. "Did they leave the restaurant together?"

"No, he left first." Montoni glanced around for confirmation.

"You're quite sure of that?"

"Yes."

"How long before she left?"

Montoni hesitated. "I'm not sure. Fifteen or twenty minutes, perhaps." Several others nodded in agreement.

"Did anyone else leave the restaurant before the body was discovered? Did any of you?" The young gendarme translated, since everyone needed to hear the question. The lieutenant's eyes swept over the group. No one responded.

"Tell me, please, who is the person who reported the missing handbag?"

I raised a finger and identified myself. The lieutenant asked for a description of the bag. "It was large, made of quilted red leather, with a silver chain. Very stylish."

"Are you certain she was carrying it with her when she left the restaurant?"

"Yes, she had it on her shoulder."

"Can anyone else confirm that?" Shelley Bennett put her hand up.

The lieutenant turned back to Montoni. "Do you know where the brother lives?"

"Villefranche, I believe."

"And Madame La Font?" Before she got an answer, she turned sharply to the good-looking gendarme. "Sergeant Navré, if you please? You and the young lady, step back a way. I can't hear myself think." The rebuke was directed at Angie and the translator. They'd been talking in English, heads together, but too loudly.

"Quite right," said Professor Curry. "Have a hearing aid, you know. Hard to understand you, with background noise like that." His hearing aid had been ringing all evening, but apparently he hadn't noticed that.

The lieutenant tilted her head impatiently. "Monsieur Montoni, what else can you tell me about Madame La Font? She had the same surname as her brother. Was she single?"

Montoni scratched his eyelid. "I think so. She lives in Sisteron. Lived, that is. She worked in a medical center. I'm not sure what she did there. She wasn't a doctor."

"Did she live alone?"

"I don't know about her personal life," Montoni replied.

"All right," said the lieutenant. "Who else spoke with Madame La Font? Beyond an introduction, you understand." The sergeant translated, but no one responded.

Montoni took up the slack. "Of course there was conversation during dinner."

"What was discussed?"

It surprised me that Jane Curry was the first to answer: she looked so mousy. She spoke in English and Navré translated. "We talked a little about gardening. When I told her I was the manager of the Blackwater Garden Club, back home in Southampton, she invited me to her gardening society in Sisteron. I didn't know if it would be possible, working around the schedule of the conference."

There was a lull. "Who else was at her table?"

Montoni, Bruce Curry, and the Bennetts raised their hands.

Ben Bennett spoke up. "I'm afraid I rather dominated the conversation. We discussed the talk she was going to deliver."

"Was there anything in that discussion to distress Madame La Font?" pursued the lieutenant.

"I wouldn't say so, no," Bennett replied. He blinked while talking.

Professor Curry's ruddy face whipped toward Bennett's. "I say, man, you badgered the woman senseless. Wouldn't shut up. She told you to stop."

"What is your name, sir?" asked the lieutenant, turning to Bennett, apparently having understood Curry's outburst in English.

"Benjamin Bennett, of Drexel University in Philadelphia. I'm working on a new biography of Van Gogh. It will be published in the fall. Madame La Font was here to speak about her grandfather's knowledge of Van Gogh's last hours. Of course we had things to discuss."

"Did your questions upset her?"

"That's not true." Bennett looked toward Professor Curry. "She simply preferred not to speak about her paper until she delivered it. That was to be tomorrow morning."

"Did she converse with anyone else?" Lieutenant Auclair paced the room, scrutinizing faces.

"She stopped at our table briefly," said the Dutch professor, when the lieutenant paused in front of him. "To greet Monsieur Didier, I recall."

"Yes, that's right," Professor Didier answered. "Isabelle's an old acquaintance. We were students in Bordeaux at the same time. She came over to be civil, you know. We greeted each other, that's all." Throughout this answer, he looked at Hans de Groot, not the lieutenant.

She demanded his attention. "Your full name, please."

He raised his eyes to the ceiling. "The name is Daniel Didier. Professor of art history at the University of Bordeaux."

The lieutenant stared at Didier until he lowered his eyes and met hers. She then pivoted to face the English speakers. "So. We come to the end of dinner, and suddenly Madame La Font goes outside. Is that correct?"

"She said she needed some air. For a moment she looked woozy," Jane Curry said. "She thought she had too much of the dessert wine."

"Which was?"

"An excellent Baumes-de-Venise," said Montoni. "We all drank it."

"What happened next?"

Maggie spoke up. "My dog followed her out and came back without her. He was barking. He was agitated. We went outside to see what the trouble was, and that was when we found her, slung over the fountain."

"Her head was in the water," Toby added.

"And you moved her onto the ground?"

"That's right. At that point I didn't know if she was still alive. My wife tried to revive her, but it was too late."

"Did anyone else touch the body?"

"No," Toby replied.

"You're certain?" She looked at Toby steadily.

"Yes. I don't think anyone did."

"*Bon.* Have you got everything, Lucien?" the lieutenant asked the assisting detective, the one taking the notes.

"Yes, Lieutenant."

"Does anyone have anything else to add?" She waited but no one spoke. "Very well. You'll be at your conference—for how long?"

"A week," answered Montoni. "We're staying at the Hotel des Glycines, on the Route de la Colle. Our conference sessions will be at the Maeght Foundation."

"Understood. We will need to see your passports and identification papers, so we will accompany you to your hotel." She turned to the older gendarme. "Please organize the company for their return to the hotel. The shuttles are in the parking lot." She turned back to her partner. "Lucien, remain with the body until the medical examiner and the technicians have done their work and the body has been removed."

"Yes, ma'am," the detective replied smartly.

Montoni and the others who had shared a table with the victim followed the lieutenant out the door. The older gendarme asked the people from our table to follow him. With a strong flashlight, he led us down the narrow lanes to the car park and saw to it that we boarded as quickly as possible. The only stragglers were Angie and the translator, who were chatting away outside the van door, until he gave her a hand up and then sat beside her. I marveled at the change in Angie—a half hour ago she'd been near tears. That's Angie, though. Her moods can shift dramatically. The attention of a good-looking gendarme of her own age and height had certainly raised her spirits.

During the ride to the hotel, there was hardly any talk, except between Angie and the sergeant. She was whispering to him in the seat in front of us, and I was frustrated because I couldn't hear them. What was she thinking? Wasn't she on the verge of becoming a nun? Flirting wasn't exactly on the program. Maybe it was an automatic reflex. Angie has always been attractive to men, and she's had a long string of boyfriends, mainly unsuitable ones. But not when she was living in a convent. I wondered if Sister Glenda noticed.

Glenda had been given the front passenger seat, behind the driver, and Maggie, who had helped her get in, sat beside her, with Emmet at her feet. It would be awkward, but maybe later I could ask Maggie whether she picked up any of Angie's conversation with the handsome sergeant. The best thing was to ask Angie herself, but she sure would be annoyed. Big and little sister dynamics.

Our hotel was only a quarter mile beyond the village walls, but it was on a steep hill and was too far to walk at night, at least for the older conference participants. I was grateful that the van brought us speedily "home." The hotel lights looked welcoming.

The first shuttle had preceded us, so Montoni was already there with his table partners, and so was Lieutenant Auclair. We walked in as he was asking her, "Can you tell us if the conference can proceed tomorrow?"

"Certainly," she replied. "You may go about your business. If we need to interview some of you further, we'll work around your schedule." She asked him for a copy of the program.

After the last shuttle arrived, the lieutenant gave us her parting words, with the assistance of Sergeant Navré: "As I said before, we don't know what happened tonight. Until we do, I caution you all to be careful and on the alert. Please report any suspicious activity to me. The sergeant has handed out my card. It has my number. Don't hesitate to call if you have any information that might be useful. Don't decide that your observations are insignificant. Let me be the judge of that. Finally, please provide your passport or identification papers before you retire for the night. We'll copy the information we need and return them to you. Thank you for your cooperation. Monsieur Montoni, would you instruct your people on what to expect tomorrow morning?"

Montoni looked at a loss. Shelley Bennett cut in: "We were going to have breakfast here at seven thirty and then take the shuttles to the Maeght at nine fifteen. Why not stick to that?"

"Quite right," said Professor Curry, as if approving a solved equation.

"Yes, fine," agreed a flustered Montoni. "I'll have to adjust the schedule, but we'll follow the program as best we can. You all have a copy. Will that be all right, Madame Richarde?" His question was addressed to our hostess.

"Of course, monsieur. Till seven thirty, then. Or when you rise. Breakfast is open between seven and ten. Do you all know your rooms and have your keys?"

That was true of all but Daniel Didier and his colleague Jacques Godard. They had driven together and had arrived only in time to join us in the village for dinner. Madame Richarde wished the rest of us good night and went to fetch the keys to the room the French professors were sharing.

Toby was at my side. It had been a trying night, and I was looking forward to a comforting hug. We rose and looked around for Angie and Sister Glenda, who had the rooms next to ours. Glenda was talking with Montoni. Angie was off in a corner saying good night to her dashing gendarme. I gave her a wave, and she dipped her head toward him and took her leave. When she moved to join us, Sister Glenda did likewise, stopping to say her good nights to Maggie and her dog. Glenda leaned over to pet Emmet and set his tail wagging. He had forgotten whatever disturbing sensations had been aroused by his discovery of a corpse. He had recovered completely. We humans had not.

What's death to a dog, I wondered?

It was the summer of 1890. We lived in Paris then. When school ended, Papa would send us all to Auvers-sur-Oise to escape the heat. We used to swim in the river and enjoy the cool evenings in the pleasant town, which was close enough to the city so Papa could come up by train and stay the weekend. That's what the husbands did. The mothers and children stayed all summer and the fathers visited on the weekends. So there were other boys my age from Paris, and I fell in with them. There were two brothers I remember well, René and Gaston Secrétan. Gaston was older than most of us. A shy boy, he often kept to himself. His younger brother, René, I can see now, was a bit of an oaf. But at the time, we all followed him around. He was brash and boastful. Girls liked him—at that age they don't know better—so we followed his lead. What was he, sixteen, like me? In some ways he acted older, in others just the opposite. For instance, he had an American cowboy outfit that he wore all the time, with fringes and a big hat. That year, or maybe the year before, Buffalo Bill had come to Paris with his Wild West show. Cowboys and red Indians were all the rage. René even had a gun, an old pistol that he got somewhere, and he went around shooting birds and rabbits, pretending they were savages. Of course, we all wanted a turn with that pistol. That damned gun. That was the start of everything.

3

I SLEPT BADLY and awoke before six, while Toby, my personal ten o'clock scholar, burrowed deeply under the duvet. I decided to take a soothing soak in the claw-footed tub. French bathtubs can be surprisingly deep. I'm too short to make a graceful leg-swing over a rim that high. So I backed my way in, holding tightly to both sides. I was glad to splash in without an embarrassing fall that would require calling for help. The foot and a half of hot water relaxed my tight muscles. When the water grew tepid, thoughts of Isabelle's drowning made me shiver. I made the effort to climb awkwardly over the stile of a rim and into the comfort of a bathroom heated by towel warmers.

Before seven, I was down the stairs and out into—the dark. I had forgotten it was almost the winter solstice. But I was glad I'd ventured out. From the hotel terrace outside the front door, the walls of Saint-Paul glowed like fire, the effect of deftly placed spotlights. The tower at the top of the town was even more brightly lit. Four stars still pierced the inky sky. I was starting to make out the buildings as a faint light began to gather. I love the words "dawn" and "*l'aube*." In whatever language, the experience of dawn is indescribable. I was glad I hadn't slept through this one, and I wanted to watch the sun rise over the village. It was chilly, though, and I had that massive hunger that hits the second morning after an overnight flight.

Turning toward the hotel entrance marked by footlights like candles, I saw Maggie and Emmet on their way back from a potty trot in the dark. She called to me and we agreed to share a breakfast table. Toby would arrive at the last minute, I was sure. Sister Glenda said she and Angie would come down at eight so they'd have time for morning prayers.

Since Maggie and I were the first customers, we had our choice of tables and took one looking out at Saint-Paul. So I *could* see the sun rise and the lamps go out. At that early hour we had the complete attention of the waitress, who showed us how to boil our own eggs, plunging them into a hot-water machine and timing them with a little rack of sandglasses—three, four, and five minutes.

While we waited for our eggs to cook and our croissants to arrive, I poured myself coffee and Maggie steeped her tea. We didn't say much. We were tongue-tied by the death the night before.

I tried my best. "Did you sleep well?"

"I was shattered last night. Thank God, I slept like a seal on the strand."

"Not me. More like a goldfish gasping for air."

In friendly silence, we fetched our boiled eggs and sat down to eat. Halfway through my croissant, slathered with apricot jam, I recovered sociability. "Emmet's up early. For a hungry dog, he's behaving well."

"Routine is everything, for children and for dogs. Even on the road, Emmet is served Royal Canine bits in gravy at six thirty sharp. He wolfs them down and then wants his walk."

"Where do you get the gravy?"

"It's like beef bouillon powder. You add water and stir."

"Marvelous. I'm glad to start the day with you both."

"You won't be, when he starts breaking wind. The lad has a toot like a foghorn. Brutal."

Under other circumstances, I would have spluttered my coffee laughing, but I was too heavyhearted for that. Maggie was more resilient. As other guests arrived, she commented slyly on their appearance and gestures. Some were from our conference, but it was a couple we didn't know who got a roasting from Maggie. I guess she didn't want to skewer our colleagues thoroughly until she knew me better.

"Will your gorgeous sister grace us with her presence this morning?" she asked.

"My gorgeous sister is praying with Sister Glenda at the moment." Maggie gave a wry look, as if to say, "Oh, really?"

I tried to explain. "I know Angie doesn't look like the religious type, but she is."

"Religious enough to shut herself up in a cold convent, far away from handsome young men?"

"That's just the problem. She's religious, but not ascetic. I don't know if this convent thing can last."

"From the sound of her *craic* with that fine gendarme, I doubt it." Maggie gnawed on her second croissant.

It took me a second to recall that in Ireland *craic* means a bit of good fun. "Did it sound as much like flirting as it looked?"

"I'll say. Eloise and Abelard couldn't be more cozy. Of course, we're hoping that what happened to Abelard won't happen to the manly sergeant." Abelard ended up minus his male equipment.

"Eloise stayed in the convent, though, didn't she? Maybe Angie will too." I sighed, pouring myself another cup.

"What makes a lively girl like her want to give herself away to praying with a bunch of daft nuns?" she asked. "Your Sister Glenda excepted, of course."

"Glenda's nuns aren't the kind we grew up with. They've broken away from the Vatican and own their own convent. They're ecumenical. And their mission is supporting the education of low-income women. Glenda teaches at a community college and lectures on daytime television."

"And what about the lovely Angie? What will she do?" Maggie refreshed her tea.

"As work? I'm not sure. She's been a model and then a hairdresser, so she doesn't exactly have experience for the mission. But Angie's inventive. She volunteered to spruce up poor women to help them prepare for job interviews, and the nuns liked that."

Maggie scooped some raspberry jam from its little pot. "That's grand! But couldn't she do that without taking those terrible vows of chastity and poverty?" She spread the jam on her croissant.

"I don't know. I have to say, I can't see Angie sticking to those vows. She loves fancy finery, and I can't keep track of how many boyfriends she's had. The trouble is, she has the worst taste in men. She's found every sleaze in Massachusetts and had her heart broken by him. Married men, potheads, con artists, crooks, would-be crooks. It's too depressing to talk about."

"So she's putting herself behind bars to ward off temptation?"

"I'm afraid that's part of it. And there's another thing." I put down my cup. "I think she needs mothering. You see how happy she is under Sister Glenda's wing?"

"Have you lost your mother, then?"

"Not at all, she's alive and well. But she doesn't do much mothering. Not the conventional kind. Mom's funny, smart, well read, curious about the world. She's everything you'd want a friend to be. But she's not very maternal. Angie and I love Mom to pieces, but I think Angie missed having that warm, protective doting that little kids need."

"Are you not asking for a saint of a mother?" She munched the last of her croissant and dusted her hands.

"Maybe. Maybe Angie is too. Having a mother superior—in more than one sense of the word—may be just what she wants."

"Speak of the devil, here she comes now." Maggie put down her napkin and grabbed for Emmet's leash. She gave me a wink and said, "Why not have a family meeting? I'm off."

Angie came in without Sister Glenda. Fresh from her morning prayer, she looked like one of Perugino's angels. When she worked at the beauty salon, she wore her blonde hair long, with highlights added, just to make sure she signaled sexual allure. For the convent, Angie cut her hair short to the chin and stopped adding highlights. Being Angie, she looked just as beautiful in a different way. The untreated hair was gold and wavy and glowed like a halo.

She slid into the chair vacated by Maggie and asked, "Can you stay for a little? Glenda's not coming down for a while."

"Of course. I guess she's going over her talk."

"She did that earlier. Now she's on e-mail. Some trouble back home."

"I hope nothing serious."

"One of the sisters is sick. She doesn't want to see the doctor. Glenda's such a good mother superior. She's got each of us in mind, all the time."

I couldn't pass that one up. "If she's got you in mind all the time, what do you suppose she thinks of the way you were snuggling up to that gendarme last night? You were, you know."

"You mean Roe-bare?"

I must have looked puzzled.

"Sergeant Navré. His first name is Roe-bare."

"Ah. Robert. And what does he call you? On-jee? Or Sister-in-Training Barnes?"

"You don't have to be snarky," she said, but she was blushing.

"Sorry. What's up with you and him? Do nuns at Grace Quarry have flirting rights?"

"We were just having a little fun. And besides, I'm not a nun yet."

"But you're considering it. Has Sister Glenda talked to you about having a little fun with the sergeant?"

"No. And there isn't anything to talk about. You're always the big sister, aren't you?"

"I guess I am," I admitted.

Angie poured herself a cup of coffee from the carafe in front of her and dug a croissant out of the basket. She topped off her coffee with warm milk, dunked one end of the croissant in her cup, and took a bite, scattering flakes on the table.

"You and Sister Glenda seem to be getting on well," I continued. "Is she more reserved with you at the convent?"

"Oh, no. Glenda wouldn't know how to be reserved with the garbageman. She makes it a home for everyone."

"So you feel at home there?"

"Absolutely. In a way, more than I do at home. Don't get me wrong. Home is great. I still love the family."

"You scared me there. I didn't think that going to the convent would mean leaving us behind."

"It doesn't, but I think I need to get away to really grow up—not because I don't want to see you. It's my role at home. That's what I've got to ditch." She looked at me with a firm set to her jaw, which was something new.

"What do you mean, your role at home? Everyone loves you."

"Thanks, but it's not much of an identity. To Eddie, I'm Angie the airhead. To you, I'm Angie the kid sister. Need I go on?" I raised a hand, admitting defeat. "I need time away so I can figure out who I am, at the core. And I need to know that, in order to see what should come next."

"You mean, whether you'll take final vows."

"Yes, but more than that. It's what everybody needs to do—you had to do that, didn't you?"

"I suppose. But do you really need to leave the family to do it?"

"You did. You went away to college, to the other side of the state, just when I needed you, when Mom got sick. Then you went away to grad school in California, and then you stayed there and got married." These were the facts and an accusation that caught me off guard.

We fell silent. Finally I said, "You thought I deserted you. Is that how you felt?"

"Of course I did." Angie reached across the table and gripped my wrist. "I was five years old, and the most important person in my life just disappeared. Mom was in no shape to notice I was sad, and, hey, Dad and Eddie are men. They were clueless. They made me stay at home to keep Mom company." She let go and sat back in her chair.

"Gosh, I'm sorry, Angie. I didn't realize. I just wanted to get out there in the world."

"I know that now. But when I was a kid, I didn't like it. I thought you should've stayed home. You could have gone to the community college in Gloucester."

"Dad wanted me to, you know. It wouldn't have worked. I would have felt smothered staying at home."

"Right." She raised an eyebrow conclusively.

"So you've forgiven me?"

"That's not the point. The point is that I need to do what you did. I need to get away."

"You're not going very far away to do it. Mom and Dad are about fifteen minutes from Grace Quarry."

"It's not a matter of distance. I'll see the family as often as you did when you were in school. Holidays, birthdays, vacations."

I took her point. "I guess you're right. Even now I see you guys maybe four times a year."

"And we make the most of it. Wasn't it great when I visited you in Bodega Bay? And this is awesome, being in France with you and Toby."

I felt my eyes welling up.

"Come on," she said. "Chin up. We've got an audience." Glenda was coming in the door. After a few words about the egg machine and the perfect croissants, I left them to their breakfast and climbed the winding stone staircase to our room, shaking my head at my ever-surprising sister and brooding over some of my own life decisions.

By ten past nine, the conference participants and the tagalongs were milling about the terrace, waiting for the shuttles to arrive. Precisely on time, they pulled up, halted abruptly, and opened their doors for our entry. As we careened down the drive, we caught views of the ramparts of Saint-Paul crisply defined by the morning sun. Once on the main road, we skirted the village and noticed for the first time the slopes below, dotted with houses in spite of their steepness. It was only five minutes before we reached our destination.

Nestled in a pine grove in the hills, the Maeght Foundation, with its façade of sand-colored bricks and soaring, white pagoda-style roof, looks like an emperor's dream. In actuality, the museum was the creation of a well-connected art dealer, Aimé Maeght, who moved to Saint-Paul in 1950 with his wife, Marguerite, and their son Bernard, who suffered from leukemia. When the boy died, loyal friends proposed a museum to honor Bernard's memory, and to fill it, they volunteered to donate their own works. These weren't just any friends. They included Braque, Bonnard, Miró, Chagall, and other luminaries, all of whom had been helped by the Maeghts in their struggling years. As a result, the museum has one of the world's premier collections of modern art.

The shuttles dropped us outside the museum grounds at the start of a tree-lined path that led through a sculpture garden featuring works by the modern greats. The primary colors of Calder and Miró danced in the sun. At the main entrance, statues of little green men stood in a fountain, squirting water from their male appendages. I would have laughed, but my chest was still heavy with the murder and my worries about Angie.

Montoni, who was fussing about keeping on schedule, led us inside. We followed him up a short flight of stairs, which brought us to a large, light-filled room where folding chairs and a lectern had been set up for our sessions. We'd been given space in the "town hall," the heart of the museum, where works from the permanent collection are shown. For the next week, we would be surrounded by treasures of modern art bathed in natural light by floor-to-ceiling windows looking out at evergreens and distant hills. Shades could be lowered for PowerPoint or slide projections.

The session was late getting under way. Montoni began by apologizing for the delay and then blathered on with platitudes about the shocking death of Isabelle La Font. Next he announced the revised schedule. Bruce Curry, who was pacing about with a distracted air, would speak first today, followed by Sister Glenda. Curry's talk was called "Plants and Art: The Role of Foxglove in the Paintings of Van Gogh." But there was a problem, Montoni said. Professor Curry had brought with him dried samples of the foxglove plant for purposes of demonstration, but the sack in which he carried the sprigs was missing. Had anyone seen it? No hands went up. "Professor Curry tells me these herbs can be dangerous. However, I'll let him explain." Montoni proceeded to deliver a canned introduction and took his seat. Then Curry, with jittery steps, replaced him at the lectern.

Bruce Curry had fluffy brown hair with gray tufts over each ear, in one of which he wore a hearing aid. Added to that, his round-rimmed glasses and weak chin gave him an owlish appearance. As he began to speak, his head jerked slightly. "I don't know who thought it would be amusing to steal the foxglove from my room, but it's not amusing to me, I assure you." He peered over his glasses accusingly. "In fact, it was a childish thing to do." People in the audience exchanged glances. This was not the typical way to begin a scholarly talk. "In case you don't know it, digitalis is a powerful drug. Foxglove is loaded with it. So if I were you, I wouldn't fool around with it. In fact, if I were you . . ." Here he started stammering, then bowed over, coughing.

Montoni fetched him a glass of water. Curry took a few gulps and wiped his brow with a handkerchief. Montoni patted him on the shoulder. "I'm sure all of us are upset by the events of last night," Montoni said. "That's understandable. If anyone does know the whereabouts of Professor Curry's plants, please let me know after the session, and I'll see that they're returned without revealing the source. Now, then. Are you able to proceed, Professor?"

Curry nodded. "Thank you. Indeed, I am upset. Someone here wants to spoil my talk, but I apologize for berating the group as a whole. Please bear with me." He fiddled with his hearing aid, then shuffled his papers and began again. Once he started reading, he appeared to regain his composure. His prepared text steadied him, and soon his voice became measured.

Curry's thesis was that Van Gogh's artistic vision stemmed from the effects of digitalis, concocted from the foxglove plant. The drug was in the homemade remedies he was given by Dr. Paul Gachet, who treated Van Gogh for depression in 1890, the last year of his life. Digitalis can affect vision in dramatic ways. Objects may appear to shimmer, and the patient sometimes sees a yellow halo around lights. Those ocular effects, Curry pointed out, appear in several of Van Gogh's best-known works. The slide Curry used for an example homed in on the quivering lamps hanging from the ceiling in Vincent's *Night Café*. Curry noted that while small doses of the drug can be beneficial for certain heart conditions, digitalis is toxic in an overdose. Gachet, he argued, was a quack. The doctor meant well, but his foxglove remedies only made Van Gogh more ill. Indeed, Vincent had doubts about his treatment. He wrote to his brother that the doctor seemed even more depressed than he was.

The next slide showed Vincent's *Portrait of Dr. Gachet*, in which the melancholy doctor is seated at a table in his herb garden, leaning his head on his right hand. Sure enough, on the table in front of Gachet, in a glass jar filled with water, are several stems of foxglove with their lavender-colored blossoms. Other scholars have suggested that Vincent included the herbs in the portrait as tokens of the doctor's calling, but Curry went so far as to attribute Vincent's painting style to them. It was an intriguing theory. It was also intriguing that Curry was so unnerved by his missing samples. He finished his talk to a smattering of applause.

After a break for coffee, Montoni introduced Sister Glenda, who stepped up to the podium. There couldn't have been a greater contrast between Curry's presentation and hers. From the moment she began to speak, Glenda was relaxed and in control. She spoke without notes, whereas he stuck rigidly to his text. If Curry's talk reduced the artist's vision to a pathology, Sister Glenda's expanded it into a philosophy. Her topic was "Christian Humanism in Van Gogh's Art." She began by reminding her audience that Vincent turned to art only after failing as a minister. (Apparently no one could stand his sermons.) But she claimed his approach to art sprang from the same motive that led him to the ministry: compassion for human suffering. His ability to feel the pain of others was evident from his earliest paintings (*The Potato Eaters* came up on the screen) to the very end. "We see it," she noted with a nod to Curry, "even in his portrait of Dr. Gachet, whom Vincent recognized as a fellow sufferer." According to Sister Glenda, the key to Vincent's art is contained in a letter he wrote to his brother, Theo. She looked down at her single notecard and quoted: "In a picture I want to say something comforting. . . . I want to paint men and women with that something of the eternal which the halo used to symbolize, and which we seek to give by the actual radiance and vibrations of our colorings."

With that, Sister Glenda looked at the audience and said: "With all due respect to Professor Curry, I'd like to suggest an alternative to his theory. Perhaps it is Vincent's spirituality that explains the halo effects we see in the paintings. Maybe the vibrations in his colors are meant to suggest our mystical bond with something of the eternal." Her last illustration was *The Starry Night*. The audience clapped enthusiastically, many with hands held high. Glenda grinned. Curry scowled.

At lunch after the session, we found ourselves seated with Curry and Sister Glenda. The etiquette at a small conference like this one is to circulate, especially at mealtimes, so that participants get to know each other. Jane Curry invited Maggie and Angie to join her at a nearby table, along with Klara de Groot. That left Toby and me as referees between

Glenda and Curry. Lunch was a light affair, featuring a choice of salads. Toby filled our glasses from a carafe of rosé wine that stood on the table.

"That was a fine paper," Glenda said to Curry, opening with the standard remark at gatherings such as these. "I hope you don't mind my disagreeing with your conclusions. Obviously we bring different perspectives to our work."

Curry was not about to be gracious. "You can think what you like," he grunted. "I don't see any need to bring religious hokum into the discussion. Science provides a better explanation."

Glenda didn't take the bait.

"Hokum? Isn't that a bit strong?" said Toby. Not that he's a defender of religion. On the contrary, Toby's a thoroughgoing skeptic. He calls himself an "Orthodox Reprobate." But he won't put up with a bully, and Curry was being one. Sister Glenda was traveling in our company, and out of chivalry, Toby felt called upon to defend her, whatever his personal views on the subject.

However, Glenda was perfectly able to defend herself. She said, "Come now, Professor. There's always room for another opinion. I have great respect for science, but it may not hold all the answers."

"I never said it did," Curry retorted. He began worrying a piece of crusty French bread, pulling out chunks of the doughy center.

"Of course, there are different theories to account for Vincent's style," Glenda continued, ignoring Curry's hostility much as a parent might deal with a cranky child. She reached for the decanter. "You don't have to accept my views as gospel."

I waded in. "Take that remark Vincent made about looking at nature through his eyelashes. It's in one of the letters. Didn't he say that squinting at objects helped him to see the relations between colors? Well, if you look at the world long enough through half-closed eyes, everything starts to shimmer. Maybe it's as simple as that."

"You think I don't know that passage?" Curry bristled. "What he was doing with his eyelashes was trying to mimic the effect that digitalis had on him when he wasn't on the drug, that's all. If anything, it strengthens my argument."

"Couldn't I say the same thing?" Glenda emptied her glass with a swig. "That by looking at nature through his eyelashes he was trying to replicate the impressions he experienced in a heightened state?"

"What kind of heightened state? A mystical trance, you mean?" Curry sneered.

"People do report having them," I said.

"Hallucinations, you mean. The mental wards are filled with such people."

"Van Gogh was in a mental ward, wasn't he?" said Toby. "Who's to say how he interpreted his experiences?"

Outnumbered three to one, Curry stiffened. "Oh, and I suppose *you're* to say? Who exactly are you, by the way? You're not on the program. Are you an art historian? A psychologist?"

"You know who I am. We've been introduced. Do I have to be on the program to have an opinion?"

Uh, oh. Trouble on the way. Toby has the sweetest temperament on earth, but get in his face while he's chugging along amiably, and watch out. He sat back and looked at Curry as an entomologist might examine a new species of bug. A malodorous bug. Coolly, Toby said, "What I do for a living is sell antiques."

"Antiques. And that makes you an expert on Van Gogh."

"No. But I'm entitled to an opinion." Toby's voice was level. "And by the way, *Professor*." The appellation was dripping with sarcasm. "When you were little, didn't anyone teach you how to play well with others?"

Curry flushed. Toby could have stopped there. He should have stopped there. But he didn't. He leaned forward and said, "I'll tell you what I think. You may be an expert when it comes to plants, but when it comes to dealing with people, you don't know your *cul* from your *coude*." No translation was necessary.

"I don't have to take that from you," said Curry.

42

"Oh? Does that mean you'd take it from someone on the program but not from a peon like me?"

"Why, you cheeky beggar," Curry sputtered, slamming his palms against the sides of the table and rising quickly. His chair tottered. At other tables, heads turned.

By now Toby had been thoroughly provoked. "You'll take it, and what's more, you'll like it," he said, with a sibilant curl of his upper lip. He was channeling Humphrey Bogart.

Curry didn't recognize the line from *The Maltese Falcon*. I don't know if that movie is as big with the Brits as it is with us. Besides, if you don't know Toby, you might not get it either. His Bogart imitation is only so-so.

Curry threw down his napkin and stomped out of the room.

Sister Glenda, placid as a pasha, refilled her glass.

"Toby," I whispered, "did you have to do that?"

"Have to? No." He reached for the decanter to refill his own glass. "But that guy is a—"

"Don't say it," said Glenda.

"Right," said Toby, checking himself.

I just shook my head. Once Toby gets on his high horse, he's off in a cloud of dust.

Jane had risen from the adjacent table as if to go after her husband, but instead she came over to our table and sat down in his empty seat. Embarrassment tinged her pale English complexion. "I don't know what's wrong with him. He's been so touchy lately. I'm sorry. Please don't take it personally. These days he's like that with everybody." She pulled her lips in, as if to silence herself.

"I guess it was my fault," said Toby. "I didn't mean to get him so upset."

"He's always had a bit of a temper, but nothing like this."

"When did you start noticing a change?" asked Sister Glenda.

"I'm not sure. He's been disagreeable for months." She looked around, as if the wrong person might be listening. Reassured, she continued. "He's been barking at me over every little thing. In November, I got a call from the head of his department asking if everything was all right. Bruce got into a shouting argument with a colleague at a meeting and they had to ask him to leave the room. That sort of thing never happened before."

"Has he seen a doctor?" Glenda asked.

"We have an appointment with a neurologist after we get back." She cleared her throat, as if to clear her voice of emotion.

"This must be hard for you," I said.

"It's not only his irritability. He's been forgetful, does things that he can't remember the next day, misplaces things. Like this business with the foxglove. He got terribly disturbed when he found that it was missing. I think he just forgot what he did with it."

"Could it still be in your room?" I asked.

"We looked everywhere. No. He thinks somebody stole it."

"Who would want to do that?" asked Toby.

"That's just it. Nobody."

"But *could* someone have taken it?" I wondered aloud.

"Bruce thought the maid stole it, but really, what would a maid want with foxglove? More likely, she thought a sack full of dried-up flowers was trash, and she threw it out. To hear him go on about it, you'd think somebody stole the crown jewels."

Toby asked, "Did anybody else know you had the foxglove in your room?"

Jane thought a moment, then said, "Bruce was showing the De Groots the herbs yesterday, when we were checking in. He was explaining their properties, and there were quite a few people in the lobby at the time."

Toby asked, "You keep your room locked, right?"

"Not always. Bruce is forgetful about that too." She sat up straight, reviving her poise. "I'm sorry for what happened just now. I hope it didn't spoil your lunch."

"Don't give it a thought," said Glenda. "It was good of you to come over. Perhaps you'd better see how he's doing."

"Yes. Thank you for your understanding." She rose and headed upstairs.

Toby gulped. "Look, I'm sorry. That puts a different light on things. I feel like a jerk. I hope the guy doesn't have something seriously wrong with him."

"God forbid," said Sister Glenda.

Toby and Glenda quietly nursed their wine, while I excused myself to go back to our room. I brushed my teeth and splashed some water on my face, going back over Curry's behavior. Something had been bothering me since his talk, and now I realized what it was. I rummaged in my purse and dug out the card with Lieutenant Auclair's phone number. After a moment's hesitation, I made the call. The phone rang a half-dozen times before going to voicemail.

At the beep I said *"Bonjour"* and identified myself, making an effort to enunciate clearly. I thought it would be best to keep my message short. "I'm calling regarding the death of Isabelle La Font. I suggest that you look for the presence of digitalis in her body. I can explain why. *Merci, madame.*" I repeated my name and left my number.

Vincent had come to Auvers to be treated by our local doctor. The Good Lord knows why. We didn't think much of Dr. Gachet ourselves. Vincent, they said, had just been released from an asylum. So, people in town called him crazy. He took his meals in the inn, where he had a room. During the day he painted, and when he wasn't painting, he spent most of his time with us. It must have been a strange sight. Here he was a grown man, and we were just boys, but he tagged along with us.

It was Gaston, the older of the two Secrétan boys, who befriended Vincent. At nineteen, Gaston had an interest in music and art. He told me that someday he hoped to become an artist himself. As for René, his only interests were hunting, fishing, and chasing girls. Although no older than I was, he boasted that he already had lots of experience. And perhaps he did. He knew some dance hall girls in Paris and invited them up for an outing one weekend. They arrived by train. Vincent sat with us on the bank of the river, hoping to attract their attention, but the girls would have nothing to do with him. His hair was unkempt and he was dressed like a scarecrow. And then, there was that ear. We had a bottle of wine in our picnic basket, and Vincent consoled himself with that while the rest of us squeezed and kissed the girls. Of course, René had to take out his revolver and show off by taking potshots at the fish. That made Vincent angry. With contempt, he called René "the terror of the herrings." Then he went off by himself to sit in the long grass with his back toward us. You never knew when Vincent's mood would change. One minute he would be cheerful and talkative, especially when his nose was in a glass, but in the next he would become sullen and morose.

At that age, boys can be cruel. We teased him mercilessly. I say "we," but I never participated in the taunts, and neither did Gaston. But the others—I cringe when I remember some of the pranks they pulled.

And I am ashamed to say I did nothing to interfere. For instance, when Vincent was working, he would absentmindedly suck on the end of one of his brushes. One day someone put chili peppers on the brush, with what results you can imagine. Then they put salt in his coffee, and it made him choke. Another time, René caught a grass snake and hid it in Vincent's paint box, and he nearly fainted when he reached into it. For a few days, Vincent kept his distance, but then he returned and things went on as before. Poor man! How lonely he must have been to put up with us.

4

TOBY LOOKED SHEEPISH when he returned to our room. "I know. I know. I shouldn't have let Curry get under my skin," he began.

I stopped him. "I've just done something myself that I'm beginning to regret." I was having second thoughts about my phone call. When I explained, Toby replied with a noncommittal "hmm."

"Hmm, what?"

"Well, you've stirred up the pot. For all we know, the woman died of natural causes."

"And what if the cause wasn't natural?"

"Do you really think Curry would use his foxglove to poison someone? Even if he is a bit cracked?"

"I don't know what to think. This business of Isabelle's death has got everyone rattled, including me."

"There's one thing you can count on. You'll hear back from the lieutenant."

I slumped down on the bed. Toby sat next to me and put his arm around my shoulder. "What's on for this afternoon?" he asked.

"I'm going shopping in the village with the girls. Want to come along?" The girls were Angie, Maggie, and Shelley Bennett. In the van from the Maeght, we'd agreed to go for a stroll in Saint-Paul after lunch.

"Shopping? Not a chance. But I could use some exercise." He nuzzled my neck, and pulling back said, "I know what I'd like to do. I'll check out the ramparts. Walking the walls should give me a workout." Fine, that would keep him out of my hair while I shopped. There's nothing like a husband's surveillance to inhibit a wife's natural inclination to forage.

"Just be careful," I said. "I'm going to ask if Sister Glenda would like to join us."

"She's gone to take a nap. Did you see how much wine she drank at lunch? She sure can knock 'em back."

That brought a smile to my lips. "She's a good woman. Let her have her little pleasure."

"Right. So you go off with the girls and have a good time, and I'll do my own thing. How about meeting later at the café, around five?"

"Sounds good."

I was meeting the walkers at two in the front hall. That gave me time to look over our guidebook. Without shame, I tore out the map of the village, folded it neatly so it could be reinserted later, and put it in my jacket pocket along with the cell phone and a card on which I'd written the name of the hotel and its phone number. Always prepared for disaster.

Shelley was there when I arrived, both of us early. She was eager for the walk but not well dressed for it. Her stretch pants might do for a French woman, but French women keep themselves tautly thin, whereas Shelley was *bien en chair*. In France, this means well filled out. Over the tight pants, she wore a loose top with a boat neckline, and the boat was sinking. No jacket, no shawl. I barged in, as is my failing.

"You might want something to put on later. They say it gets cool in the afternoon."

Shelley gave me an appraising look, taking in my worn Nikes, my roomy sweatpants, and their matching zip-up jacket. "I never feel the cold," she said. "I guess I'm warm-blooded."

"I like your top," I said (realizing too late the double entendre). I did like the pattern. The front was printed with an Andy Warhol Campbell Soup can, and as Shelley turned around so I could get a look at the back, there was his multicolored image of Marilyn Monroe. Her fashion idol? As she turned back to face me, her Marilyn moue gave the answer. With her thick strawberry-blonde hair and her straining-at-the-seams pants, Shelley did approximate the look of the later Monroe.

Angie and Maggie came sprinting down the hall together. Emmet trotted happily after them.

"Ohn-ee-vah!" said Angie, putting on her baseball cap.

Maggie laughed and said, "Where did you pick that up?"

"Roe-bare says it means 'let's go.'"

"And who is Roe-bare?" Maggie asked.

"Guess," I said, giving her a knowing look.

"Oho! The game's afoot," Maggie replied.

"What game?" Angie asked.

Maggie waved her off. "Okay, then, *on y va!*"

Women walkers inevitably pair off. You can't carry on a good conversation walking three or four abreast. In Saint-Paul, the alleyways they call *chemins* can hardly fit one. Maggie and Angie wanted to walk together. By default, Shelley and I became companions.

I started with a typical opener between Americans: "So what do you do?" In France it's considered rude to ask someone's profession, because the answer might suggest class distinctions. ("I deliver pizzas. How about you?" "Oh, I deliver talks at international conferences.") So the French, perhaps wisely, don't ask. But we do.

"I'm in art too in a way," Shelley replied. "I'm a framer."

"Do you work on your own?"

"I have a shop, a small one. Since my dad died, it's just been me and, if I'm lucky, an intern from one of the local schools. I used to do more business before South Street gentrified. A lot of the artists have moved away."

"So who's your client base?"

"Interior decorators and people reframing old paintings or prints, or wanting frames for photos—most of them from Society Hill just north of South Street. But some of the young artists come to me for quality work at low prices."

It turned out Shelley had done work for a friend of mine who teaches in the art department at Penn. She framed the paintings for one of Sally's shows. Sally's niche is painting spoofs. They're funny, and yet they give you a fresh take on the artists she's sending up. We started talking about Sally's work, and that led to comparing our reactions to other painters who do the mockery-homage thing. We found we both like Pol Bury's crazy blurred versions of Renaissance portraits.

"Did you notice that Bury at the Maeght?" she asked.

"No. Where is it?"

"In the front garden. It's a fabulous stainless steel sculpture. It's opposite the fountain with the green men. Everybody looked at the green men pissing and walked right by the Bury."

Smart too. Quite a combo, Shelley was.

We were already through the gates and facing the tourist office, so we went in. The first item we were given was a detailed map of the town. I hadn't needed to mutilate the guidebook, after all. We decided to ditch the culture and attend to the shopping, which would have been difficult to ignore. As we climbed the narrow walkway between tall houses connected wall to wall, we saw that most of them had been made into shops on the ground floor, and almost all were open. They had looked closed the night before, but that was because of shuttering. In Provence, houses have shutters heavy enough to deflect sun, wind, and rain. When you close them at night, your place looks like it's been boarded up for months. Now doors and windows were open and attractive wares were displayed on stoops outside.

We popped into stores selling olive oil, nougat candy, dolls, leather bags, clothing, and lavender sachets and soaps. Emmet poked his nose in every doorway. When Angie wanted to try on a peasant skirt and Maggie didn't, we switched partners. Shelley and Angie remained in the clothing boutique while Maggie and I walked up the path. We had set a rendezvous at the Café de la Place.

When Maggie and I reached the square with the Grecian fountain, we couldn't help circling it. We didn't need to talk about it. We just looked. There were three colors of stone, I could see now. The pointed cap of the urn was white, obviously restored. The rest of the urn was a sad gray. I stared at the basin in which Isabelle's body had been half submerged, listening to my heartbeat. Emmet tried to lift his leg, but Maggie nudged him away. She consulted the map. "It's just called the Grand Fountain," she said. She shook her shoulders in an exaggerated shudder.

We left the fountain behind us, continuing along the Grande Rue to the far end of the village, where a little cemetery is located outside the walls. Before passing through the gate, we climbed to a lookout with a panoramic view of the sea and the city of Nice. I turned further toward the left and saw the Alps in the distance. The clarity of the light enhanced the feeling of openness. I didn't want to leave. But when a squabbling family approached the lookout, I descended and followed Maggie through a gate and into the little graveyard. It was like any other French cemetery, apart from the view and the fact that it held Marc Chagall's grave. We soon found it, an unassuming slab. Visitors had left pebbles on the marker, a traditional sign of remembrance at Jewish graves. Some people, unsure of the tradition, had left coins. Maggie and I added pebbles of our own. Emmet found a shrub and registered his visit his way.

We headed back to the town gate by walking along the exterior base of the massive walls. I kept my eye out for Toby, but he must have been on the other side of town, unless he'd finished his walk already. Maggie and I didn't talk as we retraced our steps to where we'd started. I liked that she knew when to be quiet—Toby has that gift too. Not many do.

At the Café de la Place, we drank hot chocolate on the terrace and watched the boules match in front of the café. Old men, cigarettes dangling from their lips, were lobbing metal balls at a small wooden ball. The object of the contest is to get as close to the target ball as possible and to knock your opponent's ball out of the way. The heavy balls fell with satisfying thuds, startling Emmet. This was once the best-known boules court in the world. In its heyday you might find Yves Montand or Picasso playing here. We had ringside seats and were watching two old-timers with rolled-up sleeves disputing a call when Shelley and Angie arrived to join us.

Angie couldn't wait to tell us about the gallery that had a life-size painting of the Mona Lisa with real silver earrings pinned right through the canvas onto the famous lady's earlobes. Shelley said, "I call it 'The Desecration of the Virgin.'" She grinned at Maggie. "What are you drinking?"

"Hot chocolate," replied Maggie, raising her cup.

"Nuts to that," said Shelley. "We're in France. I'll be back." She went inside and returned a few minutes later carrying two glasses of white wine, one of which she placed in front of Angie. She sat down, put her own glass to her lips, and closed her eyes. "Mmm, that's good. For your information, ladies, there's a one-person women's room and a one-person men's room and both are open."

It had been a long walk, with hot chocolate on top of it. Maggie and Angie rose as one, so I was left holding Emmet's leash (and my water) and talking to Shelley.

"So, tell me how you got into framing," I said, resuming our earlier conversation.

"There's not much to tell. I was born in South Philly and I've never left, which is fine with me. I went to Temple for a while, but I didn't like it, so I went to work for my father."

"Are you ever sorry you didn't take the academic route, like Ben? You're pretty sharp about art."

"Are you kidding? When I see what Ben goes through at Drexel—the fifteen-hour days teaching and doing research and writing. The stupid department meetings. The agony of coming up for tenure. Then there's the pressure to go for full professor. Ben's been associate for ages, and he's a wreck trying to finish his biography of Van Gogh. He needs it to get promoted."

"I thought it was going to be published in the fall."

"It *could* be published in the fall, but not if he keeps pulling it back the way he's done."

"Why did he pull it back?"

"The first time was when that new biography came out and got all that attention by saying that Van Gogh was murdered. He had to deal with that, he said. Then a few weeks ago, when he heard about Madame La Font, he did it again. He'll have to deal with *that* now, he says."

"Maybe not. There won't be a talk."

"We'll see. I don't think he's had a single article published that he didn't pull back at least once. He's such a nitpicker. All those university people are. It makes me nervous just to be around them."

"I can relate to that," I said. "It makes me nervous to be around myself."

"I didn't mean you. But some of the others. That nutcase Bruce Curry, for one, going postal about some dried flowers. Give me a break."

I held my tongue. You don't run down colleagues when you're at a conference. I was glad to see Angie and Maggie returning from the bathroom. My turn.

When I came back, Toby was at the table, guzzling a glass of beer. He was exhilarated from his march atop the ramparts.

"You mean you actually climbed up there?" asked Maggie. She and I had reached the lookout next to the top of the wall. When I saw how narrow that wall was, I thought, "Discretion is the better part of valor." But not my guy.

"I sure did," he said. "The top of the wall is solid all around the village. You have to watch your feet, but you stop every once in a while to catch the views. They're fantastic. On one side of town you can see the Alps and on the other side the Mediterranean."

"But wasn't it risky?" asked Maggie. I had decided to keep mum.

"I was careful. There's a guard wall about knee-high to keep you from falling down the cliff. None on the inside, though. I felt like a sentry in the Middle Ages. It would be fun to do it at night." Yeah, right.

We continued chatting until the dispute grew louder between the two grizzled players who were pacing back and forth over the court and gesticulating about measurements of distance.

"*Mais, non!*" said one.

"*Mais, oui!*" said the other.

"*Mais, non!*"

"*Mais, oui!*"

I laughed. And shivered at the same time. It was still light enough for the match to continue, but it was getting cold. Toby noticed. He took a final gulp from his glass, slapped his thighs, and pushed his chair back from the table.

"Ohn-ee-vah!" said Angie.

At dinner at the hotel that evening Toby and I shared a table with Shelley and her husband. The Bennetts struck me as a mismatched pair. While Shelley was bursting with vitality, Ben looked drawn, with dark smudges under his eyes. He was of average height but meanly thin. With a few more pounds on him he might have been handsome. Fine, straight bones gave him a patrician air. He wore a rumpled blue blazer over an open-collared white shirt. The outfit made him look like a runaway from prep school—a scrawny, exhausted runaway. Talking about his subject, though, he came to life. Then he had a certain nervous energy that was attractive.

"I guess you're the person to ask," said Toby. "What's all this about Van Gogh being murdered? I thought he committed suicide."

"He did, in my opinion," Ben said after a moment. He was too fastidious to talk while he was chewing. The dinner was *steak-frites*, which in France means stringy, tough steak and French fries so perfect that you forget the meat's failings. "The sensational claims made by Naifeh and Smith don't hold up. Have you read their biography?"

Toby said no. I was in the middle of it: *Van Gogh: The Life*, by Steven Naifeh and Gregory White Smith. It's a long book, very well written. I had planned to finish it before the conference, but with one thing and another, including writing my own paper, I didn't. Of course, I'd read reviews.

"My talk is a rebuttal," Ben continued. "And when my own biography comes out, I'll spell out what's wrong with theirs in detail."

"Can you give us the basics?" Toby asked. "First of all, what makes them think he didn't commit suicide?"

Ben dabbed at his lips with his napkin. "We don't know the details of what happened. But Naifeh and Smith don't build a convincing case in filling in the gaps, and they leap to a far-fetched conclusion."

"What sort of gaps?"

"All right," said Ben, laying down his knife and fork. "I'll give you the short version, starting with what we do know and working from there." He straightened up in his chair. "At the time of his death, Vincent was living in Auvers-sur-Oise, just north of Paris. This was just after he was released from the asylum in Saint-Rémy. Theo van Gogh had arranged for Dr. Gachet to look after his brother. The doctor was supposed to be an expert on treating mental disorders, and he was friendly with a lot of artists. In fact, it was Pissarro who recommended him to Theo." Ben paused to sip his wine.

"So Vincent was living in this little room in the town inn. Every morning he'd leave with his painting equipment and go off to paint somewhere. He'd return for lunch and then go out again in the afternoon and return for dinner. He was unbelievably prolific that summer. He often finished a painting in a single day."

Ben's voice grew animated. "On this particular day, he didn't return for dinner. And as the hours went by, the people who ran the inn began to worry. Finally, long after suppertime, he staggered in, clutching his side. 'What happened?' the innkeeper asked. 'I wounded myself,' Vincent said, or words to that effect. We know that much from the innkeeper's daughter, who recounted the story years later. She told slightly different versions of that story as time went on, and there's some question as to her reliability, but let's leave that aside."

Toby had stopped eating. He sat still, riveted by the tale.

Ben continued: "So of course they sent for the doctor. Gachet rushed to the inn and brought a colleague with him. The doctors examined Vincent and found a bullet wound. They saw that his condition was serious and there was nothing they could do for him." Ben pushed his plate aside.

"Then they sent for Theo, who was in Paris. He arrived in time to comfort his dying brother. He kept vigil by Vincent's bedside until the end. The police also arrived and interviewed Vincent to see if a crime had been committed. But they concluded, as did everyone else, that Van Gogh had shot himself. At the time of his death, he was thirty-seven years old. And that's about as much as we know for sure." Bennett reached for his glass and swallowed some more wine. Though he was driven to talk, it seemed to be tiring him. He looked almost consumptive.

"What a desperately sad end," I said. "And dramatic. You told the story well."

"That's my job, remember. I'm a biographer."

Shelley had been fidgeting while her husband held forth. Of course, she'd heard this before. "You don't have to give the whole lecture," she said. "We're having dinner."

Ben looked at his discarded plate and kept his eyes there.

"No, please continue," Toby urged. "Because I don't see where the mystery's involved. The way you tell it, it's an open and shut case for suicide. Besides, everyone knows that Van Gogh had mental problems."

Ben glanced sideways at Shelley, like a whipped dog.

"Okay, don't mind me," she said, making a show of cutting her meat.

"As I was saying," Ben resumed, looking pained, "there's a lot we don't know. For example, where did Vincent get the gun? And then what happened to it? It was never found, even though the police did a thorough search for it. What's more, they couldn't find his easel and painting equipment, which he had with him that day. Who took them? Exactly what happened during the five or six hours between the time Vincent left the inn and when he came back? And why did he return and ask for help, if he had meant to kill himself?"

"Did he leave a suicide note?" Toby asked.

"No. And you'd think he would, for someone who was such a great letter writer."

That struck me as true. I'd read the moving collection of the letters Vincent wrote to Theo. Vincent was a passionate correspondent.

"Should I go on?" The remains of Ben's meal were congealing on his plate. There were equal portions of gristle and uneaten meat.

"Absolutely. Don't stop now," said Toby.

"Okay. So those are some of the unanswered questions. And along come Naifeh and Smith with their theory, and it answers all those questions, except it relies on a completely hypothetical reconstruction of events."

"A story about some teenage boys," I said, having gathered as much from the reviews.

"Yes. Naifeh and Smith dug up an obscure article in a French medical journal from the 1950s written by a doctor named Doiteau. The doctor had come across an old man who had stories to tell about knowing Van Gogh sixty years earlier. That old man was René Secrétan. According to Doiteau, René Secrétan told him about the times he and his friends used to tease Van Gogh and make fun of him.

"That summer René ran around with a loaded pistol, which he used for target practice. He was a smart aleck and a show-off. And to make a long story short"—here Ben glared at Shelley—"Naifeh and Smith think the kid shot Van Gogh during some kind of prank or maybe by accident."

"Really?" said Toby. "Did the old man confess?"

"No, he didn't. He did suggest that Van Gogh stole the gun from his bag when he wasn't looking. But he also said that he and his family had left town several weeks before the shooting."

"What do Naifeh and Smith say about that?"

"They say you have to read between the lines. They think the old man came forward to give the interview because he had a guilty conscience and wanted to clear it before he died, but at the same time he was trying to cover up his involvement. The problem with all this is that their theory is complete speculation. There's no hard evidence to support any of it."

Toby looked perplexed. "Even if that's what happened, why would Vincent keep quiet about it when he got back to the inn? Why would he take the blame if some kid shot him?"

"Ah. That's the beauty of pure speculation. If you ask me, the authors have to twist their argument like a pretzel to fit the facts. What they come up with is that Vincent didn't have the nerve to commit suicide even though he longed for death, so he decided not to blame the boy who shot him. Instead, he covered it up. Now, how convincing does that sound to you?"

"Not very," Toby admitted. "But it sure makes a good story."

"A good story? I don't deny it. But we're supposed to be biographers, not novelists. A novelist can make up anything he wants. But damn it—a biographer is supposed to tell the truth!" Bennett banged his fist on the table. His plate shook.

Shelley jumped. "Don't do that, Ben. I hate it when you do that."

"Sorry," he said, but the apology was directed to us, and Shelley noticed. "Meanwhile they have a best seller," he grumbled.

I said, "And now a woman appears claiming to have information that will shed new light on the question, and she's found dead. What was Isabelle La Font going to tell us? Do you have any idea?"

"Unfortunately, no. She wouldn't let anything slip during the dinner. I tried to press her. And now of course . . ." He didn't have to finish the sentence.

"So you'll go ahead with publishing your biography?" I asked.

"There's no reason now for me to delay it. Naifeh and Smith made such a splash with theirs, I'll be lucky if I can get any reviewers to pay attention to mine. At least I'll set the record straight. And I'll have the last word, at least for now."

"And you're convinced he committed suicide," Toby stated.

"Yes. All the signs point to it."

"Ben," I said, "what if Isabelle had come up with information supporting the other theory?"

"That it was murder? Then I'd be screwed."

"On the other hand, she might have offered an entirely different version of events."

Ben looked at me warily. "I suppose so."

I hadn't noticed Montoni coming up to our table. "I'm sorry to interrupt," he said, "but this is serious. The police just phoned." He looked at me. "They want to talk to you tomorrow morning. To all of us, actually." His glance took in the table, then the room. "To everyone at the conference, I expect, but the lieutenant especially mentioned you, Nora. Why you, I don't know, but there's been a development."

An ominous word, that. I looked up at him.

"They think that Isabelle La Font was murdered," he explained.

Bennett went pale.

"How?" Toby asked.

"They say it was a fatal dose of digitalis."

The Secrétan brothers left Auvers around the middle of July. The family owned a villa in Normandy and spent part of the summer there each year. I never saw either one of them again.

With René gone, our group had no leader and soon fell apart. Without Gaston, Vincent had no companion left but me. Even before Gaston's departure, Vincent and I had become friendlier. He didn't mind me watching him paint, and I liked listening to him talk, though his thoughts were often gloomy or difficult for me to comprehend. One afternoon while we were lounging by the river and he was sketching a copse of trees on the opposite shore, he turned and asked me about my plans. Well, at that age, I had no plans. "What are your hopes?" he said. "What do you dream of doing in life?" I couldn't think what to say. I stammered.

"That will never do," he said. "Look here, you must find work for which you are suited. That's the important thing, Maurice." I must have looked hurt, because he softened his voice and said, "It's all right. There's still time. At least you are young, at least you are healthy." He continued sketching for a while. Then suddenly he threw down his brush and cried: "What might I have accomplished if I hadn't been ill!" He kicked over his paint box. After that he refused to say anything more. I was frightened, but I stayed. We sat together quietly, side by side, staring at the water until it was the dinner hour and I went home.

5

DIGITALIS. FOXGLOVE POISONING. By morning everyone knew it. We were expected at ten for questioning. As a result, the conference was put on hold. Lieutenant Auclair and her colleagues from Grasse would conduct the interviews, but to make the logistics easier, we were taken to the Gendarmerie of Vence, which was much closer to our hotel than Grasse. The shuttles dropped us off at 9:55.

The small waiting room was ringed by armless chairs, twelve as it turned out, one less than needed. Angie volunteered to stand, which gave her an opportunity to lean against Sergeant Navré's counter. His bearing was military, as befits a gendarme, but he couldn't help responding to her proximity. He stood up a bit straighter and smoothed his hair.

I was the first to be interviewed. Lieutenant Auclair opened the door to the back offices, called my name, and led me down a long corridor, to the last room. It was a cramped, windowless square with institutional furniture: a metal desk and swivel chair, metal files, a bookcase with stacks of paper on the shelves, a folding chair for the person being interviewed, an overhead fluorescent light—obviously an underling's office, borrowed for the purpose. But the lieutenant, today dressed in a crisp navy-blue suit, carried her authority with her, and I felt cowed as I took my seat. The back of my chair was jammed against one of the bookcases, and there was hardly space on the floor for my purse.

"Thank you for coming," she began. "May we speak French?"

"Yes," I said, "if you don't speak too fast."

"Naturally." She leaned back in her swivel chair and said, "Well, madame. I'd like to know the reason for the message you left on my answering machine." She rested her elbows on the arms of the chair and clasped her hands. "What made you think digitalis caused Madame La Font's death?" It wasn't an accusation but a neutral question; still, I realized I was on delicate ground.

"It's true, then?"

"Yes, it's true. We've checked with her doctor. She had no history of heart trouble, and she wasn't taking the drug by prescription. So it must have been administered without her knowledge."

She waited for an answer to her question: what was behind my phone call? It was just a hunch but I didn't know that word in French, so I settled for: "It was simply a guess."

"Indeed? What led you to make such a . . . guess?" She looked at me with the eyes of a fox. I wasn't a suspect, was I? Surely she realized that a guilty person wouldn't have made that phone call and left her name and number. Nevertheless, I was anxious. She could tell. "Take your time," she said.

What was behind my hunch? I wasn't entirely sure. I began by describing Bruce Curry's talk, his frantic announcement that the foxglove he had brought from England was missing, and his warning that the drug derived from it was dangerous. I remembered Isabelle becoming ill during dinner and wondered if there could be a connection. Curry's demeanor was strange, before, during, and after the talk. I described his outbreak of temper at lunch and his wife's concern about his recent state of mind.

"It seemed more than coincidence," I said. "An unexplained death. Curry telling us that Dr. Gachet poisoned Van Gogh with digitalis. The missing foxglove. But really it's all supposition. I have no right to accuse him."

Lieutenant Auclair came forward in her chair. "Did Professor Curry have any reason to harm Madame La Font?"

"Not that I know of."

"But you believe he may have poisoned her as a result of a mental disturbance?"

I didn't respond for a moment. "I regret that I suggested that. I have no evidence to support it."

"But that's what you were thinking at the time of your call."

"Something like that, or that someone might have taken the foxglove from his room without his knowledge."

"For use with criminal intent."

"Possibly, yes."

"Who else knew about the connection between foxglove and digitalis?"

"We all did. Everyone at the conference. It was the subject of Professor Curry's talk. I suppose most of us knew what foxglove was, even before the talk, because it appears in Van Gogh's portrait of Dr. Gachet." I described the well-known painting.

With her eyes on her hand, she slowly tapped her manicured nails on the desk. One, two, three. One, two, three. Then she raised her head. "Who else might have had a reason to harm Madame La Font?"

"No one, as far as I know."

The lieutenant consulted a notepad on her desk. "Madame La Font was seen in a discussion at the bar with someone before dinner on the night she was killed—her brother, Yves. Her half brother, it turns out. Do you know what they were arguing about?"

"No, only what Professor Montoni told us. He thought they were discussing her paper."

"Tell me what you know about it."

"Nothing, really."

"I've been told that Madame La Font planned to reveal facts about the death of Vincent van Gogh and that these facts had something to do with her grandfather."

"So I understand."

"And her brother was not pleased at the prospect?"

"Apparently not."

"Besides the brother, who else might want to suppress such information?"

"I've been thinking about that, Lieutenant, but without knowing what Madame La Font was going to reveal, there's no way of telling."

She leaned forward and folded her hands on the desk. "What about the biographer?" She glanced at her pad. "Professor Bennett? People said he questioned her all during dinner."

"That's true, he did. What Madame La Font planned to say had implications for his work. But her talk might have helped his argument as easily as harmed it. He didn't know what she was going to say."

"How do you know whether he did or not?"

"I don't," I had to admit. "But his curiosity about her paper seemed genuine. I don't think he knew the contents."

She held two fingers on her lips and then said, "Sometimes fear of the unknown can be a powerful motive."

True enough. Some scholars are so passionate about their work that they will go to any length to protect it—but to commit murder? That seemed unlikely to me. Besides, I'd already put my foot in it with conjectures about Curry. I didn't want to point the finger at another colleague. "You'll have to ask Professor Bennett about that," I said.

"I assure you we will."

"And the brother, Yves?"

"We're questioning him. Is there anyone else we should be looking at?"

"A thief, maybe. What if the motive was robbery? Her handbag was missing when we found her."

"Yes, but she wasn't attacked outdoors. There was no sign of external trauma. Her head was submerged in the fountain but there was no water in her lungs, so she didn't die of drowning. No. The poison was in the victim's system well before she left the restaurant. Foxglove leaves are deadly whether dried or fresh. They can be ground into a powder. The digitalis was probably introduced into her food in powdered form, perhaps in a drink."

"The dessert wine?"

"Most likely. A sweet wine such as Baumes-de-Venise would mask the taste. Unfortunately the glasses were washed before we had a chance to examine them."

"We all drank it, though."

"We recovered the bottle. It wasn't tampered with. Someone could have put the powder in her glass, enough to be deadly. Madame La Font became ill, left the restaurant to get some air, and collapsed outside." Lieutenant Auclair picked up a pad and pencil from the desk and handed them to me. "I'd like to confirm the seating arrangement at her table. Can you draw me a diagram?"

"I think so." I thought for a moment and then sketched a rectangular table with circles representing the figures sitting at it. "Professor Montoni was at one end of the table, here, and Jane Curry at the other. Isabelle La Font was to Montoni's right." I pointed. "Curry sat next to her, and Ben Bennett sat across from her. Ben's wife, Shelley, sat next to her husband, facing Curry. But it was a narrow table, and any one of them could have reached Isabelle's glass. Perhaps not Jane, at least not easily— she was at the far end."

Lieutenant Auclair studied my sketch. "I'm impressed. You have an excellent memory, Madame Barnes."

"But if the drug was put into Isabelle's wine," I added, "it also could have happened when she went up to the bar to talk to her brother during dessert. As I remember, she was carrying her glass."

Auclair made a note of that. "Who else was she in contact with during the meal?"

I reflected a moment. "Daniel Didier. She went over to his table to greet him. Apparently they knew each other."

"Was she carrying her glass?"

"I don't remember. But now that I think of it, once she came back to her table, several people passed behind her. They had to. Her chair was next to the stairs leading up to the *toilettes*."

"Can you recall anyone else who went up there?"

"Didier, for one. I remember particularly because I thought it odd that he didn't smile or look at her as he passed by. There were others too, but I can't remember who." I wasn't keeping score on bathroom trips.

"I see. Do you recall if anyone besides Yves La Font left the restaurant after Madame La Font went outside, that is, before her body was discovered?"

"I'm fairly certain no one did."

"And your husband was the first to reach her?"

"Yes. We all rushed out. Maggie—that is, Professor McBride—was the first one out the door. It was her dog that sounded the alarm. Then my husband ran out, and he was the one who reached the fountain first."

"How soon afterward did you arrive?"

"A few seconds later."

"And you noticed right away that her shoulder bag was missing."

"That's right."

"In that case, no one who was at the restaurant that night could have taken her bag. Is that so?"

"Except the brother."

"Yes, but besides him? I mean the members of your conference."

"I guess not. We all remained inside until the body was discovered. But what about a tourist? A passerby who took advantage of a sick woman and stole her bag?"

"Wandering tourists don't usually steal purses on impulse. And we don't have thieves prowling the streets of Saint-Paul-de-Vence, certainly not at this time of year. No, I think the murder and the theft are connected. Why? Because we know the poison was introduced in the restaurant, yet the purse was stolen outside. Yves La Font could have introduced the poison as well as stolen the purse. There remains one other possibility. Perhaps more than one person was involved—one outside the restaurant and one inside, that is, a person from your conference."

That made sense.

"And therefore, I'd like your help."

"My help?"

"Your sister mentioned to Sergeant Navré that you've had experience working with the police in the United States. Is that correct?"

"Well, yes," I answered, wondering where this was leading. "I've worked with the sheriff's office at home a few times, advising on matters relating to art crime." I'd been a consultant in cases of art theft and fraud, and recently I helped in the investigation of the murder of Toby's business partner, a crime that involved the theft of an icon. Still, I was uncomfortable. Those jobs had been more research than detective work. I didn't want Angie bragging that I was Sherlock Holmes.

"You see, Madame Barnes, you've been helpful already. Of course, we would have discovered the digitalis in the body, but you saved us some time. You're observant. All I'm asking is that you watch carefully during the remainder of your conference. You'll be attending the sessions. You're staying at the hotel with the others. Watch what the people around you do and say. If you notice anything unusual, let me know. I'd like to keep lines of communication open between us. That's all. It's nothing formal, but it would be useful to have someone like you on the scene. Will you do that?"

This was just what I didn't need, to be dragged into another murder case. I'd been looking forward to a little downtime. And how would my colleagues take it if they thought I was keeping an eye on them? Then again, how could I refuse? I was the one who had picked up the phone and called the lieutenant. "If you wish," I said. "I'll help if I can." *Moi* and my big mouth.

"*Bon.*" She stood up to shake hands.

On my way out of her office, I saw a grim-looking Yves La Font walking toward me. A gendarme was escorting him down the corridor. As we passed, the gendarme nodded but La Font ignored me. He kept his Gallic nose held high and gazed into the distance—which was only a matter of meters.

Some of the conferees and two worried-looking teenagers were packed into the waiting room. Angie was still standing at the reception desk with Sergeant Navré, chatting away. He was smiling mischievously. He touched his hand to his cap in mock salute as I walked up. "*Bonjour,* Madame Barnes. *Ça va?*" ("How goes it?") It was going swimmingly between the two of them by the looks of it. I returned the greeting and drew Angie aside.

"Angie, please don't tell tales about me to your new friend. He's passed them on to the lieutenant and now she's asked me to help them with their inquiries."

"What tales?"

"About me working with the sheriff's office at home. I'm here to do my work at the conference, and I was hoping to have a bit of vacation too."

"But you're really good at finding out stuff, and this is so exciting, isn't it? Roe-bare's been telling me all about how the police system works in France. It's really complicated."

"Never mind the system. Just don't talk about me without checking with me first, okay?"

"Sure, if that's how you feel. But I only meant it as a compliment," she said with widened eyes. "I'm proud of you."

That softened me up. "Well, I'm proud of you too. Have they questioned you yet?"

"Still waiting, but Sister Glenda and Toby are done. Do you mind if I get back to you in a sec? I was in the middle of something with Roe-bare."

She returned to the counter. I looked around the room. Toby and Maggie were talking quietly in a corner. The De Groots were whispering to each other in Dutch. Everybody else was reading, trying to ignore the situation. One of the teenagers rose to give me his seat. I took it gratefully; I'd used up a lot of energy in that interrogation room. I got out my Kindle and tried to concentrate on reading, but I couldn't help stealing glances at my sister and Sergeant Navré.

The day was nearly gone by the time we were released, but when the van rolled up to the hotel, Maggie proposed a walk. Sitting on a hard chair in a police waiting room had given me restless legs, so I literally jumped at the chance. So did Shelley, Jane, and Klara de Groot. We wanted a change from talk about murder. We leaped from our seats and within minutes had changed our shoes, grabbed fleeces, and bounced downstairs to meet outside the entrance.

When I got there, Jane Curry was telling the others about the foliage. Emmet was turning in circles with impatience. Maggie pushed his rear to the ground and told him to sit. Jane stood a few yards back from the front steps, looking up at the face of the hotel, where leafy vines streaked with magenta grew high enough to drape the portico. "Oh, yes, you'll see bougainvillea all over this region, even growing wild on the roadside," she explained in answer to a question from Shelley. "At this time of year, the blossoms give a nice show of color, but the flowering is thin compared to what it will be in spring." Small as she was, Jane had a strong presence when she was sharing her expertise.

Emmet was eager to go, pulling at his leash, but Maggie restrained him in deference to Jane. "And it's a shame we'll miss the wisteria," Jane continued. Despite the name of our hotel (Hotel des Glycines means Hotel Wisteria), it wasn't the season for them. Woody vines on the north side of the building were entirely bare. Jane walked to the wisteria vines, and we followed. "They're ugly in winter, aren't they? Someone was clever enough to compensate, though. See there." She pointed to below the clay roofline, where there was a painted strip, a repetitive pattern of purple swags of wisteria against a pale pink background.

"Isn't that clever? When the vines are bare, you can look up at the painted border to see what you're missing. But, Maggie, watch Emmet around the vines. Wisteria berries are poisonous."

"You must be joking. Those vines look like they're about to keel over themselves."

"Don't be fooled," Jane warned. "We see it fairly often back home. A cat or dog is found in the morning . . ."

"Dead?"

"Too often. If they're lucky, it's just an upset stomach. They eat the berries, sometimes when they're ripe on the vines in autumn, or in winter when they're dried and lying on the ground. Even two seeds can make your animal sick."

"Thanks for the warning. I'll keep my lad away from them." Maggie tugged on Emmet's leash and pulled him away from the wall.

"I had no idea the plant world could be so dangerous," I said. "Foxglove. Wisteria. What else should we be worried about?"

"If I see anything else along our walk, I'll point it out," said Jane.

Klara wanted to take a recommended path from Saint-Paul to a fifteenth-century chapel near Vence, but the sun was setting, and we didn't have more than an hour till dark. Klara looked athletic enough to complete the circuit in that amount of time, but it would take Shelley, Jane, and me much longer. Maybe Maggie could do it. Her well-worn walking boots belonged to a serious hiker. In deference to the less fit majority, we scaled back our mission. Taking a back trail to the village, we headed for the cemetery and Marc Chagall's grave. Though Maggie and I had seen it, the others had not. On the way, we passed olive trees, cypresses, and pines. Our mouths watered at fruit-burdened orange trees. The splashy mimosa, in tree and bush forms, astonished all but this California girl. (I have to admit, their pompom blossoms are extravagantly yellow.) Stone walls were dotted with winter roses. Gardens were hedged by bushes thick with berries. And all along the way, Jane kept up her running commentary on the flora.

She came to a halt as we approached a stand of blue flowers poking up from a cluster of bushes. "Now there's a really dangerous plant," she announced. "As pretty as it looks, it's one of the deadliest plants in the world. That's monkshood." Each bulbous flower, on its tall stem, resembled the cowl of a monk's robe as it swayed in the breeze. Jane grasped Maggie by the hand that held Emmet's leash and guided them both to the side of the trail farthest away from the wildflowers. "Don't let him near them. One touch could be the end of him. And if the poison gets into your system, it could be the end of you too."

"They look so innocent," protested Maggie.

"That's why they're so dangerous," said Jane. She stood still for a moment. "I was just thinking of Isabelle La Font. You know, the strangest thing is that monkshood almost always kills, but its antidote is digitalis. Isn't that odd? Foxglove and monkshood are both poisonous, yet one plant can save you from the other."

Klara observed, "There's a lot we don't know about drug interactions. Or doses. In the right dose, digitalis is beneficial for those who need it. In the wrong dose it's a poison. That's true of the world of chemicals in general. It's the basis of homeopathy. That's how Dr. Gachet was using foxglove. A small amount of a potentially harmful substance can be used for good."

"And the wrong amount for . . ."

"Evil," said Jane, finishing my sentence.

We were nearing the entry to the village, where the streets are narrow, so we paired off. I stayed with Jane, hoping to repair the damage of Toby's quarrel with her husband.

"How's Bruce doing?" I asked.

"Not so well. He was rattled by his interview with that detective."

"Nobody likes to be interviewed by the police. We all need a walk like this to renew our spirits."

"I'm afraid that won't do for Bruce. He broods about this sort of thing, and when he broods, he gets more and more distraught. That could make him look even more suspicious to the police. To tell you the truth, as worried as I am, I was glad to leave him to go walking. It doesn't help to talk with him when he's like this."

I tried to be comforting. "It'll come out all right."

"I hope so. It's about the bloody foxglove. I was the one who grew it for his talk. I never should have done it."

"Do you still think someone took it from your room?"

"I can't be sure. Bruce had nothing to do with harming anyone. I'm sure of that."

The walk up to the graveyard shuffled us, and I crossed through the gate with Klara. We were the first to reach the grave. Beneath Chagall's name on the gray slab of stone, someone had placed a red, glass-blown heart in homage. It hadn't been there yesterday.

"Someone who loves Chagall," I observed. "So do I. Do you?"

Klara shrugged indifferently. "I'm not that familiar with him. That's my husband's department."

"But you come to his conferences."

"And your husband comes to yours," she replied. "Does he always?"

"That depends on the location," I answered honestly. "We both like France, and Toby has an interest in art. You don't?"

She pursed her lips. "It's not at the top of my list. Van Gogh is the exception. In the Netherlands he's a national hero, you know." Klara pronounced the name as "Van Goch," or something like that, instead of using the French or American pronunciation of "Van Go."

"As well he should be," I said.

"Not that Hans attends any of my conferences," she continued, with a sour smile. "The difference is, I can follow a paper on art, but he can't follow a paper on chemistry. In any case, he doesn't like to travel alone."

"Neither do I," I admitted. "I'd much rather have Toby with me." We started to walk back. "Do you go to a lot of chemistry conferences?"

"I have to choose carefully, or I would never get my own work done. But yes. I have a talk to give next month in Tokyo."

"And you'll go by yourself?"

"Unlike my husband, I don't mind. In fact, I rather enjoy being by myself." She strode ahead of me briskly, as if bored by the conversation. I didn't try to keep up.

We returned to the hotel under dim light, realizing we were late for dinner. Rather than miss a course, we decided to defy dress codes and dine in our hiking clothes. Entering the dining room, I saw Professor Curry towering over a seated Sister Glenda and pushing his finger into her breastbone. She was leaning back, protesting, "I did not! You're mistaken."

Emmet ran up, yipped, and started jumping on Curry. Toby, who'd been sitting with Sister Glenda and Angie, rose to his feet, as Jane rushed to her husband's side. She pulled at his arm. "Bruce, stop! What's going on?"

"You know what's going on," answered Curry, glaring at Sister Glenda. To Toby he said, "You and this nun turned the detectives against me, blaming me for the foxglove. So what if I brought it to France? I lost it—I didn't *use* it. Not to kill that woman. Somebody stole it from me."

"I didn't say you killed anyone," said Toby.

"Neither did I," said Glenda, adjusting her posture now that Curry had backed off.

Curry turned on me. "Then it was you. You told the police about the foxglove, didn't you? You did, didn't you?" He lunged at me, but Toby cut him off, pinning his arms to his side. Emmet jumped left and right, first scratching at Curry's shins, then at Toby's.

"Stop it! Stop it!" cried Jane.

"Let me go!" yelled Curry.

"I will if you promise to calm down," said Toby. "Nobody's accusing you of anything, okay? Will you try to get hold of yourself?"

"Let me go, damn it."

"I'm going to, all right? Just say that you'll stop swinging."

Curry grunted.

"All right?" said Toby.

I moved away. Maggie got control of Emmet.

Toby counted to three, then opened his arms and stepped back out of range. Curry slumped down on a chair. Jane put her arms around his shoulders and pleaded with him in a low voice. "Come away," she said. "Let's go upstairs, Bruce. Please, dear. Come away."

The room had fallen silent. It stayed that way until the Currys reached the stairs.

Hours could pass without us talking. He would paint, I would watch. I didn't know anyone could paint so fast. Vincent could begin a painting in the morning and finish it in the afternoon. During that summer he made sketches of all of us and several paintings too. I recall one painting he did of René before he left town, showing him in a red jacket while he was fishing from a small boat. The jacket belonged to me. Vincent insisted René should wear it because he refused to paint him in his cowboy outfit, which Vincent detested. When the girls came up from Paris that time, he painted them sitting on the riverbank, one of them next to me. René used that painting for target practice, though Vincent never knew that. What became of the others, I don't know. Except for the last one he ever painted. What became of that one I know all too well.

6

DANIEL DIDIER AND JACQUES GODARD were presenters the next morning. When Angie heard their talks would be in French, she dropped out in favor of shopping. Toby decided this was his morning to play boules. I must say, I also had some apprehension about the talks. Their topics were heavily theoretical. Didier's title was "The Self under Erasure: The Disappearance of the Ear in Van Gogh's Self-Portraits." Godard's paper was called "In-Self and For-Self in Van Gogh's Self-Portraits: A Dialogue with Daniel Didier." Godard and Didier often gave papers in tandem, leaving the impression they were talking to themselves.

"I call them Gogo and Didi," Maggie confided, as we were taking our seats. "They talk and talk, but nothing ever happens." She touched her heart in a gesture of mock contrition. "Aren't I awful?"

They seemed an odd pair. Didier was sixtyish, tall, and slender, with a full head of dark hair. In his Italian-styled suit, he was nothing short of dashing. Godard was smaller, younger, stooped, and balding. Up-to-the-second red-rimmed glasses called attention to a florid complexion. A brown cashmere sweater sagged over his hollow chest.

I found my mind wandering soon after Didier began his talk. I recalled that awkward moment in the restaurant when Isabelle approached his table and bent down for a kiss. What had been the reason for his cool response?

After an hour, when Didier showed no sign of concluding, Maggie leaned toward me and moaned, "He can't go on. He must go on. He goes on." When we were mercifully released for a coffee break, she asked me, "How much of that did you get?"

"I got the words, but the sentences flew into the ether."

"I believe that's the point. The imagery was colorful. But there were a bit too many disappearances and reappearances, didn't you think? For a while there I thought I was at a séance." I glanced around for eavesdroppers, but people were focused on the coffee.

We took our seats, and Maggie was at it again. "Theorists," she complained. "And here comes the other one."

We sat patiently as Jacques Godard repeated much of what Didier had said, a little more softly. That seemed to be the essence of Jacques. He was the lesser Didier. Less clever, less emphatic, and, blessedly, less long-winded.

Didier had arranged for one of his graduate students to be installed on the program as a commentator. This was the only session that had one. The young man's name was Thierry Toussaint. He spoke in English, which gave me hope I'd get a grasp on the previous two talks. In a high-pitched voice, he lauded his mentors and rehashed their papers, claiming that their dialogue shed light on a point that someone I'd never heard of had made about something complex. The obfuscation part he got down pat. This was Toussaint's professional debut and surely would be listed on his résumé. He seemed a decent enough sort, good-looking too. Godspeed, I thought. These days it was tough to land an academic job.

I gave him kudos when I saw how deftly he managed the question period. He had a knack for shutting down a questioner's diatribe by nodding vigorously and then pointing to Didier, who was always glad to take the floor. When Didier had worn out the audience, Toussaint would look to Godard and ask, "But Jacques, are you in accord?"

The questions began to clarify the talk for me, but I noticed they were getting sharper. The room began to buzz when Professor Curry started in on Didier, accusing him of hiding a flimsy argument under a scaffolding of critical jargon. It was just as well that Toby wasn't there to fuel his irritation. Ray Montoni popped from his front-row seat and announced that time was up. "The shuttles are waiting, people. You'll have plenty of time to talk with Daniel and Jacques over lunch."

Maggie leaned toward me and said, "I think I'll call him Theory-Thierry."

"Come on," I said. "I like him. He started out bowing and scraping, but when he took over as moderator, he stood up to Didier and let the room take him down. You could see the kid coming into his own, right before your eyes."

"He's not such a kid," said Maggie. "Let me have him for one night and he'll be all grown up, with a voice an octave lower."

"Let's duck down to the women's room," I said. I wanted to get Maggie away from the others, since she was in such a provocative mood. But she kept up the patter, even between stalls.

There was time before lunch to go up to our rooms, and I found Toby in ours, bundling up jackets and sweaters. "Hey, how was your morning?" he asked.

"Middling. You and Angie made the right decision."

"Well, I hope you like our next decision. We're skipping today's excursion. We're going to drive the Grande Corniche."

"You and Angie?"

"You're coming too."

"But I want to see the Chagall Museum. Don't you?"

"We can see it after the conference is over. That's what our extra week is for."

"What about lunch?"

"We'll stay for lunch, then take the van with the others to Nice. I was going to pick up the car in Nice on Monday. We'll just get it a few days early. Then it's off to the cliff road and a bird's-eye view of the Riviera."

"We'll have to rush. It gets dark early."

"We can do it. When the sun goes down we'll find a restaurant by the water, have a good meal, and get back here before bedtime."

That sounded great, but I was worried about my paper. "I hope so. I'm giving my talk in the morning."

"How 'bout if I get you back by ten?"

I signed up. We knocked on Angie's door, heard she'd convinced Glenda to join us, and hurried down to the dining room. I looked around for Maggie, and, wouldn't you know, she had pulled up a chair next to Theory-Thierry. Who knows what she might have gotten up to if Sister Glenda, with Angie in tow, hadn't put herself right opposite them. Mother superiors have instincts about that sort of thing.

In the shuffle of seating, Toby and I joined Jacques Godard for lunch. His soft-spoken manner played better at our table than it had at the Maeght lectern. We started with small talk about Toulouse, where he was a lecturer, and Bergerac, where he was born. Toby told him about our trip from Bordeaux to the Dordogne Valley a few years back. All the while I was looking for a chance to ask him about Didier. If anyone here knew what Didier's relationship was to Isabelle La Font, it was Jacques.

I made a few obligatory remarks about his paper, then asked about his work with Didier.

"You know, the world of art criticism is very small in France. Everyone knows everyone. The graduates of Paris stick together. Daniel and I share the fate of being 'provincial.' Until recently, the universities of

Bordeaux and Toulouse were beneath notice by the Parisian elite. At any rate, Daniel and I are close geographically, and that allows us to meet often."

"And of course you share an interest in theory."

"Yes. So you see, working together makes up for the lack of a thick network of colleagues. We've published two books together."

"And you've known each other long?"

"Let me see. It must be twenty years."

From there, it took twists and turns to get to Didier's link with Isabelle La Font. By the end of lunch, I knew that when Didier was starting his graduate studies at Bordeaux, Isabelle was interning there as a nurse. They met by chance at the Musée des Beaux-Arts and began a relationship.

"Daniel always remained very fond of Isabelle," said Jacques. "He could hardly sleep the night she was killed. I didn't get much sleep that night either."

"That's understandable," I said. But then I pried on. "Did he know she was going to be at the conference?"

"Yes, we talked about her on the way here. He was concerned about how they'd get on, I think, after all these years."

"What happened between them?" asked Toby. "Why didn't they stay together?"

"It ended," said Jacques simply, with a Gallic shrug. "These things happen. All I know is she moved away. Then she became involved with someone else, and so did he. Daniel said they wrote to each other for a while but never saw each other after that."

"Was Isabelle married?" I asked.

"Daniel said she wasn't. I believe it all had to do with this man she was involved with. He was married. And Daniel stayed single too."

"It must be awful for your friend," I said. "I mean, seeing Isabelle again after such a long time and then dealing with the shock of her murder." Awful, I thought, if he still had feelings for her. What if those feelings had turned to resentment? What then?

"Yes, awful." Godard fell silent, studying his glass of wine. He picked it up and drained it.

The half-hour drive from Saint-Paul to Nice wasn't particularly scenic until the city itself came into view, with its pastel-colored buildings gleaming in the sun and an azure sea lapping its shoreline. While Toby attended to renting the car, Glenda gave Angie and me a flash tour of the seafront. As we strode along the Promenade des Anglais, past belle epoque hotels and palm trees swaying in the breeze, she told us the history of the English Walkway and the story of how the Bay of Angels got its name. The Promenade was named for the English tourists who popularized Nice as a winter destination in Victorian times. As for the bay, according to Glenda, Saint Reparata, a Christian virgin in third-century Palestine, refused to renounce her faith and was beheaded. Her body was placed in a boat and wafted on the breath of angels to the bay of Nice. The city was so honored that it made Reparata its patron saint and christened its waters the Bay of Angels.

The beach, though, was more the Devil's work, at least for any sunbather with tender skin. "There's no sand," complained Angie. "It's nothing but rocks." She was right. The beach of Nice is covered with gray pebbles. But the wide sweep of the bay lifts the spirits.

For a glimpse of the old city, Sister Glenda whisked us across the street to the flower market in the Cours Saleya and then on to the Place Masséna. There, in the vast square surrounded by arcades and rusty-red Italianate mansions, we met Toby and hurried to reach the car before the meter ran out.

Our plan for what remained of the day was to see a stretch of the eastern Riviera from the heights of the famous corniches (cliff roads), but not from the most famous of the three, the Grande Corniche. We didn't have time to complete the treacherous mountain route before sunset. But we could take the Middle Corniche to Monte Carlo and return on the Low Corniche along the coast.

Toby was disappointed about missing his chance to careen around the Grande Corniche like Cary Grant with Grace Kelly in *To Catch a Thief.*

"Grace Kelly met her death on the Middle Corniche," said Glenda. "Drove right over the retaining wall and down the slope."

Angie said, "I guess that will be dangerous enough for us."

It was. Just dangerous enough to be exciting, with vistas that made you feel you'd entered heaven. Even in the silvery light of a December afternoon, the sea was dazzling. The towns, some hanging off cliffs, others nestled low along the shore, had the flat colors of Cezanne—the sandy orange of roof tiles, the olive green of winter trees, and the teal of palms and shrubs.

The way back on the Low Corniche took us through peaceful seaside villages. Hardy flowers spilled out of stone tubs and clay pots. Buildings glowed with washes of pink, or red, or white. The towns seemed timeless. They'd been visited by Roman sailors, settled by peoples who would later be called Italian or French, conquered by this duke and retaken by that one, accumulating architectural features, religious customs, and favorite foods from each.

When the sun was low on the horizon, it was time to choose a place for dinner. It seemed sensible to pick the last port before Nice, and right on schedule, we left Saint-Jean-Cap-Ferrat with its euro-millionaire mansions and entered Villefranche at twilight. Of all the ports along the Riviera, Villefranche-sur-Mer may be the prettiest. With its salmon-colored houses stacked above the harbor, its brightly painted fishing boats bobbing at their moorings, its cobblestone streets and cheerful restaurants crowding the waterfront, it's postcard perfect.

We entered the town high above the harbor, but without the car's navigation system we never would have found the port. Over millennia, Villefranche has been built up in tiers cut into a high cliff. At the bottom is the original settlement. Slanted into the cliff are mansions with wide stone balconies, as well as apartments sheathed in metal and glass. The hill is too steep for a street to run straight from the top to the bottom. Instead, the road slides along the cliff, then takes a sharp turn and sinks to the next level, then the next, and keeps zigzagging without an obvious plan. If you try to follow your nose to the port, you'll get lost. But with the aid of the GPS, we eventually found the parking lot by the Citadel and embarked on our search for a meal.

We walked the length of the quay, checking out menus posted in display cases in front of each restaurant. We picked the most appealing and made a reservation for 7:00 p.m. (19:00 in French time), which is the earliest a respectable French restaurant opens its doors. That gave us an hour at liberty. A drink before dinner seemed a pleasant way to fill the gap. We retraced our steps and picked the Cosmo, a café and brasserie with a glass front. The clients had a view of the port, and the passersby had a view of the clients. Even midweek on a cool winter's evening, the place was filled with locals—middle-aged women drinking coffee with their daughters, workmen ending the day at the bar with a pastis, lovers touching hands and forgetting to sip their wine.

We went in and grabbed the first vacated seats, trading off a dirty table for a great window view, looking out at the dock. As my eyes adjusted to the low light of the interior, I took in the other patrons—and was startled to see Yves La Font sitting with a man wearing a worker's cap. A carafe of red wine, three-quarters empty, rested on the table between them. "Toby," I whispered, pointing to La Font.

"What?" Angie wanted to know.

I shushed her. "That's Yves La Font sitting in back over there, Isabelle's brother. He was arguing with her at the restaurant in Saint-Paul the night she was killed. Don't stare." She stared. Yves glanced in our direction. "Don't call attention to us," I whispered.

Yves looked back at his companion and raised his glass to his lips.

"I don't think he recognized us," Toby said.

When a waiter came over, Angie and I ordered white wine, Toby asked for a Cinzano, and Glenda ordered Scotch. The drinks arrived and we turned our eyes on the water. By now it was dark outside.

Streetlights illuminated the port, and the lighthouse on the spit of Saint-Jean-Cap-Ferrat blinked on and off. Every so often I stole a glimpse toward the back of the room. "I'd love to know what they're talking about," I said to Toby.

"You'd be conspicuous if you got up. I'll go to the men's room and drift by them on the way back."

He returned a few minutes later. "I couldn't catch much, but La Font sounded peeved."

"What's the other guy like?"

"Rough-looking. A drinking buddy, I guess."

We learned nothing else before it was time for dinner. The brasserie was still crowded and Yves was still sitting with his friend when we left and walked to the restaurant.

La Grandmère Germaine had the reassuring air of a classic French bistro: crisp white tablecloths and sparkling cutlery, enticing aromas wafting from the kitchen, and a brace of hovering waiters, even though at this early hour we were the only diners. On the patron's advice, we paired goose-liver mousse with *vin doux naturel*—the poor man's Monbazillac. As soon as we put down our forks, a flutter of waiters arrived with our main course. Toby and had I ordered the sea bass grilled with fennel; it was delivered on a side table. With a flourish, the waiter lit the bass on fire—a douse of pastis and a flame, he explained. Sister Glenda's and Angie's tureen of bouillabaisse arrived in a haze of garlic. They were assured that the fish in the soup had been caught that very morning in the Villefranche bay.

Sister Glenda was telling Angie about the morning session and sharing her impressions of Thierry Toussaint. Angie had her head in her soup, but occasionally she nodded to indicate that she concurred with Glenda's assessment. "He's a bright young man," said Glenda. "He may be Professor Didier's protégé, but he's hardly a puppet. He hinted that Didier has never advanced beyond the heady days of *soixante-huit*."

I translated for Angie: "*Soixante-huit* means 1968, the year when students protested in Paris and the revolution of the sixties began." I turned to Glenda. "So you think Thierry realizes that Didier never got beyond poststructuralism?"

"What's poststructuralism?" asked Angie.

"Let me guess," said Toby. "It's what came after structuralism."

"What's structuralism?" asked Angie.

"Ask your sister," said Toby.

"Never mind," said Glenda. "The point is that Didier used to be at the cutting edge of his field but he isn't anymore."

I scraped my plate for the final few flakes of sea bass. "You don't think that Thierry will suffer from being Didier's student?"

"Not necessarily. Didier made his reputation decades ago, but all it takes is a recognizable name like his to make a university notice his student's job application."

Angie wiped her pretty mouth and interjected, "But if Didier's old-fashioned, won't that be bad for Thierry?"

"Look at me," said Sister Glenda. "I'm as old-fashioned as they come. The difference is that in my world, beliefs don't go out of style. Besides, it's up to Thierry. If he's got what it takes, he'll learn all he can from his mentor. Then he'll become his own man."

I had the impression that Sister Glenda wasn't talking only about Thierry. She was also saying something she wanted Angie to hear about their relationship.

For dessert Angie chose a sorbet perfumed with roses, Toby a cup of berries tossed with candied sage. Glenda and I shared a Soufflé Grand Marnier. Dramatic, caloric, and scrumptious. Toby ordered coffee but ignored the chocolates that came with it. They didn't go to waste.

By the time we were ready to leave, the restaurant had filled up. On our way to the car we had to pass the Cosmo, and out of curiosity, I looked through the window to see if Yves was still inside. He was, but now he was sitting with someone else, and that brought me to a halt. "Toby, look!"

"Daniel Didier. What's he doing there?"

Yves and Didier were hunched over a table in close conversation, and both were scowling. Apparently their voices were raised, for though I couldn't hear them outside, people at nearby tables were frowning in their direction.

As we watched through the window, Yves pushed his chair back and stood up—and so did Didier. But as Didier got to his feet, Yves shoved him, hard enough to send him backward, crashing into another table. Didier said something to the man he banged into and drew himself up. Yves took a menacing step toward Didier, and that brought the bartender out from behind the counter to separate them. Instantly the big, burly bartender had one palm on Didier's chest and one palm on Yves's, pushing them away from each other. Didier raised his hands in surrender.

Yves shoved the bartender's restraining hand away from his chest. And just as he did so, Didier saw an opening and threw a punch at Yves that glanced off his cheek. Then the bar erupted. For a minute it looked like a rugby huddle. Soon several men plus the bartender were pushing the combatants out the door. Didier tumbled to the pavement right in front of us. Yves reeled but kept to his feet, as did a third man. I recognized him as the one Yves was drinking with earlier.

"Go home, all of you!" shouted the bartender. "Or I'll call the police."

Yves said something defiant. The third man looked sullen. Didier got to his feet and started straightening his clothes.

"Are you all right?" Toby asked him. Didier seemed at first not to recognize Toby. Then he nodded and said, "*Ça va.*" His hands hung at his sides.

The three men, none of them young, were breathing heavily. "Go home," the bartender said again. He turned and went inside.

Didier started walking down the middle of the street. Yves and his drinking buddy hung back near the entrance to the café. They eyed us resentfully.

"Looks like it's over," said Toby, watching Didier walk away. "I guess we should get on home. Why don't you go to the car? I'll keep an eye on things here for a minute."

Glenda, Angie, and I started toward the parking lot, but after a few yards I halted because I saw Yves and his pal disappear into a side alley. I waited for Toby, and he began coming toward us. But then there was a shout and the thud of running feet. Yves and his pal darted out of another alley farther down the quay and cut Didier off. They threw themselves at him, and the three went down, rolling close to the edge of the quay. Toby ran toward them.

When I reached them, Toby was pulling the third man off the pile. Didier was on the pavement taking a pounding from Yves. Toby's opponent was bigger than he was, but Toby was younger and quicker. The guy took a wild swing at Toby, missing completely. Toby bobbed, then stepped in and threw a right, which caused the man to lean away, off balance. As he swayed back, Toby caught him on the side of the head with a looping left-handed punch, and the man went down.

He was in no hurry to get up. Meanwhile, Toby pulled Yves off Didier, whose face was bloody. Spectators were gathering. Someone called out that the police were coming. Yves shook Toby off and helped his pal to his feet. Before anyone could stop them, they disappeared into the alley from which they had emerged.

"Are the police really coming?" Toby asked the spectator who had shouted.

"No, I just said that to make them stop."

"Then we better call them," said Toby.

"No!" cried Didier. "That's not necessary." He was sitting up, holding a handkerchief to stanch his bleeding nose. "We don't need the police. Just help me up."

Toby gave him a hand. "Are you sure? Can we take you home?"

"Thank you, but I have my own car." Didier was adamant. He was standing now, wiping his face with his bare hand. He had a scrape over one eyebrow and scratches under the other eye. "It's not as bad as it looks," he said. "As you see, I can walk."

"Can you drive?"

Didier waved his hand dismissively.

"What happened?" asked Toby, placing a hand on Didier's shoulder. Shaking off Toby's hand, Didier headed to a row of cars parked along a wall.

With misgivings, we let him go.

That was an impressive left hook," Glenda observed on the drive back to Saint-Paul. "He thought you were going with the right jab."

"Don't tell me you're a fight fan," said Toby, eyeing her in his rearview mirror.

"Can't get enough of 'em. Friday nights on ESPN."

"Isn't fighting wrong?" asked Angie in a shocked tone of voice.

"Oh, yes. It's wrong." After a moment, Glenda added: "I'm not perfect, you know. I have my vices."

All Angie could say to that was, "Oh."

"I didn't know nuns were allowed to have vices," Toby said.

"Depends which ones," said Glenda. "We're human."

Angie was silent on the rest of the ride back. I was too. I was worried. I don't like to see Toby getting into fights.

It was after eleven by the time we reached the hotel. As we were undressing for bed, I said, "Toby, that makes two fights in a row. Yesterday it was Curry, and now this."

"Curry wasn't a fight. It was the opposite of a fight. I restrained him."

"It was still a physical confrontation."

"Well."

"And tonight you got into a real slug fest."

"I couldn't just stand there and watch those two beat up on him, could I? What did you expect me to do?"

"We should have called the police."

"By then you could have picked up Didier with a blotter." Toby sat on the bed, removing his shoes. "By the way, have you asked yourself what Didier was doing there in the first place? It isn't likely they met by chance."

"Are you saying he set up a meeting with Yves?"

"Or the other way around. Maybe Yves set up a meeting with him." He stood up, unbuttoned his shirt, and hung it in the armoire.

"The lieutenant said there may have been two people involved in the murder. You think Yves and Didier were working together?"

"Could be." Toby shucked off his pants.

"Then why were they fighting?"

"A falling out between conspirators?" He pulled his undershirt over his head.

"I don't see the connection," I said. "Yves didn't want Isabelle revealing information about their grandfather, so he had a motive to silence her, but what's his link to Didier?"

"Good question." Toby sat back down on the bed and pulled off his socks. "Hey, you're not really mad at me for taking a poke at Yves's buddy, are you?" Now he was down to his briefs, and today they were powder blue. I suppose they use a different word to describe the color of men's underpants. The point is, they looked adorable.

"I don't want to see you get hurt."

"Look. Not a scratch." He stood up and did a slow turn in a circle. "But you should see the other guy."

That made me smile in spite of myself. "Come here, you brute," I said.

One morning when Vincent was painting in the fields, he spoke to me about the doctor's daughter. I wonder what she thinks of me? he said. Her name was Marguerite Gachet. She was closer to my age than his. I had only seen her from a distance but I thought she was pretty. I never see her by herself, Vincent said, but the doctor has invited me to their house tomorrow to paint her portrait. I will speak to her then. I want to paint her seated at the piano. She plays like an angel, you know.

The next time I saw him, a few days later, he was downcast. Did you speak to her? Yes, I did. But she reported our conversation to her father, and he scolded me. He told me that I am a patient, not a suitor, so I am not to see his daughter alone. He thinks an emotional attachment would be harmful to me in my current condition. And harmful to Marguerite. The doctor says I must paint every day and think only of my work. Perhaps he is right. What could I offer any well-bred girl except misery? I must paint, only that. I must paint and paint and paint.

7

I N THE MORNING I phoned the lieutenant to tell her about the fight. She thanked me for my account and said, "In fact, I was planning to call you today. According to the conference program, you'll be in Vence tomorrow afternoon?"

"Yes, to visit the Matisse Chapel."

"Could you stop by the gendarmerie afterward? You can tell me more about what happened at Villefranche. Then I have something else to ask of you."

"Of course." We agreed on a time to meet. What now? I wondered.

I skipped breakfast in order to go over my paper before the morning's session. Toby brought me a croissant and coffee. By the time we boarded the shuttle to the foundation, I was ready. A good night's sleep had helped me focus. A little canoodling hadn't hurt, either.

The audience seemed larger than on previous days. The Maeght Foundation had been publicizing the sessions, and walk-ins from the museum had swelled our ranks. I scanned the room for Didier but didn't see him. I did see Jacques and made a mental note to inquire about Daniel during the coffee break. My fellow panelists were Maggie and Benjamin Bennett. Maggie and I had been scheduled together, and Bennett was added, since his talk had to be canceled on the day of the police interviews.

I knew my paper wasn't groundbreaking, but I hoped the audience would find it interesting. My topic was "Vincent's Quarrel with Impressionism." People often think of his work as part of that movement, but there are notable differences in Vincent's style. The Impressionists, for example, wanted to record visual data as accurately as paint would permit. Monet was fascinated by the play of light on surfaces and strove to reproduce the colors he saw with fidelity. But Vincent wasn't interested in surfaces—he wanted to go deeper, to express emotion. He said in one of his letters that he wanted to use color arbitrarily in order to express himself more forcefully. He devised thick, swirling brushstrokes to achieve that end as well. And he succeeded brilliantly: no one in the history of painting has ever conveyed emotion with more power.

I began with the most famous instance of his arbitrary use of color, the blood-red background of his *Self-Portrait with Bandaged Ear*, painted after he cut himself. Since I knew that Maggie planned to talk about Vincent's portrait of Mademoiselle Gachet playing the piano, I used a slide of that work as my main example. In that painting, Marguerite Gachet is shown in profile, her hands extended over the keyboard. Vincent depicts the wall behind her as covered by green wallpaper with a pattern of orange dots. On the floor beneath her feet is a carpet composed of red, green, and yellow strokes. But we know from photographs of the room that the actual wall was painted white, and the floor was bare; it had no carpet. Vincent was painting not what he saw but what he felt. In the end, I concluded, Vincent left Impressionism behind and created a new style, which evolved into Expressionism.

I received a respectable round of applause, halfway between polite and gratifying. Fair enough. At the break, I made a point of finding Jacques. He was standing at the table in the back of the room where coffee and pastries were provided. We exchanged a few words about my paper, and I asked, "How's Daniel this morning?"

"Pretty sore, but I don't think he was seriously hurt last night. I left him still in his bed."

"Did he tell you what happened? We don't even know what the fight was about."

"I don't either. But Daniel asked me to thank your husband for coming to his aid."

He moved off when a trio of American girls came over to talk to me. They were spending their junior year abroad in Aix and they'd just finished a course on Cezanne and Van Gogh. By the time I'd answered their questions, Montoni was calling the session back to order.

"Eros and Empathy: The Depiction of Women in the Art of Van Gogh and Gauguin"—that was Maggie's title. Her view was that Vincent never reduced women to mere sex objects; instead he identified with his female subjects. Maggie compared Vincent's work to that of his friend Gauguin. She claimed that Gauguin's languid Polynesian beauties were emanations of his fantasies, while Van Gogh saw women as sensitive beings like himself. As evidence, she showed us several of his moving sketches of the prostitute named Sien, whom Vincent rescued from the streets and lived with for a time. Even his nude drawings of her humanize her feelings. One called *Sorrow* has her sitting naked on the side of their bed, her head bowed on her arms, which are folded on her knees in a posture of dejection.

The central part of Maggie's talk focused on Vincent's portrait of Marguerite Gachet playing the piano. She conjectured that he had fallen in love with the young woman by the time he painted her. Maggie used her pointer to call our attention to the artist's depiction of a lone candle in a holder attached to the piano. She then compared that image to Vincent's use of candles in the "portrait" of Gauguin's chair, which he painted as a gift for Gauguin, who was coming to live with him in Arles. At the top left of that painting, a small metal wall sconce holds a single candle, surrounded by a ghostly halo of golden light. Maggie saw the isolated candle as a symbol of Vincent's solitude. In contrast to this vulnerable candle on the wall, a large candle sits in a colorful ceramic holder on the chair reserved for Gauguin, waiting to welcome him.

Maggie juxtaposed the two paintings on the screen. She was sure that, as in the portrait of Gauguin's chair, the isolated candle on Marguerite's piano symbolized Vincent's intuition of her loneliness and his yearning for a relationship with her. The doctor may have understood Vincent's meaning all too well, she added. In a letter to Theo, Vincent wrote that Dr. Gachet had agreed to permit him to paint two portraits of his daughter, one at the piano and another at the organ. But the second sitting never took place. Clearly, the doctor changed his mind. The audience loved the talk.

Ben Bennett was the final speaker. His paper, as announced, was a refutation of the dramatic claim made by Van Gogh's latest biographers that Vincent hadn't committed suicide. The arguments he laid out were those he had shared with Toby and me over dinner. In the discussion afterward, he seized on Maggie's suggestion of a thwarted love affair between Vincent and Marguerite Gachet. That, he declared, was exactly the kind of incident that might have pushed Vincent over the edge and prompted him to take his own life. And it made the new theory of an accidental shooting all the more unlikely.

Judging by the question-and-answer period, our session had been provocative. Parts of the conversation carried over into lunch at the hotel. The three panelists sat together, joined by Angie, Shelley, and Emmet. He was poised on his chair next to Maggie, as usual, and he was acting the perfect gentleman.

As soon as she sat down, Angie asked, "Was Dr. Gachet's daughter in love with Van Gogh too?"

"Nobody knows," said Maggie. "But it's interesting that she never married."

"I bet that's because she was in love with Van Gogh. It was cruel of her father to keep them apart. And then Van Gogh committed suicide, like you said"—she looked at Bennett—"and the poor girl mourned for him the rest of her life. Don't you think that's what happened?"

"It's a reasonable assumption," said Bennett.

"That's what love can make you do," said Angie. "It can."

"Are you speaking from personal experience?" asked Shelley.

"I've been in love. Plenty of times. But nothing good ever came of it."

Shelley snorted. "It rarely does."

"Hey, I wouldn't say that." Bennett elbowed his wife.

"I wasn't talking about us," she replied, in a tone that suggested otherwise.

"So is that why you're going into a convent?" Maggie asked Angie.

"There's a lot more to it than that," Angie said. "And I haven't made a final decision."

"I'm glad to hear it. Because if you go through with it, you won't get another crack at love. Men aren't all alike, you know. Although they're pretty much alike when it comes to one thing." Shelley gave a throaty laugh. "That's what I like about 'em," Maggie continued. "By the way, what do you hear from your dashing gendarme?"

Angie blushed.

"Maybe we should change the subject," I suggested.

"Yes, please," Angie said. "Have you heard about the fight last night?"

"What fight?" Bennett asked.

"You tell them, Nora." Angie pointed her fork my way.

I don't like being pushed into talking, but I had little choice. "We were in Villefranche last night and we ran into Yves La Font and Daniel. They were in a bistro talking with another guy, and a fight broke out. Daniel got the worst of it, from Yves."

"Until Toby came to the rescue," Angie said.

"No kidding? Was Didier hurt?" asked Bennett.

"Jacques says not very."

"And what about La Font?"

I started to say I didn't know, but Angie talked over me. "How would we know? He made a quick getaway, into the old town."

"I wouldn't say 'getaway,'" I corrected Angie. "That makes him out to be a criminal. He was escaping a fistfight. We aren't even sure who started it."

Angie scoffed, puffing her cheeks. "He's the violent type, if you ask me. Who's the most likely to have killed his sister? Him, of course—to keep her from spilling family secrets. Isn't that what we're all thinking?"

"We don't know that yet," I said.

"Speak for yourself," said Shelley. "This business of everyone being under suspicion is ludicrous. It's time for the police to arrest that man and be done with it."

Maggie's brows raised in mock shock. "Whatever happened to 'innocent until proven guilty'?"

"Okay," admitted Angie. "So the police need proof. I'm glad your paper's done," she said, looking at me. "Now you can concentrate on the investigation."

Bennett pulled himself up straight. "What have you got to do with the investigation?"

Again, Angie talked over me. "Nora's helping the police."

I tried to signal Angie to stop, but she plowed right ahead. "She's wicked smart. We had no idea in the family. We couldn't believe it the first time we heard Nora was involved in solving a case. She even saved me from a kidnapper last year. Why—"

This time, I talked over my sister. "Angie's being dramatic. Toby and I were trying to recover a lost painting, and things got out of hand."

Angie dropped her utensils with a clank. "Out of hand? I'll say. When you've got a maniac pointing a gun at you, you're not thinking, 'Oh, dear, things are getting a little out of hand.' You're thinking—"

"Come on, Angie. You saved yourself, remember?"

Angie smiled, remembering the scene. "It wasn't the first time I ever kicked a guy in the cojones."

"It'll be the last time if you go into a convent." Maggie couldn't restrain herself. "You won't get near any more cojones."

Angie ignored the quip. "What I'm saying is Madame Auclair particularly asked Nora to be on the lookout for suspicious behavior."

"The lieutenant asked all of us to do that," said Maggie.

"Yes, but Nora's the only one who's worked with the police before. The lieutenant knows that. I told her."

"Don't make a big thing out of it," I protested. "I agreed to report anything that might be helpful, that's all."

"And to be her eyes and ears at the conference," Angie asserted with sisterly pride.

"Is that so?" Shelley said. "Like some kind of embedded reporter?"

Her husband took a sharper tone. "An embedded reporter lets the troops know what he's doing. An informer doesn't."

"Now, Ben," said Maggie. It was a mild admonishment, such as she'd use with Emmet if he whined at the table. "Where I come from people shoot informers. Nora's not an informer. All she's saying is that she'll let the lieutenant know if she sees or hears anything odd. We all would, wouldn't we?"

"You could have said something about it sooner," Shelley said to me. "I guess I better watch my p's and q's around you." That stung.

"Leave the woman be," said Maggie.

"Just saying," Shelley said with a shrug.

As lunch broke up, Shelley brushed past me and told Maggie she'd take a pass on the Renoir tour, which was scheduled for the afternoon. "I'm a material girl," she said. "I've only just started on the village shops."

I was fretting about Angie outing me as a snooper. She resisted my invitation to go out for some sun on the terrace, on the excuse that she didn't have her sunglasses. I was forced to say, "Angie, I need to talk with you." She looked left and right, as if seeking an escape route—but she followed me out to the terrace, where we were, thankfully, alone.

"I know, I know," she said. "You don't like me bragging about you."

"Of course I don't. But that's not the worst of it. I didn't want to get dragged into this in the first place. But now you've completely destroyed my usefulness to Lieutenant Auclair. By the time we get in the van, everybody with ears will know what you said. They'll be on their guard. Nobody's going to act naturally around me now, least of all anyone who has something to hide."

"I didn't think of that."

"No, you wouldn't. You don't seem to have any appreciation of the position I'm in. Believe me, I'm stressed out." Angie gave me an inquiring look. She really didn't understand. So I continued. "Look, the lieutenant put me in a bind. If I refused to help, I'd look like someone who didn't give a damn about the murder. But if I started watching and reporting back to her, my colleagues would think I was a snitch. Now do you see my dilemma?"

"Boy, you are stressed out."

"If I am, it's your fault." Angie flinched as if slapped and tears welled up. I got a hot feeling in the chest and knew I had to end this conversation quickly. I mumbled "sorry," but she turned and walked away. I went back to our room.

I lay down on the four-poster bed and hugged a pillow for comfort. Pretty soon Toby came in and took the pillow's place. I spilled my tale and Toby listened patiently. "All right. You need to patch things up with Angie. As for the others, forget them. Why should you care what they think? When this conference is over, people will remember only two things about it: the murder and their own paper. You'll be a mote in their memory."

He was right about that. And he was right about my insecurity around my colleagues. Why should I be so worried about what people thought of me? Maybe it was time to say the hell with that. Bringing Isabelle's killer to justice was more important than my social standing, and if I could help the lieutenant do that, I would.

I reviewed what I had come up with so far. Nothing concrete. But I knew that Yves La Font and Daniel Didier had both been close to Isabelle, and both had a falling-out with her. Either one might have been angry enough to take her life. Who else had a personal connection with Isabelle? Ray Montoni may have spent more time with her than he let on. There was a vagueness in the way he spoke about how she was added to the conference program. Then again, the motive for the murder may have been professional, not personal. Bennett, for one, had a vested interest in hearing—or preventing—Isabelle's talk. Her information might have undermined his chance for publication. There was also Bruce Curry's behavior to consider, along with the fact that he provided the foxglove that was implicated in Isabelle's death. Suspects weren't lacking, but the way forward was unclear.

Toby brought me out of my reverie with a squeeze and said, "Did you drift off? Come on, it's time to go see Renoir's fleshy beauties." He patted me on the rear and helped me to my feet. "Feel any better now?" Strangely enough, I did.

On our way south toward Cagnes-sur-Mer, the sky was blue and cloudless. In the van, I sat next to Klara de Groot. "Shelley told me you've been helping the police," she said right off the bat. "Have you learned anything useful to them?"

So the word was getting around. "No, and I'm not a gendarme in disguise. My sister likes to exaggerate. I don't know any more than you do."

"Ah." Klara nodded, twisting a lock of hair around a thumb. "Well, I don't know anything at all." She turned to the window. The van took a labyrinthine route, winding up the hill called Haut-de-Cagnes. We drove through the twisting, narrow streets of a middle-class neighborhood clinging to the summit. The stucco houses must have had Malibu-quality views of the Mediterranean.

Soon we turned into a narrow lane, which led to a modern visitors' center. Guides met us at the vans and invited the less sure-footed to seat themselves in a motorized cart, which carried them up the steep path to Renoir's home. The rest of us followed Ray Montoni on a hike up the hill, past a huge olive grove, a circle of fruiting orange trees, and a tropical garden, which in midwinter took its beauty from the different textures of palms and cacti. From the beginning of the walk, we had glimpses of the famous house. The afternoon sun shone directly onto its lime-stone face. Cream-colored shutters set off French windows on both floors, and a wide balcony looked out over the sea. Renoir, who led a working-class life in his youth, had enough wealth by his late sixties to build the home of his dreams.

The center of that dream was Renoir's desire to work as passionately as ever, painting curvaceous young women even as he aged. For eleven years, until his death at seventy-eight, he was as productive as at any other time in his career. Toby and I lingered over the most important room, his studio. In the back of the house, facing away from the distraction of the sea, stood Renoir's easel, built to accommodate his rheumatoid arthritis. The lip for the canvas was low, just above the level of the chair's arms, so that Renoir could paint sitting down. The chair's front legs had a double base, so he could lean toward the canvas without tipping over.

In another room, we saw the wheelchair he used in his last years. It had arms that extended into poles to make a chairlift. A silent film flickering against the wall showed the aged Renoir sitting in the wheelchair with his hands bandaged tightly, so that he could wield the paintbrush without dropping it. The gaunt artist, hampered by a thick coat buttoned to the neck and struggling to raise his brush, made a touching contrast with his model, a robust young woman whose nakedness was covered casually by a blanket.

We returned to the family rooms, where we admired paintings and sculptures that Renoir produced at Haut-de-Cagnes. My favorite was a painting of the house as seen from the olive orchard. It might have hung in the Musée d'Orsay, but its impact was greater here, where it was painted.

A path in front of the house led to Renoir's most famous sculpture, the *Venus Victorious*. We found her at the center of an orange grove. Apart from being nude and as plump as I expected her to be, she was black, not white; short, not tall; and languid, not military. She had no weapon in hand but trailed a bedsheet instead. Her victory was in love, not war. While I was gazing at her, Toby pulled me to him and gave me one of those juicy kisses that had sealed our courtship. Renoir can have that effect on you.

We walked hand in hand as we entered the olive orchard, where wide spaces between trees gave a sense of openness. The trees, however, pulled against that joyous feeling. Their distinctive misshapen branches reminded me of Renoir's arthritic hands.

Under one crippled tree at the far edge of the field stood a couple with a dog. That is, they struck me as a couple—I'm not sure why. As soon as they saw us, the pair pulled apart, and Emmet came running toward us. Maggie waved and called to him. The man turned around, and I saw that he was Ray Montoni. What's Maggie doing with *him*? I thought. I could see Maggie putting the moves on Thierry, who was a "winning lad," as she said, but portly, hairy Ray Montoni? I decided I must be wrong.

Emmet circled around us and, like a sheepdog, herded us toward Maggie and Ray. We were stumbling by the time we reached them. "My boy is fairly dancing for his afternoon walk," said Maggie. As if on cue, Emmet positioned himself strategically over Ray's left foot and prepared to pee. "Emmet!" Maggie cried. "Come!" She reached out, clipped a leash to Emmet's collar, and rushed him under the next tree, where he went to town.

"You just had a close call," said Toby.

Montoni seemed flustered until he saw that Toby was pointing toward his shoe. "Yeah. Gotta be careful around that dog." He started trudging back in the direction of the house. We went along with him. In a transparent attempt to change the subject, he said to Toby, "I hear you got into a fistfight last night."

"It was no big deal. We drove to Villefranche for dinner and we saw Didier get into a brawl with Yves La Font and some other guy. It was two against one. I helped break it up, that's all."

"What started it?"

"Nobody said."

Since Montoni already knew about the fight, I assumed he also knew I was in contact with the police. I had nothing to lose by asking him a few questions, so I did. "Did you know Didier once was involved with Isabelle La Font, romantically?"

"Really? I was aware they knew each other but not that it was anything romantic. Who told you that?"

"Jacques Godard mentioned it. I was wondering whether Didier had something to do with getting her invited to the conference."

Ray scratched his cheek. "When Isabelle first got in touch with me, she told me she learned about the conference from him. Didier was already on the program. I don't know whether he suggested she could present here or she suggested it to him. Does it make a difference?"

"It might. Do you remember what she said when she contacted you? Was it by letter? Phone?"

"She phoned." He was somewhat out of breath now that we were walking uphill. "She said she had come across important information that had a bearing on the question of Van Gogh's death. She wondered whether our conference might be the best place to make public what she had learned. An academic setting, you know? Not the press."

"And you added her to the program just like that?"

"No." He halted. "I e-mailed Didier. He said she was a reliable person, not a crank. He supported the idea of inviting her to the conference."

"Without seeing her paper?" I asked.

"I asked her to send me a proposal, and she did, but it was very general. She wanted to keep the contents under wraps until she presented here. I've already gone over all this with the police." He looked at me in a knowing way, which confirmed my guess that he had been told about Angie's disclosures. He certainly showed no surprise that I was peppering him with questions. He resumed climbing, slowly.

"Now if you'll excuse me," he said as we neared the house, "I've got to round up our folks for the return." He waved to people up on the terrace and walked off.

Toby," I said, when we were back in our room getting ready for dinner, "when we first saw Maggie and Ray standing under that tree, did you get the impression something was going on between them?"

"What? No. Maggie and Montoni? Don't be ridiculous. Whatever gave you that idea?"

"I can't put my finger on it. Maybe I was just imagining things."

Toby grinned. "All those sexy Renoir pictures. And that statue. That's what did it."

I smiled, remembering our kiss.

Years later, after Vincent became famous and his pictures appeared in books, I would try to remember which of them I had watched him paint. But I remembered only a few. I was just a boy and knew nothing about art. I was interested in Vincent as my friend.

One I do remember is the field with crows. It was a large painting, showing a field of wheat swaying in the wind. In the painting, the sky is dark, as if a storm is coming, and black crows are flying everywhere. But in reality it was a hot, sunny day, and there wasn't a bird in the sky. I asked Vincent why he was painting crows and a stormy sky when the weather was fine and the sky was empty. He said nothing, but there were tears in his eyes. Later, when we were walking back to town, he told me he had quarreled with his brother, when he went to visit him in Paris. His brother and his wife had just had a baby and didn't know if they could continue sending him money to live on. I'm just in the way, Vincent said. He seemed sadder than I'd ever seen him before. Then he said, it's all over for me. From that day on, he got worse.

8

DINNER AT THE COLOMBE D'OR was a prospect to whet any appetite—for food, for ambiance, or for art. In the years when Saint-Paul-de-Vence was just being discovered by artists, La Colombe d'Or was the hotel where they met to eat and drink, and the bill was often settled with a painting fresh from the easel. As a result, priceless canvases grace its halls, the dining room, and the sitting rooms. Who better to appreciate them than a dozen art historians? I'd been looking forward to the evening, which was billed as the social highlight of the conference.

I dressed as well as I could, given the limitations of a roll-on suitcase. I gave my Mary Janes a spit polish and put on the black traveler pants and a velvety top that I'd worn to all our dinners. To that I added my finest fake diamond earrings (bought at an airport shop) and brushed my hair back so they'd show. Toby said I looked good and suggested that we walk to town. The sky was overcast and the road was dark, lit only when we passed windows of houses where supper was being cooked. The way ahead was clear, though, since the clock tower glowed from afar, its spotlights lit since nightfall. We arrived at the boules court and had time to huddle there, gazing at the ramparts. They seemed dauntingly high, because the walls were lit from below, with the light growing faint at the top, reflecting a few wisps of fog grazing the parapets.

Just left of the ramparts, a simple stone building was lit in the same way, with a spotlight emphasizing a statue of the golden dove after which the restaurant is named. I was feeling the cold by the time we approached the hotel's stone arch, guarded by an upscale version of a bouncer. With a glance, he decided we were the right sort. We stepped onto the terrace, where a tall Calder mobile mounted guard over a swimming pool. I pictured the pool on a hot summer day, with Picasso splashing his latest love and Orson Welles struggling to slip his whale of a body into the water.

A gust of wind propelled us into the restaurant—or rather, into the lobby, which doubles as a bar. Cocktail tables and low stools invited early arrivals to take an aperitif. At the farthest table, Daniel Didier sat alone, writing. He didn't look like he wanted company, but he couldn't easily avoid inviting us to join him. He slipped a notebook inside his jacket. His face remained sober.

"You don't look too bad, considering," said Toby. He took in the bruise above Didier's right eye and the scrapes under his left.

"Thanks to you," said Didier.

Toby gave a self-deprecating nod and mumbled the French equivalent of "no problem."

"You called the police afterward, didn't you?" asked Didier.

"Actually," I admitted, "I was the one who called."

"I wish you hadn't, Madame Barnes."

"I'm sorry," I said, "but it seemed necessary. The fight involved Madame La Font's brother."

"In any case, I spent half the morning at the gendarmerie." He flipped his hand in the air with such vehemence that his glass tipped over. To avoid getting wine on his clothes, he jumped his stool back. Almost at the same time, a young man arrived to take our order. He pulled a pristine white towel from over his arm and proceeded to mop up the spill.

Awkward as it was, we stayed at the table. Toby said, "We didn't mean to cause you any trouble."

"Unfortunately, you did. Yves and I have a history."

"Because of your relationship with his sister?" I asked.

"Godard talks too much. But yes."

"He sure was bent on giving you a beating," Toby said. "Did you run into each other by accident?"

Didier eyed me, as if to say he'd be willing to discuss the fight with Toby but he wasn't so sure about me. Nonetheless, he went on. "By accident? No. He called me at the hotel and asked me to meet him in Villefranche. He lives near the port. He wanted to put pressure on me for information about Isabelle's paper. I told him I had no more information than he had."

The young man returned with our drinks and a replacement for Didier's spilled glass of wine. "You mean Isabelle didn't tell you anything about her presentation?" I asked. My skepticism showed, I'm sure.

Didier looked at me coolly. He took a sip. "She didn't share the details. We hadn't been in touch for years."

"I take it Yves didn't believe you," Toby said.

"No."

I didn't believe him myself.

Didier put down his glass. "Then the idiot accused me of killing his sister. That's how the fight started. He never liked me. He never liked Isabelle that much either. He was only her half brother, you know. They had different mothers."

Didier reached into his jacket for a pack of cigarettes, withdrew one, tapped it on his wrist, and lit it. He blew a billow of smoke the size of a thought cloud in a cartoon. Then he continued. "Yves was always jealous of his father's second family—the new wife, Isabelle, and her younger sister. He felt the girls got all the attention and were spoiled. He used to hit Isabelle up for money. That was still going on when Isabelle and I were a couple. I didn't like that, and I let him know it."

"Did you ever fight?" Toby asked.

"Once. In Isabelle's third year at nursing school, her internship, Yves came to Bordeaux to take her out of school. By then his step-mother was dead and his father had cancer. Yves wanted Isabelle to come home to care for their father. She was torn. She wanted to stay with me and finish her degree, but she wanted to comfort her father too. There was an argument. Just like last night, Yves got belligerent. He punched me. Threw things. We wrestled. In the confusion, Isabelle got pushed and hit her head on the corner of a table." His voice rose. "Yves reported me to the police."

"Even though it was an accident?" Toby asked.

"You think the law is fair? I have the arrest on my record. The police knew that when they questioned me today. Now they think I'm habitu-ally violent—just the sort who might attack an old girlfriend."

"Didn't Isabelle stand up for you?"

"Yves convinced her to leave, to nurse her father. Once she made up her mind, she resented my interference. She took his side." He took another swallow of wine and put his glass down slowly. "That was the end of us, and she never got her nursing degree."

I could understand Isabelle's plight. I'd been in a similar position when Angie wanted me to come home from college.

"She wasted the rest of her life in Sisteron. She took care of her father until he died, and then she stayed on managing a clinic for some un-grateful doctors. Now she's dead. Yves is to blame. For everything."

"For her death too?" Toby asked.

"Who else? I'm convinced of it. He stalked her to the conference. He tried to control her every action. It infuriated him that she decided on her own to tell their grandfather's story. That's why I agreed to meet him when he called. I thought I might pick up something that could be used as evidence against him."

"And instead he tried to pin the murder on you," Toby said.

"The bastard. That's why I didn't want you to report our fight to the police." Didier angrily stubbed out his cigarette in an ashtray.

I wanted to find out more about Isabelle's sister. Where did she live? Had she been notified of Isabelle's death? But at that moment the rest of our gang entered, making a hubbub as they gave up their coats and crowded into the bar. That gave Didier an excuse to leave us. He joined his French colleagues. By prearrangement, everyone was offered champagne, and everyone accepted, since the welcoming toast, like the dinner, was paid for by the conference. Ray Montoni lifted his glass high, and we followed. He took a showy swallow. He seemed a bit sloshed already.

Whether it was the thought of Isabelle's death or the testy interchange with Didier, I couldn't get the champagne down. You shouldn't ever force yourself to drink, I thought. I put down the glass and took a self-led tour of the photographs hanging on the walls and then thumbed through the guestbook pages signed by James Baldwin, Jean-Paul Belmondo, Simone Signoret, Jacques Brel, and other icons of the last century.

The hostess who led us to the dining room wore a voluminous striped skirt, topped by a lacy Provençal blouse. The liveliness of her costume countered the severity of the waiters' black vests and pants. She flashed individual style, while her men worked anonymously. She gave each guest a warm welcome and used discreet gestures to tell her staff which guests to put at which tables. I was glad that our "family" was kept together. It gave me a chance to make up with Angie.

The handsome room helped settle me. Dark walnut paneling on the walls rose five feet high, and in the space above that, paintings hung in profusion, each lit softly from below. That was the extent of the light in the room, apart from candles and a fire in the hearth. I played a silent game of trying to identify the paintings. I thought I saw Miros, Picassos, a Chagall, and a Matisse. To tell the truth, when it comes to their simpler, playful works, it isn't easy to tell the difference. A small painting of a garishly red lobster was definitely a Soutine. It made me queasy.

I asked Toby to order for us both. The meal was good but not memorable. Toby tells me we had something called socca, a chickpea flour pancake rolled with goat cheese and ratatouille, and then duck breast with figs in honey and thyme. I do remember the dessert, a selection of little winter tarts: walnut, lemon, and almond.

As my eyes scanned the room, I saw that Maggie was surrounded by the three French bachelors: Didier, Godard, and Thierry. I wondered whether chance or a bribe had produced that grouping. For this, the most formal occasion of the conference, she had left Emmet behind with Madame Richarde. Perhaps Maggie didn't want him to see her flirting with other men. Maybe she was thinking of their shoes.

Montoni was seated with the Bennetts and the De Groots. They were engaged in animated conversation. By contrast, the Currys dined apart at a small table for two. He appeared to be sulking. I noticed that when Jane touched him on the forearm, he shook her hand off. The rest of the company chatted agreeably through the appetizers, made sounds of satisfaction through the main course, and sighed over dessert. Once all plates were empty, the hostess invited our group to take coffee in one of the sitting rooms.

When we were comfortably ensconced, Maggie proposed an after-dinner parlor game. "It's called the 'Trolley Problem,'" she explained. "A British philosopher named Philippa Foot came up with it. It's a test of what you think is the right thing to do. Would you like to try it?"

"Sure," Montoni said. No one objected.

Maggie stretched out her legs and crossed them at the ankles. "Okay. Here's the setup. Imagine a trolley that's lost its brakes, and it's barreling down on five people who are tied to the track. Never mind how they got there. If you do nothing, the trolley will hit them and the five people will be killed. You're standing next to a switch that can divert the trolley to a sidetrack. If you throw the switch, the five will be saved.

But there's a catch. There's one person tied to the sidetrack. If you throw the switch, he will be killed. What should you do?"

There was a moment's pause as people deliberated. The first with an answer was Klara de Groot. She put down her cup. "I think you should throw the switch. One person will be killed but five people will be saved."

"I guess I'd come to the same conclusion," said Bennett.

"Quite right," Curry agreed. "Jeremy Bentham. Utilitarianism. 'Act to produce the greatest good for the greatest number.'" Several heads bobbed in approval.

"Does anyone have a different opinion?" Pointedly, Maggie looked at Sister Glenda.

"What would I do? I would pray for deliverance of the people who are tied to the tracks."

"But not intervene?" asked Maggie.

Glenda looked at her hands. "I couldn't purposely take a life. It's not up to me to play God."

"Nora?"

"I don't know what I'd do. I'd probably stand there paralyzed until it was too late to make a choice."

"A lot of help that would be," Shelley observed. "I can understand where Sister Glenda's coming from. But the rest of us live in the world. We have to do stuff when it's necessary."

"I take it you would throw the switch," said Maggie.

"Of course."

"What would you do?" Montoni asked Maggie.

"I'll tell you. But first, for a tally, how many would throw the switch?" People started to raise their hands.

"Excuse me," Didier interrupted. "But your Anglo-Saxon philosophy bores me. Forgive me if I don't participate." He tamped out a cigarette and departed.

"The arrogant frog," muttered Curry.

"I don't agree with Daniel," said Jacques, ignoring the ethnic slur. "It's an interesting question."

"Then let's see how everyone feels," said Maggie. "How many here would throw the switch? A show of hands?" Eight. The Currys, the De Groots, the Bennetts, Montoni, and Thierry.

"And who would not?" Three: Sister Glenda, Angie, and Toby.

"I agree with Sister Glenda," Angie explained.

"So do I, but not for religious reasons," said Toby. "I'm thinking of the guy on the side track. Doesn't he have any rights? Who am I to volunteer him for sacrifice?"

That sounded persuasive to me, but so did the argument about the greatest good.

"That's three against," said Maggie. "And how many undecided?" One. Jacques Godard.

"Nora, you didn't vote."

I'd been thinking how marvelous Maggie must be as a leader of classroom discussion. "Sorry. Undecided."

"Now it's your turn," Montoni said to Maggie. "You're the leader here. So what would you do?"

"Well, the first time I heard the debate, I agreed with the majority. But 'the greatest good for the greatest number' isn't the only ethical principle that applies. According to Immanuel Kant, you should treat every person as an end in himself and never as a means. If I pull the switch, I'm treating the man on the sidetrack as a means to an end. Kant would call that wrong."

"So you wouldn't pull the switch," said Angie.

"I don't think I would."

"Hmm," mused Hans de Groot. "I see the point. You have two moral principles in conflict, so how do you decide? I would say that even though I regret the harm to the person on the sidetrack, it's still better to save the five."

"Good man," Curry asserted. "No doubt about it."

"You seem very sure of that." Maggie sat forward in her chair and placed both hands on her knees. "Well, here's a variation of the problem. There are still five people tied to the track and a runaway trolley is bearing down on them. But this time you're standing on a footbridge overlooking the track. The trolley will pass below you. If you had something heavy to throw onto the track, you could stop the trolley. You look around, but the only heavy object in sight is a fat man, who is leaning over the railing. If you push him, you know he will die, but his body will stop the trolley and save the five people tied to the track. Would you push the fat man off the bridge?"

This time I immediately knew my answer was no. Pushing a bystander seemed obviously wrong. Plus it was risky. What if the fat man put up a struggle and threw *me* off the bridge?

Klara de Groot echoed my thought. "I wouldn't push the fat man. The result would be too uncertain."

"Is the fat man a Republican or a Democrat?" Toby wisecracked. I had an image of Governor Christie flying through the air and broke into laughter. "Seriously," Toby went on, "don't you have to know something about these people in order to make a choice? Say the fat man was a brilliant surgeon and the five men on the track were condemned murderers?"

"You don't have that kind of information," Maggie said.

"Besides," Curry added, his voice harsh with irritation, "you can't make decisions like that based on your judgment of people. That would be purely subjective. You need a logical principle, and you should stick to it. I say the greatest good for the greatest number. So, yes, I would throw the switch, and yes, I would push the fat man."

"Even if he were your father?" asked Toby. "Or your son?"

Curry became flustered. "Now you want to make me look ridiculous. You keep doing that."

"I'm not trying to offend you," said Toby. "Just trying to make a point."

"At my expense." Curry addressed the room. "This man keeps provoking me. I'm not going to sit here and take any more of his insults. Come, Jane." Grasping his wife by the wrist, he tugged her out of her chair and pulled her toward the hall. Jane gave Maggie a helpless look, but she went with her husband.

"Well," said Maggie. "I see I'm beginning to lose my audience. The point I was leading up to is that while most people say it's right to throw the switch, they say it's wrong to throw the fat man off the bridge, even if they can't explain why. But from an ethical point of view, the situations are exactly the same. It must be the idea of physical contact that makes people squeamish about pushing the fat man to save the others. Interesting, eh?"

"I've got another scenario," said Shelley.

"Be my guest," said Maggie, sitting back and crossing her ankles again.

Shelley squared her shoulders. "This time, say you're walking on a train trestle high above a ravine and suddenly a train is coming at you. There's nowhere to escape except a small platform a few steps ahead of you. The platform only has room for one person, but there's a fat man already standing on it. So, do you push him off to save yourself?"

Angie looked shocked. No one volunteered an answer. "Would you?" Maggie asked Shelley.

"I just might."

"You wouldn't," said her husband.

"If it was him or me? Don't be too sure."

"But would it be right?" asked Maggie.

"You know what?" Shelley replied. "In a real emergency, people act on instinct. Afterward they come up with reasons for what they did."

After that quip, the party wound down. On our way out we had to pass through the bar again, but it turned out not everyone was ready to call it a night. Bruce and Jane Curry were sitting at one of the small cocktail tables, sipping port. Montoni and the Bennetts decided to linger and made a threesome at a separate table. The rest of our troop exited into the cool night air, where the shuttles were waiting to return us to the hotel.

Toby looked up at the ramparts. In the spotlights, the ancient walls glowed like moist amber. "You know, there's something I've wanted to do since the day we got here: walk the parapets at night. This is my chance."

"Are you crazy?"

"I knew you'd say that. Look, we probably won't be here again at night. I can do the whole circuit in twenty minutes. I've already done it."

"That was in daylight."

"Yes, and now I want to see what the village looks like at night from up there. I'll be careful, I promise." We went back and forth, and after some sweet cajoling, I gave in. I know. I shouldn't have.

"Forget something?" Montoni asked, looking up as I reentered the bar.

"It's Toby. He forgot to grow up." I explained what was happening.

"You can have a nightcap with us while you're waiting." Ray pulled an extra chair up to the table. "What would you like?"

I ordered a pot of tea and made a trip to the restroom downstairs. I wasn't gone long, but when I returned, Shelley and Jane were alone in the bar, and Shelley was patting Jane's shoulder.

"What's going on?"

Jane looked miserable. "It's Bruce. As soon as you left, he said your husband had made a fool of him, and he ran outside. He said they were going to have it out."

Shelley read the alarm on my face. "Ray and Ben went after him," she said. "But Ray's had a lot to drink, and Ben doesn't like heights. I don't think they'll be much help if Bruce gets to the ramparts."

"Can you warn Toby?" Jane asked. "Does he have a phone with him?"

Damn it, he didn't. I was the only one in the family with a phone that worked in France. "Did they all leave together?"

"Bruce had a head start," said Jane. "Ray and Ben argued for a minute over what to do."

"I better go. Maybe I can catch up with them."

It's a good thing I wasn't in high heels. I bounded onto the terrace and ran past the man guarding the gate. His chin jerked up. Four guests had just run out the door. That wasn't how an evening at the Colombe d'Or was meant to end.

Out of the corner of my eye, I noticed the glow of a cigarette and saw Didier standing in the doorway of the café opposite the restaurant, looking across the boules court, watching.

Which way to go? The other day, when Maggie and I were walking outside the village wall, we saw a flight of stairs leading from the path to the top of the ramparts. We didn't try it, for several reasons. The steps were uneven, worn down by centuries of weather. They were narrow too, as if made for smaller feet than ours. The left edge of the steps was braced against the wall, but the right edge had no railing. An iron bar blocked the stairway. A youngster might take that as a challenge to leap over. Maggie and I had decided to obey the warning. I wasn't eager now to attempt what I hadn't dared in the light of day.

Within the village, there were several flights of stairs leading to the ramparts, but how to locate them in the dark? Then I remembered that the lookout near the cemetery was level with the parapets. It was at the farthest end of town—an uphill climb—but I knew I could get easy access from there. I hoped that if I ran fast enough, I'd catch up with Ray and Ben.

The distance seemed endless. I tripped on uneven pavestones and ran into a ground-floor flowerbox as I rounded a corner. When I reached the square at the end of the path, I was frustrated to see that the lookout was dark as a closet. The town fathers must have decided to discourage nighttime wall walkers. The weak glow of a cloud-covered moon cast only enough light to mark the top of coal-black walls, almost indistinguishable from the ground in front of them.

The phantom image of Toby on the ramparts, struggling with Curry, kept me moving forward, even when I saw the white sign I remembered from my first visit to the lookout. In the darkness, it was only a blur. In daylight, the message had been clear: "Dangerous to mount walls. The village refuses any responsibility in case of accident." I blindly mounted the steps to the lookout, and going by memory from my previous visit, turned left and felt my way to the iron barrier, here so low that it almost said, "Oh, all right—go ahead."

I stepped over the bar and felt around to get my bearings. With my right hand, I held on to a thin, stone guard-wall at thigh height. I was leaning over a virtual abyss. Fear brought my left hand next to the right. Secure there and on my well-planted right foot, I swept my left foot to the side and then behind me. I found the edge of the wall and estimated that the top of the rampart, my walkway, was about two feet wide. I prayed that it wouldn't narrow and that the guard-wall wouldn't drop so low that I couldn't use it for balance. In the daytime, a daredevil like Toby might not need it. He'd just prance along. But this was night-time, and when I tried walking forward, keeping only my right hand on the guard-wall, I felt like I was balancing on a wire.

I couldn't go on like that, so I faced the guard-wall with both my hands holding its top and inched sideways, like a sneak-thief on a window ledge. I took twenty steps that way—I was counting. Then I began lifting my right hand every couple of steps and swinging my left hand forward to give me balance. I must have looked like an orangutan to anyone with night vision. I was moving carefully and listening for someone ahead of me. I could see better as I moved along, perhaps because I was approaching housing and streetlights.

Gingerly, I picked my way along in the direction of the village entrance. On my left I passed a flight of stone stairs descending to the road inside the ramparts. If the others had come up on that stairway, they would be far ahead of me by now. On my right, the guard-wall was jagged and uneven. In places it had eroded, leaving gaping holes. I could topple right over it, into the ravine. And to make matters worse, tendrils of fog drifted along the narrow walkway. I called Toby's name but got no response.

I had gone some distance by the time I caught a glimpse—far ahead—of a figure moving even more slowly than I was. I called out, "Toby!" He stopped for a moment and then took off at a reckless lope. That wasn't Toby. I struggled to follow him and called again, "Professor Curry! Is that you?" I picked up my pace, all the while trying to peer ahead through the gloom.

I lurched and gasped. I had stumbled on a medieval pothole, a spot where the surface of the walkway was broken. I grabbed the guard-wall and brought my feet back to balance. In that crouched position, I heard footsteps on my right. I tried to rise and turn in that direction, but before I could see who it was, he slammed me back against the wall. My feet started to slip out from underneath me. In panic, I swirled round to grab the guard-wall again, but the force of my turn was too great, and I felt myself going over, my legs kicking to find a purchase.

Somehow I managed to hold on to the top of the guard-wall with one hand. Desperately, I reached up with the other hand and got hold of a jagged piece of stone. Thank God, the stone was firm and I didn't lose my grip. But I was dangling over the ravine.

Dread drove me to dig my left knee into the wall while my right foot clawed until it found a rough piece of stonework big enough to support the toe of my shoe. Resting my weight on it relieved the pressure on my hands, but I didn't have the strength to pull myself up. There was no way I could maintain my position. I screamed as I do in dreams—without breath, silently, failing to call out. For a moment, I despaired. Then I breathed in and made a body-breaking effort to raise myself up. That didn't work, and I called, "Help!"

My fingers were cramping and losing their grip. My left knee was slipping toward the ravine. I kept calling out. Finally someone shouted, "Where are you?"

"Here! Here!"

"Hold on. I'm coming."

In another moment a pair of big hands gripped me by the wrists and began pulling me up. The hands belonged to Ray Montoni. With his effort and mine, my waist reached the top of the parapet, and we struggled until I slumped onto the walkway. Fearing another fall, I positioned my back against the guard-wall and slowly lengthened my body out. I was taking no more chances with balance. "Thank God you came along," I gasped. "I was falling."

"What happened?"

"I'm not sure. Someone rushed by me and pushed me over the edge. I could have been killed."

"Was it Curry?" Ray asked.

"I didn't see." My shoulders ached, and my knees felt scraped. But that was nothing to my hands. They were on fire. "Where are the others?" I managed to ask. "Have you seen Toby?"

"I haven't seen anyone. Ben was lagging behind me, but he's not here now."

"What about Curry?"

"No sign of him either."

"Which way did you come from?" I asked. Ray pointed in the direction I was heading. "You didn't pass Curry? I thought I saw him running ahead of me. I know I saw somebody running that way. You didn't see anyone?"

"No. Maybe he climbed down. Look, are you hurt?"

"A little."

He helped me to my feet. "Are you able to walk?"

I took a few steps, testing. "Yes. We need to find Toby."

We inched our way ahead until Toby suddenly emerged from the mist, hurrying toward us. "Nora! I heard you shouting. What are you doing up here?"

"Curry said he was going after you. We were afraid he'd find you and there'd be trouble."

"There's trouble, all right. I just spotted him back there," Toby gestured behind him. "He's at the foot of the ramparts. I don't know if he's alive or dead."

The days went by until it was nearly the end of July. Vincent was painting in a field just beyond the walls of the chateau on the outskirts of town, and I was sitting under a tree, daydreaming as usual. He seemed in better spirits that day. Late in the afternoon he called me over. Wear your red jacket tomorrow, Maurice, and I'll put you there. He pointed to the middle of his canvas. That's where I need a splash of color. He was pointing to the right of several yellow haystacks in the distance. Farther to the left was a house. The top of the painting was blue sky. On the bottom were rectangles of green and yellow for the fields.

We met the next morning as arranged. He showed me where to stand and told me to pretend that I was digging. Then he walked back across the plain to his easel. After an hour, he was finished. Now there was a little red figure in the distance, digging with a hoe next to a haystack. What do you think of it? he asked. I complained that nobody could tell it was me. Well, then, let's do another. He turned his easel around and asked me to lean against the tree, which I did, with my hands in my pockets and my red jacket unbuttoned. This time he stood only a few meters from me. He fixed a clean canvas to the stretcher. Now take your hat off, he said. And that's how he came to paint my portrait.

9

WHEN WE REACHED HIM, Curry was sprawled on the pavement, moaning, his left leg twisted at a brutal angle. "Hang on," Toby told him. "We'll get help."

My cell phone was in my handbag back at the restaurant, but Ray had his. He dialed 112, the emergency number in France, and got an ambulance on its way. While we waited for it, I knelt by Curry, put my hand to his cheek, and talked to him, thinking this might help him stay conscious.

Ray moved closer to Toby to talk confidentially, but in the midnight silence his words sounded clearly. "I don't know what happened, but it looks like Curry pushed your wife over the wall. It's lucky I arrived when I did."

"What?" Toby turned around and reached for me.

He held me so tightly that I gasped as I explained, "Somebody ran into me from behind and I was pushed. I lost my balance. I couldn't swear it was Curry, but it must have been. Ray pulled me up. He saved me."

"Oh, my God!" said Toby. "Thank you. Thank you, Ray." He clasped me even harder. "This was my dumb idea. I'm an idiot. I thought it would be fun to come up here at night."

"The trouble is," said Ray, "you weren't alone. Curry came after you. He said you'd made a fool of him and he wanted to even the score. On the ramparts if need be."

"But why attack Nora? He has issues with me, not her."

"All I know," said Ray, "is that he was in a rage when he left the bar."

"It might have been an accident if he was rushing to get by me." I had other thoughts but kept them to discuss with Toby later, in private. Curry wasn't the only one who could have pushed me. Ben Bennett had been on the ramparts too, and now he was gone. I recalled his hostile reaction when Angie revealed that the lieutenant had asked for my help. And what about Daniel Didier? He watched me running out of the restaurant after the others. He could have followed me onto the ramparts too.

"Are you sure you're all right?" Toby asked.

"Basically. I'm banged up and my shoulder hurts, but I'll be okay."

He held me close until flashing lights announced the arrival of an ambulance. In less than five minutes, the medics had picked up Curry and were headed to the hospital in Cagnes-sur-Mer, one of the best in the region and the closest. As the ambulance pulled away, sounding that awful ump-ah that they use in Europe, we started back to the restaurant to break the news to Jane. Montoni said he would take Jane to the hospital to be with her husband.

"Don't say anything to her about what happened to me," I cautioned. "She has enough to worry about."

Back in our hotel room, I gave Toby a fuller account of my mishap. "So yes, it could have been Curry, but it's also possible it was someone else."

"Someone who doesn't want you nosing around." Toby looked grim. "If that's the case, you're in danger."

I slept badly that night, disturbed by a recurring dream. In the dream I was falling, not from the ramparts, but from a bridge over a railroad track into the path of an oncoming train. Just before I hit the track, I'd wake up. By five o'clock I was done for the night and lay in bed with an aching shoulder, waiting for dawn.

At breakfast, the air crackled with whispers, as people divulged to each other what they'd learned about Curry's fall. We seated ourselves with Maggie and Jane. "Bruce says he slipped," Jane was saying, her features tense with distress. "It's a good thing he fell to the street side." She touched a tissue to her eye. "He broke a hip, and his leg has two fractures. They'll operate this afternoon. He would have died if he'd fallen over the other side."

"He was lucky in that," said Maggie.

"Maybe it's a blessing in disguise," Jane continued. "Now that he's in the hospital, they'll run tests to see what else is wrong with him." She looked up at Toby. "These character changes, the lack of control. I asked them to look for a cause. At least in the hospital he's safe."

Maggie put her hand on Jane's and suggested she get some sleep before returning to the hospital. Leaving the room, Jane looked unsteady. Maggie was at her side, ready to give aid.

Shelley came down and took the chair that Jane had left. Noticing that she had no place setting, since Jane had used it, she took a cup and spoon from a nearby table. She poured coffee from our carafe, left it black, and sipped it.

"Isn't it awful?" she said. Ben's just sick about it. He wishes he could have been more help."

I recalled that when we returned to the Colombe d'Or last night, Ben was sitting with Shelley in the bar. He said he became dizzy after he followed Ray up onto the wall, so he climbed down as soon as he saw a stairway. Was he telling the truth?

And then there was Didier. This morning he sat grim-faced, alone at a window table, nursing an oversized cup of café au lait. Shelley saw me peering at him. "He's a snotty one, isn't he? What was he up to last night when he walked out on us? That's what I'd like to know." Silently I echoed her thought.

We waited for Ben, but he didn't appear for breakfast. "I guess he's sleeping in," Shelley said eventually. "He wasn't feeling well this morning." She finished her coffee and followed the others out.

We skipped the morning session at which Montoni and Hans de Groot were giving papers; it wasn't exactly collegial of me, but I could read them later. Instead we drove to Vence to report the events of last night to Lieutenant Auclair. Angie insisted on coming with us. I knew why: she was hoping to run into Sergeant Navré at the gendarmerie. Sure enough, he was at his desk behind the counter in the waiting room. Navré beamed when he saw her. However, he put on an official air as he ushered Toby and me into the lieutenant's office.

Auclair, who was reading a file, stood up to greet us and startled us with the news that they had just arrested Yves La Font. "We found Isabelle's handbag in a garbage bin behind his house. He tried to burn it." She sat back down and swiveled her chair to face us.

"Does that mean you think he's the killer?" I asked.

"He admits stealing the bag but denies having harmed her. He claims that when he left the restaurant that night he was angry with his sister, so he walked around outside to cool off. When he returned, he found her slumped over the fountain, dead."

She pulled a page from the file, which apparently contained his statement, and summarized. "He swears he thought she died from a heart attack. Then, he says, he saw her bag and thought her paper about their grandfather might be in it, so he took it before anyone else could find it. But there was no paper in it. At least that's what he claims. For now he's been charged with theft, and we're holding him on suspicion of murder."

She rocked back slightly in her chair, folded her hands on her lap, and looked at me. "We need more proof. What more can you tell me about this fight he had the other night with Daniel Didier?"

"You still think Professor Didier is mixed up in this?" asked Toby.

"That's what I'd like to find out, monsieur." She switched her gaze back to me. "Of course I want to know exactly what happened to you last night, but first tell me once more about the fight you witnessed in Villefranche. Could you go over it again, please?"

I related what I recalled, beginning with spotting Yves and Didier together in the café. Toby filled in details about the scuffle. "Didier told us it started when Yves accused him of killing his sister," said Toby. "In return, he accused Yves."

I added what Didier had told us about his previous clashes with Yves over Isabelle, including the incident in which Yves reported him to the police for domestic violence. "Her injury was an accident, he said."

Lieutenant Auclair arched an eyebrow. "It didn't happen that way," she replied. "I've seen the reports. There were several complaints made against Monsieur Didier over a period of time. And they were filed by Isabelle La Font, not her brother."

Toby gave a low whistle. "That changes things, doesn't it?"

"We shall see. He's been summoned for further questioning." Lieutenant Auclair closed the file and looked at me for a moment. "Now, what in the world were you doing on the ramparts of Saint-Paul last night?"

"It was my fault," Toby started to explain.

I interrupted and took over, recounting Curry's gripe with Toby, the pursuit on the ramparts, and my harrowing experience of being pushed and rescued. I told the lieutenant about finding Curry at the foot of the wall, and I described his injuries. "I never actually saw the person who jostled me. I think it was Curry, but I don't know."

"Who else was on the ramparts besides your husband and Monsieur Montoni, the one who saved you?"

I explained about Bennett.

"And Professor Didier? Do you know where he was at the time?"

"When I left the Colombe d'Or, he was standing in the doorway of the café across the street. He saw me run into the village through the main gate."

"He could have followed her," said Toby.

"It's more likely that Professor Curry knocked me over by accident."

"But if it wasn't Curry," Toby persisted, "it was no accident. My wife could be in danger. People at the conference know that you asked her to watch what was going on and report to you."

Lieutenant Auclair put down her pad and pencil and sat up in consternation. "I very much regret if I've put you at risk. I'll look into this immediately." She picked up the desk phone and spoke rapidly into it. I gathered she was sending someone out to interview Curry at the hospital. When the call was finished, she replaced the phone in its cradle, took up her pencil, and tapped its eraser on her desk. After a pause, she said, "I was going to ask you to perform another service for us, Madame Barnes, but under the circumstances, perhaps it would be best if I didn't."

"Yes, you mentioned there was something, when we spoke on the phone."

"Whatever it is, you shouldn't be involved," Toby said to me, switching to English.

The lieutenant understood. "Perhaps your husband is right."

"Please, Toby. I can speak for myself. What were you going to ask?"

She looked at us both, tapping the pencil again. "If you feel at all uncomfortable, I will understand perfectly."

"Go ahead, lieutenant." I placed my hand over Toby's.

"Very well," she said. "On Sunday your group is planning to visit Saint-Paul-de-Mausole in Saint-Rémy. Is that correct?"

"That's right," I replied. "It's the asylum where Vincent van Gogh was sent."

"Are you aware that Saint-Paul-de-Mausole still functions as a mental institution?"

"Yes, so I understand." I'd read in my guidebook that the ancient monastery, which was converted to a psychiatric hospital in the nineteenth century, still treats patients today. They accept only female patients, and they live in a modern building next to the old asylum. The patients follow a course of art therapy intended to help them cope with their emotions—a program inspired by the hospital's most famous inmate.

"Well, then," continued Auclair, "it may interest you to learn that Isabelle La Font's sister, Juliette, is a patient there. She's been in and out of the clinic over the years. I'm not sure of the reason, perhaps depression. But according to the director, she's doing well at the moment, and he encourages visitors. If I can arrange it, would you be willing to talk to her?"

It took me a moment to grasp what she was saying. Isabelle La Font's sister was being treated at the asylum that once housed Vincent van Gogh. Extraordinary.

"We needed to locate Juliette La Font in order to notify her of her sister's death. That's when we discovered where she was. But she refused to talk to my colleague from Saint-Rémy who delivered the news. She seems to have a phobia about police."

"But why would she talk to me?"

"You're not a police officer. You're a professor of art history—and art is her passion. I'm told it's all she wants to talk about. According to the director, Saint-Paul-de-Mausole is the only facility of its kind she agreed to go to, thanks to its artistic program and its connection to Van Gogh. It seems she feels a bond with him."

"Because of her family history? Does she know anything about her grandfather and Van Gogh?"

Lieutenant Auclair shrugged. "What interests me is what Juliette can tell us about her sister's relationship with Yves La Font. That's why I ask if you would you be willing to talk to her."

I turned to Toby and nodded so slightly that the lieutenant couldn't see it. But Toby did.

"We also hope," she added, "that Mademoiselle La Font will want to meet you because you were with her sister on the night she died. The director thinks such a visit might be therapeutic for her. Why don't you talk it over with your husband before you decide and let me know."

I agreed to think about a meeting. The truth is, I'd made up my mind to accept the assignment. I couldn't see how talking with Juliette

La Font would put me at greater risk. The person who might object was Yves La Font, and he was in custody. Besides, my curiosity was aroused. What if Juliette knew the story about their grandfather that her sister was prevented from disclosing? Would she be willing to reveal to me the secret that had died with Isabelle?

Back in the waiting room, Angie and Sergeant Robert Navré gave me something else to think about. They were having an intimate tête-à-tête. He leaned on his side of the counter and she leaned on hers, facing him. They seemed drawn toward each other like a pair of magnetized paper clips. You can tell when a man and a woman are cooking up an assignation, and these two had something going. An old woman sitting with her purse on her lap was watching them with a benevolent smile. She might have been observing a pair of birds in the forest pecking on a limb. Or building a nest.

After lunch at a café, we drove a short distance to the Matisse chapel, where we planned to meet our group on their afternoon excursion. Matisse, known for his bold colors and appetite for life, surprised his contemporaries by taking on a religious project late in his career. After centuries of dark cathedral art, the Impressionists wanted fresh air. They went outdoors to paint a world filled with sunshine, showing ordinary people having a good time. Then along comes Matisse in his old age and decides to take modern art back to church.

My reveries came to a halt when the lady in the GPS said, "You have arrived at your destination."

"She must be wrong," said Angie. "This is a residential area. There's no chapel here."

"I think that's it." I pointed to a boxlike stucco building.

Toby tilted his head so he could see from the driver's seat. "Can't be. It's got to be that one with the tower."

"Let's park and see," I suggested. Toby pulled up in front, and we saw a tiny sign for La Chapelle du Rosaire. "Let's get in fast," I said, "before the group arrives. I'd like to get a feel for the space when it's empty."

The soft-spoken woman who answered the door conducted us to the lower level. She knocked on a wooden door and opened it slowly, to reveal a marble floor lit by color spilling from stained glass windows. The entire left wall of the chapel glowed with generous masses of blue, green, and yellow light. By contrast, the rest of the chapel was stark. The walls were covered with gigantic black line drawings on white tile. Color was reserved for the stained glass windows.

"Giant tulips!" Angie whispered.

"Palm fronds," a voice behind us whispered back. An aged lady sat in a wooden chair just inside the door. The large wooden cross on her cord necklace signaled that she was one of the nuns. She invited us to look around the chapel, and she offered to answer questions. We roamed in silence until the arrival of our conference friends filled the room with chatter.

The sister never rose from her chair, but she commanded attention, and quiet descended on the visitors as she explained Matisse's intentions and interpreted his iconography. She gave her performance twice, first in French, then in English. When she called for questions from our group, Shelley asked, "Why would the nuns hire a man who was known for painting nudes?"

The elderly nun pursed her lips but then spoke gently. "We did not seek out Monsieur Matisse. He came to us. I was young then, a novice, but I met him."

"What brought him here?" Shelley asked.

"He lived across the street from us. Some years earlier, when he was in Nice recuperating from a cancer operation, he placed an ad in the newspaper. It said: 'Artist seeks young, pretty nurse for daily care.' A girl fresh out of nursing school answered the ad. She changed his bandages, took art lessons from him, and became, as they say, his chaste model. He was shocked when she announced that she was going to enter the convent. He tried to talk her out of it, but she was sure." The nun seemed proud of that.

"Years later, as God willed, her order sent Sister Jacques-Marie to our convent here in Vence, where Matisse had settled for his old age. When Sister heard the convent wanted a chapel, she started designing one, and she brought her sketches to Matisse for comment. Her drawings lit a fire in his imagination, and within a short time, he made the project his own. You see before you the result."

Sister Glenda picked up the thread. "Matisse didn't practice his faith, but just look—he created a great ensemble work of Christian art. Some even compare it to the Sistine Chapel." Sister Glenda's arm swept from the brilliant windows to the stone altar and finally to the Stations of the Cross represented by abstract figures on the tile wall.

Shelley looked unimpressed. She turned her back on Glenda and our guide. "'Chaste model,' my ass," she said, to Maggie. "It's obvious she was his mistress."

"Why else would they go out of the way to tell you she wasn't?" said Maggie.

"*Honi soit qui mal y pense,*" pronounced Glenda.

The visitors moved into the adjacent exhibit hall, but Angie held me back. "What's that mean, what Sister said?"

"Uh, 'Shame on people who have dirty minds.'"

"That doesn't sound like Sister Glenda."

"Well, she was a little more polite."

"What's the big deal if Sister Jacques-Marie did sleep with Matisse?" asked Angie. "What counts is what you do after you take your vows, not what you did before. Right?" When I didn't comment, she repeated her question.

It sounded like special pleading to me.

I awoke with a start. An explosion of thunder still reverberated. Heavy rain drummed against the shutters. I raised my head to see the clock on Toby's bed table. It read three o'clock. Toby groaned and rolled over. In moments, his slow breathing told me he was out again. I fluffed my pillow, turned it over to the cool side, and tried to sleep, but it was no use. I lay in bed, thinking, drifting off into a dream, and then jumping awake with fear.

After several such cycles, I heard muffled sounds coming from the corridor. I had the impression that a man and a woman were fighting. I got up and crept to the door. I put my ear against it but couldn't make out the words or recognize the voices. Then I heard a door slam. I opened our door a crack and peeked out, just in time to see a wisp of white nightgown and the heel of a slipper disappear around the corner. Montoni's room was just down the hall from us, and the *Ne pas déranger* tag hanging on his doorknob was rocking back and forth. Well, well. Ray had been entertaining a female visitor, and there had been a spat. Maggie?

While I was speculating, the light in the hallway abruptly increased. Someone had turned on the light at the bottom of the stairwell. I heard footsteps on the stairs and pulled back, leaving my door ajar only a sliver, so I could barely see out. A tall figure, moving furtively, crossed in front of the door. It was Angie, dressed for outdoors, her coat dripping, tiptoeing in at three in the morning.

By the time he was ready for lunch the next day, my portrait was nearly finished. Already you could tell it was me, with my red jacket, blond hair, and crooked nose, which the other boys made fun of. As usual, Vincent carried his equipment back to the inn, and I went home to eat with my family. Because Papa was with us, the Sunday meal took longer than on weekdays, and that's why I was late getting back.

Vincent was pacing impatiently in front of his easel. He seemed distracted. I thought perhaps he had taken too much wine at lunch, but something else was wrong. He yelled at me, which he had never done before. The words made little sense. His eyes looked strange.

Suddenly he reached into his paint box and pulled out the gun. I could see right away that it was René's old revolver. How Vincent ended up with it, I don't know. Be careful! I shouted. You never knew when that thing would go off, it was so unreliable. Did he mean to frighten me? Shoot me? Instead, he raised the gun to his temple.

I was terrified. Without thinking, I threw myself at him and reached for his arm to pull the gun away. Let me do it, he cried. We both tumbled to the ground. With one hand gripping his wrist, I tried to pry the gun from his fingers with the other, and managed to grasp the handle. I pushed away from him and got to my feet. Now I was holding the gun, and I thought the danger had passed. But Vincent sprang at me, seized my hand, and began forcing it toward his chest. Let me do it, he cried again. I was big for my age, but he was a man and stronger. With both his hands over mine, he forced the gun closer, reaching for the trigger with his thumb. But I wouldn't let go. Then, my God. I felt the explosion. Vincent clutched his side and staggered against the easel, knocking it over, along with the painting. He swayed for a moment, looking at me. Then he fell to his knees, moaned, rolled over on the ground, and lay still.

I only wanted to save him. But instead I shot him. I was holding the gun in my shaking hand.

10

EMMET TROTTED into the breakfast room as if he owned it, head raised, nostrils aquiver, nails clicking briskly on the tile floor. He was followed by his mistress. I was already on my second cup of coffee. "Top o' the morning!" said Maggie, putting on her brogue. Her eyes looked puffy from lack of sleep. She folded herself languidly into the chair next to mine. Emmet circled around ceremoniously and nestled against her leg, resting his snout on his forelegs.

I gave the server across the room a signal, and she came right over and poured some tea. Maggie added milk to the brim. Just like my grandmother. Very Irish.

"Only one cup," she said. "I'm waiting for someone."

Then I didn't have much time. "Maggie, this may be none of my business, but tell me the truth. Was that you I saw coming out of Montoni's room in the middle of the night?"

She looked puzzled. "Which night are we talking about?"

"What do you mean? Last night, of course."

"Then, no."

I sat back in my chair.

"Last night I was with Thierry. Ray was Wednesday night."

"You're kidding me!" I said, too loudly. Then I toned my voice down. "You mean you're sleeping with both of them?"

"Slept. Just once." I stared at her. "Apiece, that is, not together," she added by way of clarification. There was a pause. "Ray, I admit was a mistake. But Thierry's a sweet boy."

"But . . . You're old enough to be his mother," I sputtered.

"Not at all. Don't exaggerate, Nora. Anyhow, nothing will come of it. I won't corrupt him, if that's what you're worried about." I must have looked dazed. "Well, you asked for the truth. Look, fooling around is one of the perks of coming to these conferences. I don't carry on like this at home. People would talk."

"People would talk here. I'm talking."

"Yes, you are."

"I'm sorry. Look, I don't mean to judge you. Really. I'm just trying to take this in."

"When you've finished taking it in, let me know."

My life is sheltered, I thought. Bodega Bay's in California, but it's not Sin City. To shift the subject, I made some awkward remark about the Matisse chapel, but Maggie had my number. "Go on, ask me more. You're dying to, now, aren't you?"

"Of course. Your nightlife is a lot more interesting than mine."

"Don't say that. Toby's a fine man." She said it with a lascivious lilt.

"Hey, get your own guy!"

"I did. Twice."

"Ray isn't 'your own guy.' He's married, isn't he?"

"He told me he was getting a divorce."

"That's more than I know. Anyway, if that wasn't you last night, he slept with somebody else."

"I knew he couldn't be trusted." She laughed at herself. "Then again, neither can I. No double standard here." She raised her teacup as for a wedding toast.

"I see that you're having fun. But don't these one-offs get tiring after a while? Wouldn't you like a more permanent relationship?"

"Marriage suits you obviously. Maybe it doesn't suit me."

"What about companionship?"

"Don't forget Emmet. He's loyal." She reached down and scratched him behind the ear. "As for a man, I thought I had a good one last year until he ran off with one of my graduate students. That's the reason I'm on leave, if you must know, to pick myself up. Here comes Thierry." Maggie got up. "You'll have to excuse me, dear. I agreed to meet him for breakfast."

Thierry's smile made him look even younger than before. Perhaps to hide his shyness, he bent down to stroke Emmet's head. Maggie pointed toward a table for two and signaled to her man and her dog to join her. As I watched them walk away, all three looked happy. Emmet was wagging his tail, and Maggie for my benefit wagged hers. She winked at me when she sat down.

My mind returned to last night. Well, if Maggie wasn't with Ray Montoni, who was? I had picked up signs of tension in Shelley's relationship with Ben. Had her frustration with him sent her to Ray? The Bennetts and Montonis lived in Philadelphia, so she may have taken up with Ray before the conference. I looked around the room. Jane Curry was having coffee by herself. Now, there was another woman with a problem husband. Could she have turned to Ray for comfort, while her husband lay in the hospital? Would she have done that?

As I mulled over these possibilities, the De Groots entered the breakfast room. Normally, Hans was cheerful, but today he looked sullen. What about Klara? If she was an errant wife who had just been found out, she looked awfully calm. Maybe Hans was simply grouchy from lack of sleep. I probably hadn't been the only guest disturbed by the storm. But then my overactive imagination conjured a scene of Hans awakened in the middle of the night by a thunderclap, only to discover that his wife wasn't in their bed. As quickly as the thought occurred to me, I dismissed it. At least I was sure of one thing. Whoever was sleeping with Montoni, it wasn't Sister Glenda.

That turned my thoughts to Angie. What had she been up to last night? A whispered summons from Madame Richarde, who appeared at my side and asked me to follow her, led to the answer. Coffee in the library is not part of the breakfast deal at Hotel des Glycines, but Angie has a way of getting what she wants. She was sitting on a couch with a tray on the coffee table in front of her. Madame Richarde gave Angie a conspiratorial look and left, closing the door firmly.

"What's this?" I asked. "Am I being ambushed?"

"Don't be so suspicious. Just sit down." She patted the place next to her on the couch. "I need to talk with you—privately."

"Getting Madame Richarde to lock us in a room together seems a bit dramatic. What did you tell her?"

Angie calmly poured herself coffee. "We're not locked in. And I told her the truth."

"Which is?"

"I said I have a love problem, and I have to talk with my sister. She was very understanding. She told me how to say it in French: *un problème d'amour.*" She pursed her lips into a secret smile and opened her eyes wide like a Kewpie doll. For a woman with love problems, she appeared awfully merry.

"Is this about Robert?" She looked coyly at her cup, as if to hide her smile. "So you *are* in love with Robert. Is he in love with you?"

She looked up, and I saw the Angie of twenty years ago—a child of delight, feeling joy in every hour of the day.

"I think so. He says so."

"He says what, exactly?"

"I feel like you're badgering me. I'm trying to get your advice, not the third degree."

"Okay, Angie. I'll try not to grill you, but if you'll tell me what he said about his feelings, that will help me give you advice."

"You know, 'I love you. I adore you.' It sounds so sweet in that accent of his."

"Are you sure he means it? He just met you. Maybe he's practicing the phrases they taught him in English class."

Angie's face fell.

"You're smitten, aren't you?" My voice was light, but my chest was heavy. I love my openhearted sister, and I feel for her when she gets hurt by callous men, which happens absurdly often. Did she need a warning to slow things down? I waited, reminding myself to just listen.

"I really like him."

"Tell me about it."

She sighed. Then she took a breath and started what seemed a rehearsed presentation. "First," she said, "we'll be leaving here in two days. That's not enough time to finish falling in love, even. I'm starting to be heartbroken already. If this is really love, then I should stay here or come back fast and give it a chance."

"But you don't speak French. How would you get along here? How would you support yourself?"

"I have some savings." She put her hand up. "But let me finish. The second problem is that I'm not a hundred percent sure that Roe-bare is as much in love with me as I am with him."

I had my doubts too.

"Third, this comes at a bad time. I'm supposed to be making up my mind about whether to become a real novice. I'm facing a vow of chastity."

"Yeah, I'd say that's a problem."

"You're always sarcastic. Cut it out."

I felt cornered. "Have you told Sister Glenda? She's your mother confessor, right?"

"Oh, God. I got up all my courage and told her yesterday morning. It was so hard. But then all I had to confess was that I was attracted to him. Now I have to tell her we've done the deed." She waited for my response. "You're not surprised?"

"Listen, Angie, I was up last night at three o'clock in the morning. I heard you come in."

"You did?" She hung her head.

"Does Sister Glenda know about last night? She's right next door to you. Maybe she heard you leave and return."

"Maybe. I don't care. I'm going to tell her anyway. I have to. I promised to. It's part of living in a convent. You open your life to your mother superior."

"What do you think she'll say?"

Angie gazed into the distance. "I think she'll say what she said yesterday: that I'll know God's will when He grants me the grace to know it."

That was the official answer. I wondered what she really thought.

Angie turned to look me in the eye. "I'm supposed to pray for God's grace. Will you pray for me?"

"Sure, if you'd like me to."

Angie threw her arms around me, which is awkward when you're sitting with your knees wedged between the couch and the coffee table, but we managed a long sisterly hug. Pain cut into my shoulders, but I kept holding her until we began breathing at the same rhythm. We drew back from each other, feeling consoled. Angie faced some tough days ahead of her, and I couldn't do much to help. I did say a little prayer for her. It couldn't hurt.

Having finished his breakfast, Toby was propped against the bed pillows reading. I clued him in. "It's what I've been telling you all along," he said in a tone of irritation. It's best not to get into a serious discussion with Toby first thing in the morning. Plus he was still grumbling about my decision to meet with Juliette La Font. We'd settled the matter last night, but his concession was grudging and now spilled over into this conversation. "Your sister was never cut out to be a nun. She happens to like men. What she wants is to be a 'nun with benefits,' but they don't offer that option in the convent."

"She thinks she's in love."

"Thinks. And if this romance doesn't work out, the same thing will happen again when the next guy comes along. Face it. This fantasy of hers of becoming a nun was always just that, a fantasy."

"Maybe so, but Angie has to find that out for herself."

Toby grunted and went back to his book. I decided to leave it at that and wait for his mood to improve. It usually does as the day wears on. Meanwhile I got myself ready for the morning session. Toby was planning to skip it, as were the other nonacademic guests. It was the annual meeting of the Society for Vincent van Gogh Studies. To present at the conference, you had to be a member. Naturally, I joined.

The society members assembled in our usual room at the Maeght, which today seemed too large for our number. The main item on the agenda was the election of officers, which can be a sham in small organizations like this one, where the titles are parceled out to the handful of people who show up. Ray called the meeting to order. He had another year to go as president but announced that he was stepping down in order to finish a project he was working on. He was anxious to get it done, he said, and was behind schedule. He informed the group that Ben Bennett was willing to assume the presidency for the coming year, should he be nominated. So he was, by Hans de Groot; and facing no opposition—these things generally being prearranged—he was duly elected. Ben looked pleased. Next, Hans was reelected secretary/treasurer. Since the position required work, no one else wanted it. The board of directors was reappointed by acclamation. It wasn't clear to me what the directors did, but their names were on the letterhead. In fact, the left margin of the letterhead had names and titles ranging vertically from top to bottom.

Having managed things to his satisfaction, Ray then asked if there was any new business. Maggie's hand shot up. "I'd like to suggest an addition to the slate of officers," she said. "The society could use an international secretary, someone based over here who could promote membership and publicize future conferences and activities. I'd like to propose the creation of that office. And I'd like to nominate Thierry Toussaint for the position." She locked eyes with Montoni, and it seemed for a few awkward moments that they were engaged in a wordless conversation on an entirely different topic. Eventually Ray blinked.

"Is there a second?" he asked in a somewhat subdued voice. I raised my hand. "Is there any discussion?"

"It's a good idea," said Jacques, who was sitting next to Thierry. The kid had performed well. Why not give him a title he could add to his resumé when he went out on the job market? That seemed the general sentiment.

"All those in favor?" asked Ray. "Any opposed? Motion carried."

I wondered how they could possibly fit another name on the letterhead.

"I move to adjourn," said Maggie, beaming in Thierry's direction.

"Is there any other business before the committee?" asked Ray. His brow was moist, although it wasn't noticeably warm in the room. No one stirred. "Then a motion to adjourn is in order. Those in favor?" A dull murmur rose from the gathered scholars.

As the room emptied, I glanced outside to check the weather and caught an unexpected movement out of the corner of my eye. I turned my head and looked out the east-facing windows to the Giacometti Sculpture Court, one of the museum's highlights. I'd been looking at Giacometti's spindly bronze figures all week, but not with this backdrop of silvery fog. His wraithlike *Walking Man* was fixed in midstride in the center of the court. Facing him stood six emaciated figures lined up in a row, arms at their sides as if at attention. They were called *The Women of Venice*, though they looked just like the man. The only way to tell women from men in Giacometti's work is that the women are always motionless and the men are always walking.

Now, however, one of the women moved. Her feet came forward. Her head swung back. She was levitating. Or rather, she was upended by two workmen clothed in identical blue smocks. Three more blue men reached out to carry her corpse-like off the terrace. One had her by the shoulders, one cradled her head, two supported her at the waist, and another had her by the feet.

What is this—some kind of performance art? I wondered. I slipped out to the hall just in time to spot the workmen carrying the rigid woman down a staircase. They moved like pallbearers. The impression of a funeral was reinforced by the fact that at the bottom of the stairs a long wooden box stood open like a casket. With bowed heads, the men lowered the *Woman of Venice* into her coffin.

"What are you doing?" I asked one of the workmen.

"We're sending her to Rome, for an exhibition."

Now it made sense. But the image of the statue as a dead woman had rattled me. It brought back a picture of Isabelle laid out at the foot of the fountain. All at once I felt faint.

When I got back to our room, Toby looked up at me and said, "Hon, are you all right?"

I related my uncanny experience. "It looked like they were carrying a corpse."

"Come here." He put his arms around me. "Can I get you something? A glass of water?"

"Yes, thanks."

Toby went to the sink and filled a glass for me. "What you need is a distraction. Maybe the perfume factory will be just the ticket." Today the group was going to the Fragonard Museum in Grasse, followed by a visit to the perfume factory that also bears his name—the artist was a native son. Toby was right, I needed a distraction. And what could be better than shopping?

It was pouring when we set out. Rain sloshed off the roof of the van ahead of us, splashing across our windshield. The back road was slippery on the curves, but the vans managed to slither around the loops, hold the road on dips, and ascend with steady power. Still, we were relieved when we pulled into the parking lot at the height of the peak on which

Grasse stands. Ray sensibly had scheduled the museum visit first. Any normal woman could spend many hours at a perfume factory. There's much to learn and scores of scents to sample. Ray realized that if we started at the factory, we'd never leave in time to do justice to Fragonard's paintings. So it was going to be Art first, Perfume later.

Ray advised that we stay in the van while he arranged entry to the museum. There was a rustle, as umbrellas were found and jackets were zipped, but the bustle stopped when the door was pulled open. Ray stood there, shivering and sheepish. "I'm sorry, folks. The museum's closed. Renovations."

Nobody spoke. What could we say? Shelley knew what to say. "Jesus, Ray! You took us to this godforsaken place without checking that it's open?"

Ray clamped his lips together and turned his attention to the rest of the passengers. He cleared his throat and announced, "Okay. We'll go straight to the perfume factory. Wait till I tell the other van."

The change of venue was quickly executed, and since the factory gives tours all day, 365 days of the year, we were welcome—including Emmet. I was disappointed not to see the Fragonard paintings but excited by the prospect of my first tour of a factory, never mind one that offered perfume samples. I assumed that all the women would feel the same, even Sister Glenda. Klara, the chemist, would love it. I wasn't sure about the men.

The Parfumerie Fragonard doesn't look at all like a factory. From the street, you see a handsome three-storied building, painted sunflower yellow, and lightened by rows of high windows with light blue shutters. It looks more like a city mansion. Though the entryway at the back is a recent addition, much of the interior keeps the appearance of an old and noble house. Floor-to-ceiling windows in rooms large enough to dance in speak of eighteenth-century balls. Gold-framed mirrors invite elegant ladies to check their maquillage. Each of many tables, which in other days would have been laid for tea or lunch, displays a line of perfume, with its attendant lotions, soaps, colognes, and powders. The flower associated with a particular perfume is featured in an appropriate bouquet—modest for lily of the valley, lush for gardenia. I was eager to roam the display rooms, but we were told that this pleasure was reserved for the end of the tour, when we could also sample (and buy) the perfumes.

Two young women in identical black suits, high heels, and red lipstick were waiting in front of an elevator door beyond the display rooms. Each guide took six of us. Bowing ever so slightly, ours introduced herself as Ms. Lin, from Taiwan.

"How'd you get this job?" asked Shelley.

"My given name is Fang," the young woman said. "It means 'fragrant.' From an early age, I was interested in perfumes. I was hired in the industry in Taiwan, and my company asked me to work at Fragonard for a year."

"Were you trained in chemistry?" asked Klara.

"And in business. MIT," replied Ms. Lin.

Ms. Lin's passion for her field made for a lively tour. First, she taught us how to identify the natural ingredients of perfume. For that purpose, she brought us to a row of numbered boxes. She challenged us to sniff through the hole in the box and guess the ingredient inside. We had a list of possibilities: rose, lavender, lemon, peach, strawberry, cinnamon, coffee, and sandalwood. The winner would accurately match each box number with its ingredient. You'd be surprised how hard it is tell sandalwood from cinnamon (my downfall). Klara, with her chemical expertise, was done in seconds. Maggie and Shelley dithered and laughed and guessed out loud. Ms. Lin encouraged Ray and Daniel Didier to join in, but they stepped back, leaving the game to the women. Throughout the process, Emmet's nose twitched with curiosity. He was on his best behavior, though—no jumping toward even the doggiest aromas.

After telling us about "the Nose," the expert on fragrances who creates new perfumes, Ms. Lin escorted us to his work station and on to the laboratories of his assistants. Then I understood why dogs were allowed on the tour. The work areas were completely sealed off by double glass panes. Without fear of contamination by our presence, middle-aged women in floral-print aprons performed the tasks of manufacturing and testing. In one meticulously clean room, they emptied vials of pale liquid into glass pipes that swirled and bent, eventually splashing into steel vats. In other equally immaculate rooms, they poured gold fluids into amber bottles. In another room, a team of workers in hairnets boxed cream-colored ovals, soap for a powder room. Down the way, women molded pale pink soap into roses the size of a fist. The happiest room held hundreds of small yellow ducks. A Rubenesque girl sat bent over, painting orange beaks and big black eyes on the soap duckies.

Ms. Lin herded us back onto the elevator and escorted us to the display room, where she handed us over to a white-coated beauty who was to be our "sampling guide." She was French, chic, and flirtatious. "You are all our welcome guests," she said, "and especially you, messieurs. The husbands don't always participate in the sampling. I have something special for you."

Didier interrupted. "Thank you, mademoiselle, but we are not the husbands. They are in the other half of our group." He tilted his head toward the elevator, which was ejecting Sister Glenda and Angie, followed politely by the husbands (Hans, Ben, Toby) and the bachelors (Thierry and Jacques).

"Then we shall all go together." She signaled to her colleague, who led us to the display area for men's colognes. "Every man has his own scent," our guide said. "A cologne must not mask it but deepen it. There is a cologne that suits your deepest nature." She lingered over the last word. At that moment, every man, with the exception of Didier, was under her sway.

"Don't be afraid to experiment," she urged, looking straight at Didier. "I'm going to show you how to find your true scent." Didier stepped back. Without even an "excuse me," he turned and walked away.

Taking no notice that she'd lost a customer, the guide continued. "The first step is to determine which scent gives you initial pleasure."

She paused for effect. "So that you don't become confused, you must follow the proper procedure." She and her colleague handed each person a rectangular white packet, the size of a fat cigar, filled with long, slim paper sticks. Each stick had the name of a fragrance. "Don't spray the cologne on yourself. Not to begin. Instead, spray the fragrance on the stick with its name. Give it a moment to set, and then sniff it. If you like the smell, put the stick on the little dish in front of you." There were different-colored dishes up and down the counter, just ready for the men to get to work.

"Discard the ones that don't please you." She pointed to a chrome box with a slot in the top. "Then go back and retest the sticks in your dish, until you have narrowed down to two." She looked around to see that we were listening and inclined to follow her instructions. I was distracted by the names of the men's scents. Beau Gosse (Handsome Kid) was perfect for Maggie's Thierry. Suivez-moi (Come Hither) fit Ray's nighttime behavior. And I knew which one I wanted to describe Toby: Toujours Fidèle.

When I attended again to the voice of our sampling guide, she was saying, "You will then be at the point of decision. Spray a small amount of one of your two selections on your left wrist and the other on your right wrist. Do not inhale them until they have fully set. The product must blend with your essence, gentlemen. It will be worth the time to find the fragrance that projects . . . you."

Her speech divided the men from the boys. Ray, Thierry, and Ben started their work at the counter. Toby eyed Hans de Groot and Jacques Godard, and they headed for the exit and the café next door.

It was now the ladies' turn. We moved to the section of women's perfumes, which was of course many times larger than the men's. The discourse we were treated to was longer than the version for the men. The guide pointed out each fragrance by name and announced its base note and its minor notes. She then left us to ourselves, to go through her prescribed program. Most of us set to work, but Sister Glenda kept Angie on a rein. I saw her read through the list of perfumes. She stopped at the name "Miranda."

"That's interesting," she said. "Three of the perfumes are named after women: Miranda, Émilie, and Sorenza. Why don't they use the most appropriate name of all?"

"What's that?" Angie replied.

"Magdalene. The French would say Madeleine. She's the patron saint of women, fallen and otherwise. She's also the patron saint of perfumers." Glenda indicated the surroundings. "And hairdressers." She pointed to Angie, who was a hairdresser before she entered the convent.

"Really? There's a special saint for hairdressers?"

"And fallen women," Glenda repeated. Angie looked at her shoes.

Shelley was hard at work at her sampling process. Seeing that I was not, she grabbed my elbow. "Give me a hand," she said. "I'm looking for something that will rekindle Ben's you-know-what." She had already put a stick on her red plate, and now she sprayed perfume from a fancy bottle onto her left wrist. She rubbed it in and raised her wrist to touch her nose. "Do you think this would work? It's called Défi. That means 'dare,' doesn't it? I *dare* you to try it."

Never one to refuse a challenge, I looked through my sampling sticks and found the one marked Défi. Shelley handed me the bottle and I sprayed from it onto the stick. I sniffed. "That may be a bit much for me."

"I don't care if it's too much for you. Is it enough for Ben? I'm not looking for subtle here."

"It's definitely not subtle."

"Oh, come on, you can't really tell until you spray it on your wrist and rub it in."

I wasn't keen on spending the day smelling like a streetwalker, but Shelley was hard to say no to. I held the atomizer poised to spray.

Just then, Emmet, who had been so good for so long, decided to bolt, heading for a dainty poodle at my side. She was the companion of the artfully coiffed woman next to me. Emmet brushed by me on such a tear that I tripped and lost my balance. I caught hold of the counter to steady myself, but the bottle of Défi fell to the floor, shattering into shards. Startled by the noise, Emmet did an about-face and returned to the puddle at my feet. He sniffed, looked up at me and sniffed again, and then started lapping up the spilled perfume. "Emmet," I said, "that's not for you!"

Maggie swept down to snatch at her dog. "Emmet, Emmet!" She pulled him by his collar to her side, hissing, "Heel!"

Meanwhile, the poodle had arrived to sample the spilled perfume as well. The little mince wasn't about to let some Irish tramp get all the goods. Maggie and her French counterpart struggled with their respective pets. The little ones suddenly appeared docile. Then Emmet whimpered and rolled on his side. The poodle fell over, shivering. Simultaneously, they moaned softly. Emmet regurgitated some fluid. The poodle fell silent and stiff.

"Emmet!" cried Maggie. He pawed the air, but in another moment, he stiffened too. Sister Glenda put her arms around Angie.

Maggie looked up at me, stunned. "They're dead," she said.

Then Shelley collapsed.

It didn't look like a faint. It looked worse.

I panicked. I wanted only to run away. Who would believe me? I had killed Vincent and would go to prison. And it was the painting that condemned me, proof that I was there. So I tried to hide everything, not thinking beyond the moment. I put the gun in my pocket and snatched the painting from the easel. I pulled it off its stretcher and rolled it up. Then I folded the easel and carried everything into the field and looked for the biggest haystack I could find. I swept the top of the hay off and put the easel and painting on the pile and covered them over. I went back for Vincent's paint box. I hid that in another haystack and threw in the gun as well. Then I returned to where Vincent lay. He had not moved. Blood oozed from his shirt. I was sure he was dead.

How I spent the next few hours, I don't remember. When I got home I said I was sick and refused supper. My mother sent me to bed, where I lay awake, thinking terrible thoughts about prison. I knew I must move those things hidden in the hay, or else they would be discovered. So in the middle of the night, when everyone in the house was asleep, I crept out and returned to the place where Vincent had fallen. But he wasn't there! That meant someone had discovered the body. By morning, the whole town would know about Vincent's death.

Fortunately, the haystacks had not been disturbed. I removed any evidence that could point to me if the police came to search the area. I broke up the easel and put the pieces, along with the pistol and paint box, into a canvas sack, and I carried it to the river, where, weighted with stones, it sank.

But the painting? I can't adequately explain that even to myself. I think in the beginning I kept it to remind me of my sin. It accused me, and it seemed a sacrilege to discard it. Then, as the years went by and Vincent became famous, I knew it would be an act of vandalism to destroy it. So I kept it hidden.

Imagine how I felt when I learned that Vincent had survived the night. He regained consciousness, so they said, and dragged himself back to the inn, where the police interviewed him. I expected to be arrested at any moment, but they never came. Had Vincent said nothing about me? It took two days for him to die, two days of suffering from that wound. The town was full of talk, but none of it about me.

11

THE LIEUTENANT'S VOICE was breaking up, but I could make out that Shelley was in the hospital in Grasse. "The doctor says . . . improving . . . to see her now." It was raining again this morning, coming down hard, and the storm was interfering with reception. I walked my cell phone over to the window to see if I could get a stronger signal. It helped. "Fortunately, it seems she will recover."

"Was it the perfume?" I asked.

"Evidently."

"Do you know what was in it?"

"Not yet. I've ordered a full chemical analysis, but it will take at least twenty-four hours. Also an autopsy on the dogs for their stomach contents. But the preliminary blood work . . ." The line crackled, then cleared. "They found digitalis in Madame Bennett's blood . . . a trace amount but in such small quantity that it shouldn't have produced an adverse effect."

It occurred to me that if Isabelle's poisoner had tainted the wine of everyone at her table, tests might show that they all had traces of the drug in their systems. Shelley and her husband, Montoni and the Currys might all be carrying digitalis in their blood. Then I thought of a simpler explanation. "Maybe she was taking it by prescription."

"We'll soon find out. In any case, whatever made her ill was something else. I'll know more tomorrow. Meanwhile Fragonard is treating the incident as a hostile act by a disgruntled employee. The newspapers in Grasse are reporting that story. The factory is in the midst of a labor dispute with their workers, and the management thinks that someone may have tampered with a bottle to frighten customers away. An act of industrial sabotage." Something like that, I recalled, happened in the States. Someone put cyanide in batches of Tylenol capsules, and seven people died. The person who did it was never caught.

Then I remembered there was a small Fragonard outlet in Saint-Paul. Anyone at our conference could have bought the bottle there, tampered with it, and placed it on the shelf at the factory.

"I realize that," said the lieutenant when I voiced my thought. "First Isabelle La Font is poisoned, and now we have a similar incident involving a member of your group. It seems more than a coincidence."

"Are you saying this was a personal attack?"

"It's best not to jump to conclusions. Even so, do you remember who was standing near Madame Bennett when she was sampling the perfume?"

I closed my eyes and tried to recapture the scene. Maggie, Klara, and I were closest to her, Jane Curry too. I thought it odd that Jane had come with us on the trip to Grasse, given that her husband was in the hospital mending from his operation. She did spend the morning with him, but she said he kept ordering her to get out of his room. "He's in a bad state," Jane said. "I mean, in his mood. His bones will get better, but he's not in his right mind. The doctor said I should leave Bruce on his own today and they'll do tests."

At the perfumery, Jane was unable to relax and get into the tour. She kept to herself, saying little. Others asked questions and made comments, but she didn't. And I don't remember her sampling perfume. It was natural that her mind would be elsewhere, with her husband. But then, could she have kept herself inconspicuous because she was orchestrating a poisoning? Did she have any reason to hurt Shelley?

"What about the men?" asked the lieutenant. "Where was Monsieur Didier?"

"By then the men were at the café."

"But before they went there?"

"Didier was in the sampling room with the rest of us, but he left abruptly, when the sampling guide started her pitch." Was that because he'd set the scene in motion and wanted to be out of the way, beyond suspicion, literally? What about the others? Anyone could have placed that bottle on the table. But how could anyone predict who would pick it up?

Then I recalled Ben wandering around the women's display area before he left with Ray and Thierry. Could he have poisoned his wife? Someone who knew Shelley well enough might predict she'd try a perfume named Dare. And Shelley was consistently nasty to Ben. It wouldn't be the first time a mild-mannered husband exacted revenge on his shrewish wife.

The lieutenant seemed aware of my distraction and kept silent, perhaps hoping I would offer my thought. When I didn't, she asked, "Did you see anyone offer the bottle to Madame Bennett?"

"No, she was holding it when she called me over." Shelley was the one who handed the bottle to me—what if I'd been the target? Was Shelley trying to poison me? No, she sprayed herself first. She wouldn't have done that if she knew the perfume was poisoned. It was a muddle. Maybe the theory of a random attack by a factory worker made sense after all, coincidence or not.

"I'll let you know if there is any change in her condition," said the lieutenant. Then she confirmed the arrangements for my visit to the asylum, which was scheduled for the afternoon. She wanted to know whether I was still willing to speak with Juliette La Font. Of course I was.

"Excellent. She's expecting you. Present yourself at the reception desk when you arrive and the director will meet you. His name is Dr. Salles." There was a pause on the line. "One more thing, Madame Barnes. About Fragonard, I'm not sure what's going on. You will be careful, yes?"

Saint-Rémy-de-Provence is less than two hundred kilometers from the Riviera. Though we were taking the autoroute, Montoni figured on three or four hours, given the rain and a stop along the way for lunch. Ben was with Shelley at the hospital in Grasse. Jane was spending the day in the hall outside her husband's room, in Cagnes-sur-Mer. Didier was at the gendarmerie being interrogated, and Maggie, heartbroken over losing Emmet, remained at the hotel. Thierry stayed behind with her to offer consolation. The remainder of our troop set out in the gloomy rain to visit the lunatic asylum where Vincent had been confined. Along the way, I reviewed what I knew about his stay there.

There are many theories about Vincent's illness. Some think his disorder was schizophrenia, some say manic depression; others attribute his condition to malnutrition, lead poisoning from his paints, the abuse of absinthe, or the late stage of syphilis. Freudians have their own opinions. The first doctor to offer a diagnosis was an intern at the hospital in Arles, where Vincent was treated after he slashed off part of his ear in a state of delirium. He concluded that his patient had "a kind of epilepsy." Soon after Vincent was admitted to the asylum at Saint-Rémy, its director, Dr. Théophile Peyron, accepted that diagnosis, and some recent scholars agree with it.

They suggest that Vincent suffered not from the familiar kind of epilepsy that erupts in physical convulsions but from a more insidious form that generates attacks accompanied by anxiety, hallucinations, and loss of consciousness. Those were the symptoms Vincent described. Brain disorders ran in the Van Gogh family. One of Vincent's aunts, an uncle, and two cousins were epileptics. Two other uncles, his grand-father, and his sister suffered from some kind of mental illness. Vincent's younger brother, Cor, committed suicide, and there were suspicions of other suicides in the family going back several generations. Whatever the exact nature of Vincent's affliction, it was probably genetic.

Vincent had been considered odd since childhood, but as he matured he suffered full-blown fits, which occurred during emotional crises or perhaps caused his emotional crises. In any case, the fits grew worse during his stay in Arles. The ear-slashing episode occurred a few days before Christmas of 1888. Vincent spent two weeks in the hospital, then was released. Within a short time, neighbors complained to the police about his wild behavior. When he didn't, or couldn't, change his ways, the police used force to return him to the hospital. This pattern was repeated over several months. He finally agreed to seek help and had himself committed to the asylum of Saint-Paul-de-Mausole on the outskirts of Saint-Rémy, a few miles from Arles.

The asylum is in a converted monastery nestled in a pleasant valley at the foot of the Alpilles mountain chain, near the ruins of the ancient Roman city of Glanum. The Romans selected the site for its healing waters, strategic advantage, and beauty. The monastery of Saint-Paul-de-Mausole, built in the eleventh century, takes its name from a Roman mausoleum. Van Gogh became a patient there in May 1889 and stayed until the following May. The doctor and nurses treated him kindly. They even encouraged him to paint during the periods of calm between his attacks. He did some paintings in his room, on an easel set in front of the window. In time, he was allowed to take his easel out on the grounds; he painted the flower gardens, the buildings, and the gate that kept him safe. The regimen agreed with him. His stay led to tremendous productivity—nearly 150 paintings and almost as many drawings. But in the end he wanted his freedom back and asked for his release. From there, he left for Auvers-sur-Oise to seek the help of Dr. Gachet, and three months later he was dead.

It was two o'clock by the time our van turned onto the little road leading to the gates of the monastery. The drive had been rough, through splashing rain, as trailer trucks churned ahead of us on the highway, throwing muddy spray against our windows. Lunch at a rest stop along the autoroute didn't offer much respite. The fare was no worse than what you'd get at an American counterpart along the interstate, but no better either. In France you have higher expectations.

We parked alongside the wall of the monastery and hurried through the gate, trying not to get soaked. I recognized the circular stone fountain on the path leading to the arched entryway to the main building. Vincent depicted it in paint and in charcoal. Once inside, we walked along a corridor bordering a lovely cloister, which I recognized from another one of his paintings. The walls of the corridor had that clammy smell of old wet stone. The supporting columns of the cloister were finely shaped, and the quadrangle they enclosed contained low green shrubbery. It was a peaceful spot, designed for contemplation. Vincent had spent hours here, and I could picture him sitting on one of the flat stone surfaces spaced between the pillars of the colonnade.

The corridor led into a large hall, which in former times served as the refectory. Now it was used as a reception area and exhibition space. There was a ticket counter and a little shop displaying books about Van Gogh, picture postcards, and the like. While Ray paid for the tickets, I glanced at the exhibition of paintings done by current patients in the art therapy program. They were the work of amateurs, and it showed. Most tried to imitate Vincent's style, with baleful results. But one woman had made portraits of her fellow inmates. They were unforgettable—faces distorted by anxiety, anger, fear, delusion. Just one of her subjects, a gaunt painter before her easel, evidenced hope. She wielded her brush like a trowel, as if trying to dig herself—paint herself—out of her mental grave.

As my companions lingered over the paintings, I approached the woman behind the counter and gave her my name. "Ah, *oui*," she said, her face indicating recognition. "I'll tell the director that you're here." She pressed a button on the desk phone and spoke a few words into the mouthpiece. "Come this way, please, Madame Barnes." I signaled Toby to let him know that I was leaving. She led me back through the corridor to the cloister and pointed to a door at the end of a hallway. "Go right through there, please. He's expecting you."

Dr. Salles got up from behind his desk to welcome me, and we exchanged introductions. He was a slight, elderly man with sparse white hair. What was it about his face that gave it a kindly mien? Perhaps the crinkles on his brow from decades of professional concern. He wore a woolen suit.

"It's very good of you to permit a stranger to visit your patient," I began. "Thank you for arranging it."

"Not at all. It's important to maintain good relations with the police, isn't it? If I can be of help, so much the better. What's more, Juliette is looking forward to meeting you. I spoke to her this morning."

"I'll do my best not to upset her. I promise."

"That's good of you. You must be sensitive. She was badly shaken by the news of her sister's death. But now she's eager for information about what happened. I'm quite sure she will be glad of your visit."

"I hope so. What exactly is the nature of her illness, Doctor?"

"Such information is private, madame. I cannot disclose medical details without the patient's authorization. I am able to say this much, however. Her condition comes and goes. In the past month, she's been much better. I was hoping to release her, but now it may be prudent to keep her with us a little while longer. She's been coming here for years, you see. For the peace and quiet and for the painting. It soothes her. Sometimes she stays weeks, sometimes months. When she returns home she can manage well enough for a period, but inevitably the cycle begins again. You will find her completely lucid, but fragile."

"Is there someone at home to care for her?"

"She was living with her sister, but now, alas . . ." He waved a hand disconsolately. "It's going to be hard for Juliette to accept that her sister is gone. There's a kind neighbor who lives next door but otherwise she will be alone, I'm afraid. She receives government assistance, but it's emotional support that she requires now."

"I understand. I won't stay long. Thank you again."

"Not at all. Shall I let them know you're on the way?"

"I wonder if I could take a quick look at Vincent's room first?"

"You haven't seen it?"

"Not yet, we only just arrived."

"But of course! I'll tell the nurse to expect you in a quarter of an hour. Naturally you must see Vincent's room. Go back to the reception hall and take the stairs to the second floor. It's marked. The first room on the left."

"Thank you again, monsieur."

"Not at all, madame. A pleasure." He bowed and showed me out.

There was no one in the reception hall except the attendant. Our group had already seen Vincent's room while I was talking to the director. Now they had gone off to another room for the afternoon program. There would be a lecture about art therapy, a tour of the premises, and a film on Vincent's stay at the asylum.

I followed a sign, went through an alcove, and found the stone stairwell leading to the deserted upper floor, where in the old days the patients had their rooms. Vincent's room was just off the landing. I found myself alone in it.

The little room felt like a cell. It had bare walls, a red tile floor, an iron bedstead, and a mock-up of Vincent's easel. The main feature of the room was a narrow window that looked out over an enclosed garden. The window had thick bars. This was Vincent's view of the world for almost a year, and it was here that he painted his iconic *Starry Night*— here, looking through the bars at a small patch of sky. He wasn't allowed outside at night.

As I looked out at a gray sky, I could see that painting in my mind's eye. And I realized that hardly anything in it was taken from nature. It was a vision. In the foreground, Vincent painted the top of a towering cypress tree as it might be seen from a second-floor window. But there is no tree out there, and in the painting no bars block the view. He saw a village in the middle distance, its church and spire visible, but in reality no such town exists. In the painting, there's a row of mountains beyond the village. Yes, those are there, but all the rest—two-thirds of the canvas—is given to the night sky, a sky painted deep blue, not black, and lit by outsize yellow stars and a blazing moon. In the center of the sky are two mysterious curlicues of light. They look like whirlpool galaxies as they might be seen through a modern telescope, but that's not possible. Galaxies were unknown in Vincent's day. Those colliding fireballs were symbols of a cosmos in turmoil, a projection of Vincent's inner world.

As I crossed the grounds to reach the women's residence, fat raindrops battered my hood and my thoughts turned to that other starry night, the night that Isabelle was killed. What words of comfort could I offer to her sister? And could she tell me anything that might be useful to Lieutenant Auclair? I rang the bell. A matron in a starched white apron showed me in. She was holding a clipboard, and she checked my name against a list of visitors. Her manner was curt. "Follow me, Madame Barnes." She led me up a flight of stairs and down a long hallway, to the very end. She stopped at the last door and rapped the rap of someone in charge. "Juliette, a visitor for you," she said crisply. The door swung open.

Little Dancer of 14 Years. Degas's beloved sculpture flashed into my mind. Juliette stood in exactly the young ballerina's posture: arms behind her, shoulders back, chin slightly up, feet in fourth position. Either Juliette had trained as a dancer, or she was purposely imitating the famous statue—some kind of delusion?

"*Bonjour,*" I began, "I'm Nora Barnes."

"They told me about you," she replied. "Come in." As she turned to show me a seat, she looked even more like Degas's girl. She was petite, perhaps five foot two. Her long wheat-toned hair was tied low on the nape of her neck in a wide black ribbon. She wore a scoop-necked black sweater and close-fitting black pants.

"I'm sorry to come at such a private time." I'd expected the visit to be awkward, coming so soon after Isabelle's death, but I hadn't anticipated how wrong it would feel. I was about to disturb the mourning period of a delicate woman. As Isabelle's younger sister, she must have been in her sixties, but her body and face looked adolescent, almost ethereal. Still, the strain of grief on her thin face was unmistakable.

"Thank you. That's kind of you. I'm grateful that you've come. You're going to help them find out who killed Isabelle." She sat very upright in a straight-backed chair and gestured for me to sit in the only other chair.

"I'll do everything I can. I met your sister on the night she died. She was a beautiful woman and very gracious. It must be terrible . . ."

"It is, it is. She was my sister, my older sister. She was good to me."

"I'm sure she was. Did she visit you often here?"

"Oh, yes. Sisteron is not so far. When I'm well, we live together there. Lived together." Making the correction took all the energy she had. She closed her eyes. I thought I'd better let her compose herself.

"May I look at your paintings? They're so vibrant." On the walls of the small but comfortable sitting room, Juliette had hung at least a dozen paintings. There was another, just started, on an easel near the window.

"Do," she said, her head bowed so low that I couldn't see whether she had opened her eyes.

I walked around the spacious room, which had the feel of an artist's studio. There was almost no furniture against the walls—no dressers, no desk, just an armoire and a narrow bed, tucked into a corner. All the focus was on the paintings. They were forceful, glowing with the intensity that only acrylic can give. She had used the properties of the medium brilliantly. Juliette's subjects were the same as Van Gogh's, from around the asylum: the flowering almond tree, the vegetable garden, the circular fountain, the gnarly orchard, the mountains, even *Starry Night*. But the colors were in a high key. Gold dominated, then magenta and marine blue. The lines were softer than Van Gogh's.

"You did all these?" I asked. The paintings bore no signature.

"Yes. They're mine." She looked up at her version of the flowering almond tree. She seemed to be assessing it, probably for the hundredth time. I didn't see pride on her face; rather, satisfaction, sober satisfaction.

"You must find it absurd—all this copying of Van Gogh?" Juliette asked uncertainly.

"Not at all. They're beautiful—and different from Van Gogh's, actually."

"Thank you. We all do these copies. We call them our 'versions.'" "We" referred to the other patients. I'd seen their work in the gift shop, but not hers, I think. I would have noticed them. It came to me that the painting I'd admired most there was a portrait of her: the gaunt woman furiously painting herself out of her emotional prison.

She spoke again. "I'm the one who suggested doing versions of Van Gogh. I'd been doing them all my life. Van Gogh means everything to me."

"Because of your grandfather?"

"Yes. You see, I was his favorite. Yves—my brother—didn't like that. Grandfather talked all the time about Van Gogh—Vincent, he called him. They were friends, but it was a sad story—I think that's why he had to tell it over and over. It bored Yves and Isabelle. They walked away and left me there, listening to Grandfather. He showed me pictures of Vincent's paintings, in a big book. Vincent became my imaginary friend. I would talk with him, and then I began drawing with him, and finally painting with him, just like him, or so I thought. Grandfather liked that. He rewarded me with more stories. I think I know what happened on every day of the summer that he spent with Vincent."

"Do you know what happened at the end, when Vincent died?" There was an awkward silence before she spoke again.

"Did they tell you why I'm here? All my life I've had what they call periods of mania—hyperactivity, they call it now. I thought it was what artists do. I liked it. It made me more productive. Like Vincent. I read his letters and the biographies. I knew about his so-called illness, but I thought, and I still think, people didn't understand his artistic mind. However, when I reached my thirties, the manias became different. I would work in a fury, glad to be in a flow of inspiration, but after weeks like that, I couldn't sleep, I became irritable, I felt angry, and then worn out, vanquished, floored. Isabelle said I had to get treatment. I resisted, but Isabelle found this place, the place where Vincent came. I have to admit, it was perfect for me. Over the years, I've retreated here many times."

She looked up defiantly, as if she supposed I thought her crazy. I judged that I might not have much more time before she became agitated, so I'd better get to the questions Lieutenant Auclair wanted answered. "If it's not too painful, can you tell me about your sister?"

Juliette's shoulders twitched. "What do you want to know?"

"Some facts about her life. Her childhood, people who were important to her. Things like that will establish a context for the investigation."

"That's all right, then. I see." She turned and looked into the middle distance. "We were born in Sisteron, where my father grew up. My mother's family were vintners from Cahors. Mama met my father when they were both in Paris for a time."

"You were the second family, I understand."

Juliette's chest swelled and her lips clenched. "Yes. Yves came first, my half brother. But Papa wasn't married to Yves's mother. They had a difficult relationship. Yves is forever whining that Papa betrayed his mother, that he deserted both of them."

"When was that?"

"It was during the Occupation. Papa left Vevette when she was pregnant with Yves. Papa said she was impossible to live with."

"Is Vevette still alive?"

"No, she died a long time ago. My parents took in Yves when he was eleven. I was four. His mother was incompetent. She drank, and worse. She had no home for him."

"How did you all get along?"

"I was young. I liked having a brother. He taught me things—how to set a fire, how to skin a fish, all kinds of boyish things." I stayed quiet, waiting for her to elaborate.

"It was hard on Isabelle, though. Yves bullied her. She was six, not much older than me. He treated me like a pet, but he took Isabelle as an enemy. He was small for his age, and she was tall for hers. They fought as equals. He wrestled with her, punched her, pulled her by the hair. Once he tied her to the stair rail and choked her with his belt. If I hadn't heard her and made him stop, she would have died right then." Juliette's voice was changing to a sob. She covered her eyes with her hands. I gave her a moment and then followed up:

"Did your parents do anything to stop the bullying?"

"They never knew. Yves made us keep our mouths shut. We were afraid of him, by then. We spoke of it only to each other, and not till we were grown. Yves left the house when I was twelve, and when he came back into our lives, he was a grown man. He didn't hit Isabelle anymore. He was just cruel, to both of us."

"What was life like for you and Isabelle after Yves left home?"

Her face softened. She seemed to like the question.

"We still had a year together in ballet school. We'd been taking lessons since I was five and she was seven. It was a way for us to play together. Isabelle had talent. She was expressive, you know, not simply competent. Unfortunately, I had the body for it and she didn't, not after fifteen. She shot up in height and developed a woman's figure. I stayed light and flat-chested." Juliette smiled, recollecting. "So we started going our separate ways. At school she followed the academic track. She was the leader of her class, at least socially. Boys were constantly coming to the house. None of them became her boyfriend, though. She awed the boys. She was so beautiful, so elegant, so smart, smarter than them." She paused, and her face was sober.

"Did Isabelle ever have a boyfriend?"

Juliette's mouth went glum. "There was someone, in Bordeaux. Yves went there to meet him—he said he didn't like him."

"Do you know the man's name?"

"Daniel. He was studying at Bordeaux. Later he became a professor."

Now I had to decide whether to reveal that I knew Daniel Didier. Better to be honest, I thought. "I've met him. He was at the conference where your sister was killed."

"Was he? I wonder if he was the one she meant."

"I don't understand."

"Isabelle said that a professor at the conference was helping her write her paper."

"Did she mention a name?"

"No, I don't think so."

"Did she mention whether this professor was French or some other nationality?"

"She just said a professor. Didn't she give him credit when she gave her paper?"

"Juliette, it seems you don't know. Your sister died on the night before the conference started. She never gave her paper."

Juliette stopped breathing.

"Does that surprise you?"

"Yes . . . I assumed she gave it."

"You know what the talk was about?"

"Oh, yes. It was about Grandfather's letter." She spoke as if I should have known such an obvious—and relevant—fact.

"What letter?" I asked.

"The one Isabelle found when she went searching through Grandfather's things. About a year ago. It was when she heard about a new biography of Van Gogh."

"The one written by Naifeh and Smith?"

"Are they Americans?"

"Yes."

"Then that's the one. That's when she went looking through the boxes and found the letter. It was sewn inside the cover of a photo album."

"Juliette, this is very important. What do you know about that letter and Isabelle's paper? The police suspect that someone killed Isabelle to stop her from giving her talk. If we knew its contents, we would know whether anything in it threatened someone enough to murder her."

Juliette looked confused.

"Well, there's Yves of course. He didn't want the paper to be delivered. He fought with Isabelle about it. He wanted her to give the letter to him. Isabelle made sure he wouldn't get it."

"Do you know where that letter is now?" I asked.

"Yes, but I haven't finished telling you about Isabelle's life. You see, Papa had a stroke when Isabelle was in her first year of nursing school. Mama had died. There was no one to take care of Papa but me, and it got to be too much, and Yves didn't help. So I asked Isabelle to take a semester off from school and help me with Papa."

I wanted Juliette to get back to the letter, but there was no interrupting her.

"I guessed Papa would die in a few months, and I was right. After the funeral, she returned to Bordeaux, but she broke up with Daniel and came back home to Sisteron. That put an end to nursing school. She got a job as a receptionist in a medical clinic in town. At some point, she became involved with one of the doctors in her clinic. He was married, with grown children. They went on with each other for decades, until he died."

I said, "Juliette, just now when I asked you about your grandfather's letter, you said you knew where it was. Can you tell me?"

She gave a girlish grin. "I can do better than that." She went to her bureau, opened the top drawer, rummaged in it, and took out a large manila envelope. "Isabelle asked me to keep this safe from Yves. He never comes here. She meant to publish it after the conference. You'll see to that now, won't you, Madame Professor? Now that Isabelle is gone?"

Astonished, I reached into the envelope and withdrew a thick letter folded neatly in the middle. I looked at Juliette, silently asking permission to unfold the grayed sheets of paper.

"Go ahead, read it," she said, encouraging me.

The document was written in the careful penmanship of an earlier era when pupils were taught how to write properly, yet the lines were shaky, suggesting an older hand.

There was no salutation, no person addressed.

I didn't mean to shoot him, the letter began.

I can still see him clutching his side and looking at me like a wounded animal. He kicked over his easel and stumbled to his knees. The painting he was working on fell to the ground. Later they said he shot himself, but that isn't true. I did it. I wanted to help him but instead I killed him, and I've been sorry for it all my life.

During the next four years I never knew a moment's peace. I grieved over Vincent's death. Try as I might, I couldn't rid myself of guilt. I lost all interest in my studies and barely managed to graduate at the lycée. I took no pleasure in companionship and lost my friends. What girl would want a young man in such a state? My parents were at a loss, having no idea as to the cause of my unhappiness. They said I lacked an occupation, and so my father found me a position in a bank. I toiled at my desk but cared nothing about the work and had no ambition. I spent my evenings alone, drinking. I had no appetite. I was weak and fatigued.

My only solace was in prayer. I had always attended church, but now I went every morning and returned at the end of the day when my duties at the bank were over. I prayed for forgiveness—yet hesitated to enter the confessional. That I couldn't bring myself to do. The priest, a kindly man, noticed my comings and goings. He also respected my reticence. Soon we began to have long discussions about life, sin, and service to God. It was he who perceived my need for penance. He urged me to undertake a spiritual retreat when my summer holiday came, and he recommended a Franciscan monastery in the Alpes-Maritimes. His brother was a monk there and often spoke of its serenity. I was eager to go.

So it was that I found myself at the monastery of Saorge at the age of twenty, in 1894. I had planned to stay a month. I stayed nine years. At the end of that summer I took my vows. And during those nine years I found peace. I loved working in the garden, looking out at the surrounding mountains and listening to the distant sound of the Roya River rushing in the valley below. I loved breathing the cool air. I treasured each hour I spent in the beautiful penance room, where I made amends to God for my crime. In time I even learned a trade, which stood me in good stead in later years: I became a baker. I would have stayed forever had it not been for the infamous law of 1901, when the government shut down the monasteries. It took them two years to get around to Saorge, but suddenly we were expelled, almost overnight.

I barely had time to find a better hiding place for Vincent's painting, which I kept rolled up in a trunk with my other things, stored in the attic above our cells. In the attic was an exposed chimney. Behind it was a panel in the wall that gave access to a space that once had been made for workers who had to repair the roof. There was room enough inside to conceal my trunk. I pushed it in and resealed the panel. My intention was to reclaim my possessions as soon as we were permitted to return, for we expected the closing to be temporary. About that, we were wrong.

You may think you make a plan for life, but life makes a plan for you. I never did return. A year into my exile, while I was living in Sisteron, earning my bread by baking for others, I met a young woman and fell in love. A year after that we were married. In the beginning I often thought of finding some way to retrieve the painting. But gradually, as my new life took hold, I began to understand that it was better to let go of the past. I had a family now and new responsibilities. Nine years of penance— that was behind me.

One day, I am sure, someone will discover Vincent's painting of me where I left it hidden, but I will be gone by then and beyond the reach of earthly punishment or disgrace. God has forgiven me, that's all that matters.

As I write this, today is my eighty-fourth birthday. In all probability it will be my last. I leave behind this confession so the world will know how Vincent van Gogh died. I never had a better friend.

Whoever finds this letter, I beg you, pray for our souls.

Maurice La Font
Sisteron
October 9, 1958

12

"THIS EXPLAINS EVERYTHING," said Toby. We were back in our room. He was reading Maurice La Font's letter over again, his back propped against the bolster, legs stretched in front of him on the bed. A Michelin map of Provence/Côte d'Azur was splayed across his thighs. Rain slapped against the shutters. "Not only do we know how Van Gogh died, we know the motive for Isabelle's murder—to keep that hidden painting a secret. Have you any idea what it would be worth?"

"Millions. Tens of millions probably." Even unfinished, Van Gogh's last work would be the find of the century.

"Sure. That's why Yves and Isabelle were quarreling. He didn't care about their grandfather's reputation. He was after the painting."

"That's got to be it," I said. "My guess is that Isabelle told Yves about the letter but refused to say where the painting was hidden. She was afraid he'd seize it for himself. That's why he stole her handbag the night she was killed. He was looking for the letter or her paper, assuming it contained the information."

"Yes," Toby agreed. "But Yves wasn't the only one who could have known about the painting. Didn't Juliette tell you that a professor at the conference was helping Isabelle write her paper? Whoever that was would have known about it too."

"That's right. Juliette didn't know the professor's name, but it had to be Didier. According to Ray, he was the one who told Isabelle about the conference. Didier put her in touch with Ray."

Toby raised a finger. "That makes Ray another possibility. Let's say Isabelle takes Didier's advice, contacts Montoni, and tells him about her discovery of the letter. As head of the conference, Ray offers to put her on the program and help her write the paper. Does that make sense?"

"It does and it doesn't. If the killer's motive was to stop information leaking out about the existence of the painting, then Ray isn't the killer. Why would he want to put Isabelle on the program? Someone who hoped to steal the painting would avoid any public announcement."

Toby scratched his jaw. "What about Ben? He's the one whose research is directly connected with Van Gogh's death. Would Montoni have suggested she work with Ben?"

That made me sit up in bed. "It's possible. That would give Ben a double motive to silence her. One would be to keep the facts about Vincent's death a secret until he published his biography. The other would be to try to get the painting. If that's the case, he's one good liar. I would have sworn he was sweating with frustration because he didn't know what Isabelle was going to say." I touched Toby's arm. "I just thought of something else. If we're right about the hunt for the painting, the killer is waiting for his first opportunity to get inside the monastery. If it's Ben or anyone else from this conference, that would be tomorrow, when everyone's leaving."

"Suppose we got there first?" Toby scrutinized the map. He put one finger on Saint-Paul-de-Vence and another on a spot above it to the upper right, in the foothills of the Alps. "It's not that far from here to

Saorge, but the road is mountainous. If we leave at a good hour tomorrow, we could make it by the afternoon."

"Whoa. Isn't this a matter for the police? I've been working well
with Lieutenant Auclair. Shouldn't we defer to her on this?"

"Of course," Toby assured me. "We'll call the lieutenant first thing
in the morning. But meanwhile, look up Saorge on the Internet and see
what you can find out about the monastery. For instance, whether it's
open to the public."

It wasn't hard to get information. The Monastery of Saorge is classi-
fied as a national historic monument and has its own website. According
to the description, the former monastery is notable for its picturesque
site, baroque architecture, and seventeenth- and eighteenth-century
frescoes. The main building currently serves as a writers' retreat. The
monastery is open to visitors "in season" but closed in winter. Prospective
visitors are asked to call for exact dates.

We rose early the next morning to make our calls. The storm had
intensified during the night and I hadn't managed to get much sleep.
To save time, we had breakfast in our room. The tray came with a pot
of coffee, croissants, and a neatly folded copy of *Nice Matin*. The front
page was filled with news about the storm, apparently the worst in years.
There were floods in parts of Nice, mudslides in the hills, downed
power lines, and washed out roads. Not what you'd call a good day for
an excursion. Communications were disrupted as well. When I dialed
the gendarmerie at Grasse, I received a recorded message that said in
effect, "We're sorry your call could not be completed. Please try again
later."

As luck would have it, I was able to get through to Saorge. A harried-
sounding male voice answered on the seventh ring. I asked politely if it
would be possible to visit.

"The monastery is closed until March," the voice responded gruffly.
Well that was that. I put my hand over the receiver and relayed the
message to Toby.

"Tell him you're an art historian from the United States and you'd like to see the frescoes. You won't be here in March."

That cut no ice with the man on the phone. "I'm alone up here and there's damage to attend to because of the storm. I have no time for visits. I'm sorry, madame." There was a click and the line went dead.

"What now?" I asked Toby.

"Try the lieutenant again."

I was listening to a repeat of the recorded message when Sister Glenda knocked on our door and came in with Angie. Our plan had been to check out of the hotel after breakfast. "Have a seat," I said. "There's a lot to tell you." Toby and I moved to the edge of the bed, and they took our places at the table while I gave them the gist of what we now knew. "So we're trying to get through to the lieutenant but we can't. I did reach someone at the monastery, but he said they were closed."

"And we need to get up there today," said Toby.

"I might be able to help you with that," said Sister Glenda. "What's the number? I'll call from my room."

Ten minutes later she was back, suppressing a smile. "It's all set. We can see the monastery this afternoon, if you want to go."

Toby was incredulous. "How did you manage it?"

"I told him who I was and that I'm in charge of an important convent back home."

"And that changed his mind?"

"Professional courtesy," she deadpanned.

"Well, I'll be damned," said Toby.

"That could be arranged too," said Sister Glenda. She had a twinkle in her eye. Toby grinned back. "There's just one thing," she continued. "You have to take me with you."

"Me too," said Angie.

"Hold on. If we go, you two should stay here," said Toby. "The weather's terrible. Plus it's a winding road. You wouldn't be comfortable in the back seat."

"It's me they're expecting," said Sister Glenda.

"What about me?" said Angie.

"And my postulant," said Glenda, folding her arms. "Plus two of my colleagues," she added as a postscript.

Toby bit his lip and sized up the situation.

"I'll get the kitchen to pack us a lunch," said Glenda, clinching her argument.

Toby glanced at his watch and gave in. "Don't say I didn't warn you about the ride."

"What about Lieutenant Auclair?" I asked.

"Try again." I did, with the same result.

"We'll reach her on the way" said Toby, grabbing his jacket. "Sooner or later we'll get through."

Before leaving the hotel, we made arrangements to stay another night. On the way out, we ran into Maggie. I hadn't had a chance to comfort her over the loss of Emmet, and I apologized. It turned out she and Thierry were staying over too. "Then we'll have dinner together tonight," I promised. "I'm sorry we're in such a hurry. I'll explain later." I waved to her as I went out the door.

The rain had slowed to a dreary mist but the sky still looked ominous. Although the shortest route to Saorge from Saint-Paul was northeast by way of minor roads, Toby decided it would be faster to go south to connect with the A8 toward Italy and turn north at Menton. Given the conditions, the more ground we could cover using the autoroute, the better.

It was a grim ride, even from the start. Weak morning sunlight, obscured by its passage through fog, created a ghostly glare. The going was slow until we accessed the autoroute. Once we were headed east on the A8, the miles passed more swiftly, but the spray from passing trucks mucked the windows. "Better get into the right lane," I reminded Toby. On a French superhighway, the left lane is for passing only, and as soon as you're in it there's a Mercedes behind you playing bumper cars. Toby stepped on the gas and moved into the right lane, shooting in between two cars that were themselves speeding. I was grasping the armrest more from fear than for balance. I closed my eyes for a minute and listened to the rhythmic hum of the tires. Then I turned around to ask Glenda, "Do you know anything about a law in 1901 that closed the monasteries? Maurice La Font mentioned it in his letter."

"I do, because it was a calamity. It just about eliminated religious communities in France—which was its intention."

"Why did they do that?" asked Angie.

"It was a blow aimed against the church. There was a wave of anticlerical feeling at the time. The politicians claimed that centuries of government support for religious organizations made it right to confiscate their property and shift their services to the state. Saorge is an example. The monks at Saorge took care of the ill. But under the new regime they were expelled and the monastery was turned into a public hospital. That sort of thing happened all over France."

"The poor monks!" said Angie. "Imagine giving your whole life to an order like the Franciscans, working hard every day to nurse sick people—and there you're tossed out, as if you'd done something wrong."

Glenda began to tick off examples of precious works of art that had been lost or damaged when the religious communities were closed, but then she broke off. "Don't get me started," she concluded.

"It's about the separation of church and state," said Toby. "It's—"

I nudged him with my elbow, and he let the subject drop.

Before we knew it, we were approaching Menton, where we were going to turn north. "The exit's here. See it?" I pointed ahead. We made the turn and looked for signs to Sospel, the first major town on the way to Saorge. The sign was small and hand-lettered, and we almost missed it.

"Uh-oh, a detour," Toby said. Yards ahead of us, behind a temporary barrier, was a mountain of orange earth with boulders and tree branches protruding from it. There had been a landslide. The road was completely blocked. We came to a halt, with me fearing a rear-end collision, but thankfully there was no one behind us. Glenda spotted a second hand-made sign and we followed it, making several turns, anxiety rising. Without notice, we found ourselves back on the A8 with no remaining exits before Italy. We had skirted Menton, the last French town on the autoroute.

"Do you have your passports?" I asked the backseat ladies.

"No," said Angie. "It's in my suitcase."

"We won't need them," Toby said. "We're in the EU. The borders are open." Sure enough, there wasn't even a checkpoint as we crossed from one country into the other, just a small sign that said Italia. The first exit, Ventimiglia, came up immediately. The woman who took our euros at the tollbooth said, "*Grazie.*"

The GPS had been repeatedly scolding us to "do a legal U-turn," but she settled down when we started north, on the Italian side of the border. The map said we'd cross into France again somewhere in the mountains south of Breil-sur-Roya, and that would put us on the road to Saorge. In fact, we hadn't gone too far out of our way. The distance from Ventimiglia to Saorge was only about fifty kilometers, but the road was sinuous. "This is where the driving gets tough," Toby said to our passengers in the back. And it had started to rain again.

My cell phone jingled. It was Auclair. "Lieutenant, I've been trying to reach you all morning."

"Yes, I'm sorry. Our lines have been down. I'm calling about your meeting at the asylum yesterday. But first, I can tell you that your friend Madame Bennett is better. She's out of the hospital."

"That's good news. I've been worrying about her."

"They found a poison called aconitine in her system. It was in the perfume too. It's derived from the monkshood plant, and it can be absorbed through the skin. It may be fatal if ingested, so that's what killed the dogs. A human can recover from a small dose. She was lucky in that respect."

Monkshood? That rang a bell. But before I could complete the thought, the lieutenant pressed me for information about my meeting with Juliette La Font. I started to explain where we were and why, but the connection cut out. She redialed a moment later.

"Italy? What are you doing in Italy?"

This time the connection held long enough for me to tell her about Maurice La Font's letter and our suspicion that the murder was tied to a hidden painting by Van Gogh. "When we couldn't reach you, we started out for Saorge to look for it. But you can't get to Saorge from Menton because the road is blocked."

The lieutenant's voice grew stern. I covered the phone with my hand and relayed her message to Toby. "She wants us to turn back. She's dispatching a car from Vence and wants the police to handle this." That's what I thought she'd say.

But Toby was having none of it. He was like a hound tracking a scent; his blood was up. "We're more than halfway there. They haven't even started. By the time they get there, the painting may be gone. Let me have the phone."

I relinquished it, watching the road to make sure that one-handed driving didn't do us in.

Toby said, "Lieutenant, tell your men they'll have to go through Ventimiglia."

She said something back. I could hear her voice crackling.

"It will be better if we wait for the police at the monastery," Toby insisted. "We can tell them where to search."

She barked a command.

"Sorry, I can't hear you," Toby replied. "You're breaking up. What? Say again. I can't hear you. Hello? Hello?" He handed back my phone. "The line cut out again," he explained.

"Did it really, or are you just saying that?"

The slightest trace of a smile creased his lips. "So you want me to turn around?" The truth was, I didn't.

Angie said, "Don't worry, Nora. If they send Roe-bare, he'll arrive before we do. He drives like a demon."

Glenda observed, "In for a dime, in for a dollar."

So we drove on. Now that I had a chance, I began thinking over what Auclair had said about Shelley. Her poisoning must be connected in some way with Isabelle's. Both women had been poisoned by extracts from deadly plants—foxglove and monkshood. I recalled Jane pointing out a blue flower of that name during our walk and warning us of its dangers. Who else had been on that walk? Klara, a trained chemist, if that meant anything. Shelley. And Maggie, who pulled Emmet away from the flowers to prevent him from touching them. Something Jane said at the time struck me as curious, but now I couldn't recall what it was. It would come to me if I gave it time.

Toby whipped around a curve, and I woke up to our surroundings. We were enveloped by gray—an aluminum-gray sky, slate-gray mountains, and olive-gray scrub. The dingy atmosphere wasn't just an effect of the weather. The terrain we were passing through was bleak. The phrase "pre-Alps" had summoned visions of *The Sound of Music*. I'd expected green meadows atop rolling hills, calling little children to burst into song. Instead, I felt oppressed by the stolid rock face ahead and then, as the car turned a corner, dwarfed by jagged mountains towering over a cavernous black valley.

I don't believe that Angie's Roe-bare could take the turns any faster than Toby did. What we call "hairpin turns," the French call *lacets*, or laces: I picture shoelaces, zigzagging up your foot from toes to ankle. Shoelaces, once tied, lie there securely; a car on a *lacet* careens from left to right, making the passengers nauseated. Toby was bearing it fine, as the driver tends to do. But for the rest of us, tossed against the door and then against our seatmate, the ride was an ordeal. We followed the Roya River for the entire route. Most of the way, the water was shallow enough to run roughly over stones. Often it fell into cascades the color of chrome. The gunmetal river seemed driven by a force that would overcome any obstacle. It took that level of force to push through these mountains and this stony soil.

When we reached the town of Breil-sur-Roya, with its medieval square and bustling main street, it seemed the Alpine equivalent of an oasis. We stopped briefly near a park and ate our packed lunch in the car, anxious to get back on our way. We made use of the public facilities and set out again. By then the rain had relented to a mist.

The change in weather was a boon, since the dizzying Gorge of Saorge stood between us and our destination. It was a harrowing traverse, but Toby brought us safely through the winding passage between two mountains, and it wasn't long before a sign appeared for Saorge. In a few minutes, we were in a long tunnel cut through solid rock. Emerging from its vault, we saw ahead of us an almost unearthly village of white-washed buildings hanging from the side of a gray mountain, with larger snowcapped Alps behind. A sign reading Old Franciscan Convent came up immediately, and the GPS said, "Turn right!"

The narrow road was difficult to negotiate, with frequent "laces" and only a log fence to prevent a car from plunging over the side. We came to a dead end at a chapel next to which was a small parking lot occupied by a white Renault and a black motorcycle, both thoroughly muddied. From there the road appeared to continue as a footpath. A young man and woman in orange ponchos emerged from around a bend in the path and headed toward the motorcycle. A brief conversation confirmed that the path beyond the bend did indeed lead to the monastery but it was a steep climb. "Up there, a sign said it was closed," the young man warned.

We thanked them but didn't mention we had an appointment. We watched them drive off and started to climb. It was hard going, especially for Sister Glenda. The angle of the slope was forty-five degrees, or at least it felt like it. Every few yards, a stair-step, intended to ease the climb, instead proved a tripping hazard. The path itself was too narrow to accommodate a car, but someone had brought a motorbike up. It was parked to the side of one of the stone houses on the right side of the path, facing the ravine. A high stone wall edged the left side. No one was there but us. The only sound other than our footfalls came from the Roya surging through the ravine. I looked down and saw a white water-fall. We stopped to catch our breath. "It's beautiful, isn't it?" said Angie. "It must have been so peaceful for the monks here."

It's odd the way memory works. Monks here. Monkshood. Something clicked. Now I remembered what it was that Jane had told us about monkshood. At that moment everything came into focus and I was pretty sure I knew who the poisoner was. "We've got to hurry," I said.

"Let me take your arm," Toby said to Glenda. "It can't be too much farther."

As we continued climbing, the peak of a salmon-colored bell tower came into view. Then we rounded a corner and were gazing up at the gold and pink façade of the monastery. It wasn't as I had pictured it. This seventeenth-century monastery tucked away in the French Alps looked remarkably like a California mission. It had a façade of spacious arches with a square pediment perched above them and stucco walls painted in soft colors. But we weren't here to admire the architecture. We stepped carefully across the grassy yard, which was sopping from the rain. We were headed for the church stairs, but Angie pointed to a door to the right, marked *Billets*, Tickets.

Sister Glenda strode up to the massive wooden door and clanked the knocker. She knocked again when there was no response. After another moment, a voice from behind the portal said, "*Oui?*" Sister Glenda announced who she was, and we heard the sound of a heavy bolt sliding on metal. The door swung open. "*Bonjour, ma soeur,*" said a bearded young man. "Your colleagues are already here," he added, as we stepped inside the ticket office.

Glenda looked puzzled. "My colleagues are with me," she said, pointing to Toby and me.

It was the young man's turn to look confused. "From the art conference. Didn't you say that two colleagues from your conference in Saint-Paul-de-Vence were coming today?"

"Who—?" Toby began, but I interrupted.

"I think I know who. Come on, Toby." I grabbed a map of the monastery from a stack on the counter and headed through the doorway leading inside. Toby followed, leaving Sister Glenda and Angie to deal with the tickets. The doorway led into a cloister open to the cloudy sky. The arcades of the gallery rested on pillars, and at the far end of the courtyard was a well with a conical roof. A painted sundial adorned one of the gallery walls. According to the map, the gallery level housed the former monks' cells. "If there's an attic, it must be up there somewhere," I said to Toby.

"This way," he said, pointing to a door on the north wall.

Inside, a stone staircase led to the upper level. There we began to go from room to room, looking for an access to the attic. By then Angie and Glenda had entered the cloister. Angie called up to me from below. "Stay down there," I shouted, "where you'll be safe."

Toby, already ahead of me, had reached the room at the end of the corridor. I caught up with him. Inside the empty room, a narrow door stood ajar. It looked like a closet but led to a flight of wooden stairs. "Let me go first," Toby said. There was no banister, and the stairs were so narrow that he had to climb sideways, touching the wall for balance. I came up behind him.

There was a startled cry as Toby's head cleared the landing. I was beside him in a few quick steps. The attic was sharply pitched, its head-room partially obstructed by the oak beams that supported the roof. The light was dim, coming from a series of tiny triangular openings at floor level. I could see well enough, though, to confirm my suspicions. There was Shelley. But she wasn't with Ben.

Ray Montoni was kneeling beside an open trunk, having forced its hinges; a screwdriver was on the floor by his knee. Shelley stood next to him, clutching a rolled canvas. Her eyes darted around the room, looking for an exit. Ray reached for the screwdriver.

"Don't even think about it," said Toby, inching forward. "You'll only make matters worse." Ray looked panicked.

I said, "We know everything, and so do the police. They're on the way." Shelley took a step back, glaring at me.

"I don't know what you're talking about," huffed Ray, struggling to his feet. His heavy frame loomed large in this confined space, but Toby was fearless. He inched forward again.

"Don't deny it," I said. "We've got Maurice La Font's letter. We know all about the painting." Shelley clenched her fist more tightly around the rolled canvas. There was no way to hide it.

While I stared at Shelley, unable to believe her brazenness, Toby continued to advance. "You got rid of Isabelle so you could steal the painting," he said to Montoni. "You poisoned her. It was cold-blooded murder."

The word struck Montoni like a bludgeon, and in an instant, whatever defiance he was prepared to mount deserted him. His knees sagged, and he reached for a low-lying beam, to support himself. "No," he mumbled, "you've got it wrong."

"I don't think so, Ray," I said. "It was you who pushed me off the ramparts, wasn't it? When you found out I was helping the investigation. But you couldn't go through with it, so you pulled me up. That's the part I don't understand."

"I'm not a killer, that's why. Oh, God!" He made a sound like a howl. "It was her idea. It was Shelley. Everything was her idea. She dragged me into it."

"Shut up, you idiot," snapped Shelley.

"She poisoned Isabelle, not me."

"Shut up. You're lying!" Shelley shouted.

"Is he?" I looked at her coldly. "You're quite a hand at poisoning. First Isabelle with the foxglove, which you stole from Curry, and then that trick with monkshood at the perfume factory. That was supposed to get me out of the way after Ray lost his nerve on the ramparts. But you dosed yourself with foxglove first. Then you sprayed yourself with the perfume you poisoned to make it look like you were the victim. Jane gave you that idea when she told us digitalis was an antidote for monkshood poisoning. I was there, remember? And it would have worked too, if the bottle hadn't broken. Those poor dogs paid the price."

"That's a story you made up," said Shelley. "It's a fantasy. You don't have any evidence for that."

"Oh, no? How do you explain the digitalis in your blood along with the aconitine? The toxicology report is fact."

Shelley started at that news. Montoni moaned, "I told you it would never work. You thought you knew everything. I told you."

"Shut your mouth, you fat-assed idiot. Don't say another word."

"It's a little late for that," said Toby. "Now hand me that painting and then we're all going to walk downstairs and wait for the police. You can tell your story to them." Toby had been blocking the way to the stairs. Now he stepped aside and motioned to Ray and Shelley to start down. Ray, his spirit broken, began shuffling toward the steps. Shelley hung back, grasping the rolled painting.

Ray had just reached the first step when Shelley lunged forward and shoved him hard in the small of the back. He plunged headfirst down the stairs, tumbling heavily and crying out in pain. Before he hit the bottom, Shelley turned and started running toward the far end of the attic, where I now saw there was a second door. She had the painting and was ducking to avoid the beams. At the bottom of the stairwell Montoni was stirring as if trying to flee. "I've got Montoni," Toby shouted, hustling down the stairs. "Go after Shelley. Don't let her get away!"

13

I CROSSED THE ROOM at a sprint and reached the door, which Shelley had thrown open. Dim light revealed another section of attic, at the end of which was another door. I rushed toward it, slowing at the end, anticipating a flight of stairs. They were dark and steep, but I took them as fast as I could, always on the lookout for Shelley. At the bottom, I found myself in an alcove that led into a hall with doors on either side. Which way to go? I tried the first door, on the left. It opened into the refectory, with its long dining tables. I glanced at the paneling and frescoed walls and saw there was no exit, except through two large windows. I checked that the windows were secure. Through their panes, I saw a wide expanse of terraced grapevines. No one was in sight. Shelley must have taken the other door.

I pivoted, ran back to the hall, and pulled opened the second door. It gave onto the cloister. There I found Sister Glenda, leaning against the well and trying to catch her breath. One hand was pressed to her breast. The other, extended at arm's length, held the rolled painting.

I stopped abruptly. "That's the Van Gogh!" I cried. "How did you get it?"

"Left hook," gasped Glenda. She was gulping for air. "Mine isn't as good as Toby's. She got up."

"Shelley ran into us. She knocked me down," Angie complained. She was slowly getting to her feet, rubbing her knee. "That's when Sister Glenda clobbered her."

"Which way did she go?" I asked.

"Through the ticket office." Angie pointed.

"Hang on to that painting. I'm going after her."

I dashed through the office, out the door, and across the wet grass. With my arms out like wings, I held my balance while making the sharp right turn onto the descending path. Momentum sent me sliding on slippery cobblestones. I grabbed for the wall on the inside of the path. My palms shredded as my body kept moving, but I slowed myself by throwing a shoulder against the wall. My jacket took the scraping instead of my skin, and I was able to right myself. For a second I stopped, stuck against the wall, and looked down to spot Shelley. She was ahead of me by half a football field, scrambling headlong down the path.

I resolved to ignore pain and flout caution. Down I went, jogging and slipping, using the wall until it disappeared. The occasional stair-step sent me teetering and tripping, but I never fell. My whole being, body and mind, was focused on staying upright and getting to Shelley.

I let out a grunt of frustration as I saw Shelley heading for the white Renault. I picked up my pace and reached her car just after she had backed up, getting ready to turn the car around. If I'd been in my right mind, I would have stood back; instead, I charged the passenger-side window, as if I could snatch her through the glass. The lurching car threw me back. Without thought, I reached in my jacket pocket and ran to our car. The car key was in my hand, punching the lock open.

The next thing I recall is turning the first "shoelace" of the mountain. I had never in my life made car wheels squeal, but I did now.

All my attention went to controlling the car. I had to focus on the road, but I could sense a moving blur of white in the distance. Rounding the third hairpin turn, I heard the crunch of metal. Did it come from above, from below? I didn't know, but I stepped on the brake—then, feeling a skid, I switched to pumping it. My car came under control, but it was still going too fast when I saw the smashup ahead. The white car heading down the hill and a red car coming up had collided on the narrow road, and the red car was wedged sideways, entirely blocking Shelley's escape. I stamped on the brake, forgetting all rules about driving in wet weather.

The result was predictable—a 180 degree spin, halted by the force of inertia and a log fence at the ravine's edge. Later I realized that I'd knocked down part of the fence. At the time, my only concern was that I still had enough road under me to get out of the car. I eased the door open and slid out. Immediately I jumped back, seeing the right side of the car sink a foot. I had stopped at the very edge.

I looked around for Shelley. Angry shouts were coming from the red car. A man leaped out of the driver's side. A woman rolled down her passenger window and yelled toward Shelley, who was already trying to maneuver her car to get away. But she couldn't. The red car was occupying her lane, and the only way forward was into the ravine.

Foiled and furious, Shelley sprang from her car and ran right at me. I ducked behind my car to evade her attack. But she wasn't coming after me. She was headed for the break in the fence that I had created. She was going to try to escape on foot, via the ravine.

Shelley was through the break in a flash. The hillside dropped off sharply. With the agility of a high-wire dancer, she scrambled through the brush alongside the fence until the ground flattened out for a couple of yards. She got up speed and then leaped back over the fence and started running up the road, retracing the way to the monastery. Where she expected to hide, I don't know, but I counted the possibilities—behind one of the houses that hung to the cliff, or inside one if she could break in; in the woods above the path, if she could find a low section of the wall and climb it; or behind the monastery—she could cross through the vineyards and go over the hill, to who knows where. I was going to be right behind her, however reckless her flight.

"Shelley!" I cried. "Stop!"

She kept running up the road. She had a head start, but I ran cross-country in high school. I hoped that muscle memory would propel me forward, and it did. After an uphill spurt, I grabbed her by the waist just as we reached the parking lot, and she fell to the ground, taking me with her. Fear of losing my grip shot through me, but my arms tightened around her and I took resolve when I heard the raucous siren of a French police car—never more welcome than at this moment.

I straddled her, pinning her wrists to the ground.

She spit dirt from her lips. "Bitch!"

Boy, did I want to slap her—I raised my hand. She turned her face to the side and winced. There was a welt on her cheek from Sister Glenda's blow. She was done. What would be the point?

I held her there until Sergeant Navré arrived with his partner, the pug-faced officer who was with him on the night of the murder. I quickly explained the situation. They pulled Shelley to her feet and handcuffed her. "My husband is holding another suspect for you at the monastery," I told them. "Professor Montoni. He's involved in this too."

I followed the two gendarmes down the hill as they frog-walked Shelley to the police car, which was parked behind the red car, which still blocked the road. They dealt with the irate occupants, who calmed down now that the police were there, and then they took charge of clearing the blockage. Luckily, the banged up vehicles were drivable. Our rental car had a crumpled hood, twisted bumper, and broken head-light, but it would get us back to the hotel. With their help, I was able to turn it around and lead the police up to the parking lot. The couple in the red car headed down to a garage.

At the monastery, Toby had marched Ray into a room identified by the map as the penance room. The room had carved walnut paneling and that sweet, musty smell of old waxed wood. Ray sat disconsolately on a pew, babbling a confession. Sister Glenda sat next to Ray and held his hand in her lap as he slumped forward, head bent. Toby was sitting on Ray's other side, keeping him close. Toby looked up as I entered with the police. "They've got her," I told him. "She's shackled in the car." He gave me a thumbs-up.

Ray seemed unaware of our entry. His words came pouring out as if a valve had opened. He was telling Glenda that Isabelle intended to donate her grandfather's painting to the state if they found it. She and her sister thought it would be wrong for anyone in the family to profit from it.

"But Yves had a different opinion, didn't he?" Toby prodded.

"Yes. That's what they were arguing about."

"So then you got the idea to grab the painting for yourself," said Toby.

"No. No. I knew Isabelle was right. If the painting was recovered, it belonged in a museum. It would have been enough for me to be in on the discovery. It was Shelley. I told her about Isabelle's paper, mentioned the painting and where it was located—it was just pillow talk. But Shelley seized on it; she started to plot. She kept saying we had to stop Isabelle from giving her paper. I told her I couldn't. The presenters knew she was on the program. But Shelley kept at it, kept pushing me to do whatever it takes. That's what she said: 'whatever it takes.'"

He looked up at the ceiling, then shook his head in disbelief. "I told her she was crazy. We didn't even know if the painting was still there. But she had an answer for everything. She said if the painting had been found, the world would have heard about it. She was sure it was still at the monastery."

"Who came up with the idea of using foxglove?" asked Toby.

"Shelley. That was her idea too."

"But you went along with it," Toby said, with disgust. "You let it happen."

"No, I told her I was against it." Ray wiped his nose. "She ignored me. When Isabelle fell sick the night of the dinner, I knew it was Shelley's fault, but I couldn't do anything about it. It was already too late. I sat there at the table, paralyzed. Shelley had it all worked out. As soon as the conference was over, we'd get the painting and run off together. The Cayman Islands. We'd be rich, she said. I knew it was crazy, but I thought she really cared about me. Now . . ." His voice trailed off.

"Stand up, monsieur, you're coming with us," Navré announced. He and his partner had been standing in the doorway, listening. Meekly, Ray allowed himself to be handcuffed.

"I'll turn this over to you," said Toby, holding up the rolled canvas.

"Could we see the painting first?" I asked the sergeant.

"I don't see why not," he said. "Go ahead. Meanwhile, I would like to say a few words in private to your sister." Angie brightened. "Armand," he said to his partner, "take Monsieur Montoni to the car, will you? Put him in the front seat, and don't let him talk to the woman. I'll be with you in a moment."

"Let's take the painting into the refectory," I said to Toby and Glenda. "We can unroll it on a table, and there's good light."

We crossed the cloister to the refectory. There were two long trestle tables in the room and delicate frescoes on the walls. Under other circumstances we might have admired them. Now we paid them no attention. With mounting excitement, I watched Toby place the scrolled painting on one of the long tables. While Glenda carefully held down the top corners, Toby slowly unrolled the canvas until the entire painting was exposed. "Well, there it is," he said at last, his fingers pressed against the bottom corners.

We stared in silence. The majority of Vincent's portraits were painted indoors and show the subject's head and upper torso. But this one was different. Here he placed a full-length figure in the foreground of a landscape. Van Gogh's last portrait, painted with tenderness, shows a teenaged boy in a red jacket, lounging against a tree. His hands seem to be in his pockets, although the section of the painting below the boy's wrists is unfinished. The lad has a thatch of blond hair, a sharp nose, and blue eyes that squint against the bright sun. Vincent has given him a squiggle for a mouth; somehow, the wavering line conveys the boy's vulnerability. In the middle distance behind the tree, fields are suggested by blocks of green and yellow. Here and there, dots of red indicate flowers. Far off, two yellow haystacks break the horizon under a band of cornflower-blue sky.

"It's definitely a Van Gogh," said Sister Glenda, breaking the silence. "And it's a gem."

On close inspection, the canvas looked to be in excellent condition except for minor flaking along a crease. A good conservator could address that problem. Given the right frame—a simple frame painted white is what Vincent would have chosen—the work would claim its rightful place in Van Gogh's oeuvre.

We took our time gazing at the precious painting, taking in its details. Then, reluctantly, Toby rolled it up and we walked back across the cloister to the penance room. Even before we entered, I could tell something was wrong. A sallow-faced Sergeant Navré was waiting for us at the door. Angie was sitting on a pew inside. He took custody of the painting with a curt word of thanks. Where its final home would be, I didn't know, but for now the work of art was evidence in a criminal investigation. Navré was awkward with us. He asked us to report tomorrow to Lieutenant Auclair at the gendarmerie. Then, without pleasantries, he tipped a finger to his cap and hurried outside.

"What happened?" I asked Angie. She looked stricken.

"He told me he has a fiancée," she blurted. "He lied to me. I can't believe he lied to me!"

"Oh, no. I'm sorry, Angie."

She dragged her knuckles across her nose. "Why? Why does this always happen to me?" Tears fell, and I felt myself softening into tears in response. I moved to embrace her, but she threw me off.

"That's it," she said angrily. "I've had it with men." She turned to Glenda. "Sister, I want to take my vows as soon as we get home."

"Is that wise, dear?" Glenda asked, quietly.

"I hate him!" Angie sobbed. "I hate all of them!"

Glenda and I exchanged looks. "Come," she said gently, helping Angie to her feet. We started for the door.

Toby paused at the threshold and looked back with curiosity. "That's two confessions in one day. What is it about this room?"

It's a cozy room, isn't it?" said Maggie, gazing into the fireplace at Le Tilleul, the homey restaurant on Linden Square in Saint-Paul-de-Vence. "It's comforting."

Thierry, seated opposite me, put his hand over Maggie's. Emmet's death had hit her hard. I'd been hoping that a Provençal dinner would lift her spirits, but I could see that Maggie was beyond being cheered by cassoulet. Still, it was soothing to share a meal in each other's company. We were a foursome. Angie hadn't felt like going out, so she and Sister Glenda had remained at the hotel for dinner. I thought that was a good decision.

We gave Maggie and Thierry a thumbnail sketch of the events at Saorge and Ray's confession. "Whatever happened to Isabelle's paper?" Maggie wanted to know.

"Ray was holding on to it the night she was killed," said Toby. "She gave it to him to prevent Yves from getting it. He says he destroyed it after she died."

"The skunk," said Maggie. But her deepest ire was reserved for Shelley, when she learned that in addition to poisoning Isabelle, Shelley had tainted the perfume that killed Emmet. Maggie cursed her when she heard the story.

Let's focus on the menu, I said to myself. But when appetizers were mentioned, Maggie said she wasn't hungry. Thierry took her hand again, this time entwining his fingers through hers. In the singsong tones of southwest France, he implored her to share a first course of duck-liver scallops. (It sounds better in French: *Escalopes de foie gras de canard et truffe blanche*.) The final lure was Thierry's confession that as a boy he raised geese for their foie gras and learned to feed them corn mash through a tube.

"They don't mind at all," he said. "They're used to it, and it's done gently, so to them it's a pleasure, the pleasure of being fed. They are happy geese." The way he said "ah-pee geese" made Maggie smile.

Toby picked up the theme of pleasure and suggested that he and I share the apple salad with crispy baked Pont-l'Evêque cheese. I couldn't resist the idea of eating both cheese and dessert before dinner. For our main course, we weighed the merits of going native with a braised cheek of beef in red wine sauce or posing as Parisians with a galantine of chicken. The men went with the city fare and the women with country cooking.

I was grateful for Toby's social ease. Engaging Thierry first, he soon had Maggie describing the day's events in Saint-Paul while we were away at Saorge. The couple had spent the morning at the hotel, sheltering from the rain and making futile phone calls. The morgue wouldn't release Emmet's body. The hospital in Cagnes-sur-Mer wouldn't describe Curry's condition. And the hospital in Grasse denied having Shelley as a patient.

On the subject of Emmet, Maggie spat fire. "I could have killed that bloody bureaucrat. What a feckin' idiot! If he was standing before me, I would have wrung his neck!"

Thierry offered a calmer description of the phone call. "The clerk wouldn't let Maggie speak to the coroner. Maggie was—how you say? Very, very angry."

"Outraged," Maggie said. Her face embodied the term. "For God's sake! They have his blood samples, his tissue samples. What more do they want?"

"*Calmes-toi, calmes-toi,*" Thierry counseled. In English telling someone to "calm yourself" sounds patronizing. The phrase is so much kinder in French, and the way Thierry said it was consoling. So was the bottle of Bordeaux red that he selected. Sipping the velvety wine, we resolved the matter of Emmet. Thierry promised that he would help Maggie give him a proper burial when the time came.

Appetizers arrived, and we switched the conversation to our food. Thierry explained the difference between white and black truffles to Maggie, while Toby and I savored our warm cheese over a cider-dressed salad.

"Is there any news on Bruce's condition?" Toby asked Maggie.

"Yes, there is. Jane called in the afternoon. He has a brain tumor, and they're going to operate."

"Jane must be devastated," I said.

"It's better news than she was expecting. The operation's fairly safe. And Jane thinks it may return Bruce to himself. 'My old curmudgeon,' is what she called him." A pause. "Lord, that was good." Maggie smacked her lips, taking her last taste of foie gras.

"What about Ben?" Toby asked. "Have you seen him?"

"He showed up here before lunch, looking for Shelley. Apparently when he arrived at the hospital this morning they told him Shelley had been discharged and had left in the care of her husband. When he found out Ray had checked out of the hotel, he put two and two together."

"What did he do?" Toby asked.

"All he knew for sure was that his wife was missing. He tried calling the police but couldn't get through. The last I saw of him, he was heading for the gendarmerie at Vence."

"That fits with what Montoni was telling us in the penance room," said Toby. "He'd been having an affair with Shelley for years. I wonder if Ben had an inkling of it?"

At that point, our main course arrived. Toby looked sour when he saw his serving: a roll of white meat the size of a hot dog, surrounded by wiggling cubes of chicken jelly. Pretty clearly, the dish was cold—not what you want on a wet winter night after a day of mortal danger. But he tried some and cheered up at the taste. He poured himself another glass of Bordeaux and continued his report on Ray's confession.

"Ray said he met Shelley at an art opening at his school. Ben was there as a judge of Ray's students' work. From that night, Ray and Shelley were hot at it. Ray's wife guessed he was having an affair and left him. He said he was relieved—he couldn't handle two women at a time. As it turned out, he couldn't handle Shelley by herself."

Maggie shook her head. "So it was Shelley you saw coming out of Ray's room the other night. I must have been daft to even give him a thought. He's spineless."

I agreed. "He was Shelley's puppet; she jerked him on her strings."

"She's a hard character, all right. I'll give her this much, though. The woman sticks to her principles."

"I don't follow you," I said.

"Remember the trolley debate? Didn't she say she'd push the fat man off the bridge to save herself?"

"That's right, she did."

"Well, what did she do when you cornered her in the attic? I'll be damned if she didn't push him down the stairs."

"You mean Ray?" I said.

"He's chubby enough for the role. Take it from me." That brought smiles all around, though Thierry blushed.

Maggie seemed to be emerging from her funk. "Now, what about your sister? Tell me what's bothering her. She was in a desperate state when we left tonight."

I explained about Navré's engagement, Angie's shock, and her impulsive decision to take her religious vows. Maggie couldn't bear to hear it.

"She's an angel, your sister. Too good for her own good. It's a shame, but there's always a cagey man waiting to take advantage of a trusting woman. How could you let her remain so naïve, Nora? She needs someone to stop her from this folly and teach her how to take care of herself in the real world."

My reaction was defensive. "She's a grown woman. I can't make up her mind for her. Maybe the place that can teach her how to live is Grace Quarry."

"Bollocks. Her heart may be broken for now, but what she needs is a good man, not to give up on life by retreating to a convent. Look at me. I was crushed when Emmet died, the poor thing. But Thierry has given me something to look forward to." Thierry blinked. "I don't know where this thing is going, but it's better than turning your back on love. Angie isn't cut out for the convent, any more than I am. I'm going to tell the girl as much."

"I wish you would," said Toby. "I couldn't agree more."

A part of me agreed as well. I wondered what Sister Glenda was telling Angie back at the hotel. I thought of Maurice La Font, who chose the life of a monk in order to do penance, blaming himself for what had been an accident. He entered the monastery out of guilt, not piety, and in the end he returned to the world. Was Angie about to embark on a similar path? For her, the convent was a refuge from disappointment. That wasn't the best of reasons to choose a monastic life. True, she was duped by Navré, but she put herself in the way of that danger. As Toby joked, she wanted to be a nun with "benefits." And that wasn't part of the bargain.

The waiter appeared with a silver scraper and made a show of scooping crumbs from the tablecloth. He laid out clean silverware. Ah, dessert. A welcome respite from troubled thoughts. Apple tart with crème d'amande and vanilla ice cream for Toby, poached pear crumble with whipped cream and caramel for Thierry, and for Maggie and me, warm chocolate cake with crème anglaise. Yes, there was something to be said for the sensual side of life.

It was late when we got back to the hotel. We found Angie and Sister Glenda in the sitting room, which otherwise was deserted. Glenda, who had been keeping Angie company until we returned, rose to leave as we arrived. "I'm ready for bed," she said. "It's been a long day." She smiled at Angie. "Think over what I've been saying, won't you, dear?" Angie smiled back, weakly. She looked drained. We said good night to Glenda, and she went upstairs. Thierry excused himself to go upstairs as well but said he'd be back in a few minutes.

"Did you and Sister Glenda have a good talk?" I asked, taking a seat next to Angie on the couch. Maggie and Toby sank into two oversized chairs.

"I suppose," said Angie listlessly. "How was dinner?"

"Great," said Toby. "Sorry you weren't with us."

"We brought you some chocolate cake," said Maggie, taking a napkin from her bag and unrolling her stash.

"No thanks. I've already had my dessert."

"Take a taste. It's good."

Angie gave in and took a bite. "You're right. It's delicious. Thanks, Maggie."

"Listen, Angie," Maggie said, "we've been talking about this idea you have of going into the convent, and I'd just like to say a word."

Angie bristled. "I know you're trying to help, but I don't need another lecture."

"Well, I won't have another chance after tonight, and I've got something to say."

Angie let out a deep sigh.

Maggie leaned forward and barged ahead. "This is the worst possible moment for you to make a decision. You're distraught. And the fact is you're not made for it. You're a romantic, God help you, like me. You need love, that's what you want. You're perfectly normal. You've just had a run of bad luck, but you can't give the whole thing up because of it. Look what just happened. A handsome man comes along and in one week your idea of chastity goes out the window—which is where it belongs, if you ask me. Then he dumps you, and right away you're thinking of taking your vows. From the fire back into the frying pan. But what will you be thinking a month from now or a year, when the next fellow comes your way? I'm saying that—"

"Maggie, save your breath," Angie interrupted, making a stop sign with her palm. "I've just been over all that with Sister Glenda."

"And?"

"And she agrees with you."

"She does?"

"Well, not about chastity. But she thinks I'm not ready to make a decision that will affect the rest of my life. She wants me to wait. And I've agreed to."

"I'm glad to hear you say so, Angie," I said. "Whatever that decision will be, you need time to think. And I'll support you, whatever you decide."

"Thanks. That's what I need most." She reached over and gave me a sisterly hug. "The truth is, I'm hurt—I admit it. I'm also confused. I don't know what I want to do."

"That's okay," I said.

"It's fine," said Maggie. "Just don't rush into anything."

"Don't worry," said Angie. "Sister Glenda won't let that happen."

"She's a wise one," Maggie conceded. I thought so too.

Maggie looked up as Thierry entered the room, and the entire atmosphere changed. He was carrying the most adorable puppy I ever saw. "He's for you," Thierry said, depositing the pudgy ball of fur in Maggie's lap. The little fellow had a wet black nose, floppy ears, and brown soulful eyes. He yipped with excitement as Maggie picked him up.

"Oh, Thierry," she exclaimed, "he's beautiful!"

"I know he can't replace Emmet," Thierry said, "but look, he likes you."

Maggie stroked his head. "Does he have a name?"

"His name is 'ah-pee.'"

"That's brilliant. Hello, Happy." Maggie lifted the pooch to face level and rubbed noses with him. In return, Happy began licking Maggie's face like a kid with a drippy ice cream cone. She smiled with delight, and Angie burst into laughter.

Toby pulled me to him and whispered, "I'd say it was a classic case of puppy love."

"Which one?" I asked. "The dog or Thierry?"

"Take your pick," said Toby. "You can't go wrong."

Afterword

Who Shot Vincent van Gogh?

IN 2011 Steven Naifeh and Gregory White Smith made headlines around the world when their new biography, *Van Gogh: The Life*, made the startling claim that Vincent van Gogh had been murdered. The culprit, they concluded, was an irresponsible teenager in the town of Auvers-sur-Oise named René Secrétan, who was known at the time to brandish a pistol. This intriguing theory became the inspiration for our novel. Our original plan was to use the authors' account as the backstory for our plot. However, as we examined their sources, we began to doubt the validity of their accusation. The questions they raised remained compelling, and the broad outline of the theory was persuasive, but on crucial points the evidence was weak. In the end, we parted ways with Naifeh and Smith. Even so, we began our journey with them, and we remain in their debt. Whatever conclusion one draws about their theory of the shooting, their magisterial biography is an impressive achievement.

In this postscript, our aim is to review their argument and to explain how we arrived at our own conclusions. There is much we still don't know about Vincent van Gogh's death. Even at the time of the shooting, there were unanswered questions. For example, where did the shooting occur? Where did Vincent get the gun? What happened to it? It was never found—nor were his easel, paints, and the other materials he was carrying that day, including whatever painting he was working on. If Vincent had intended suicide, why did he shoot himself clumsily in the side rather than in the head? And if he really wanted to die, why did he return to his lodging to seek help afterward? A prolific correspondent, Vincent left behind no suicide note, nor had he given any hint of his intentions in the days leading up to the event.

The appeal of Naifeh and Smith's theory is that it provides answers to these questions. The authors base their argument on a series of interviews that a retired banker named René Secrétan gave to Victor Doiteau, a French doctor who maintained a lifelong interest in Vincent van Gogh's case. In 1957 Doiteau published an article in a French medical journal summarizing these conversations: "Deux 'copains' de Van Gogh, inconnus: Les frères Gaston et René Secrétan; Vincent, tel qu'ils l'ont vu" (Two unknown "pals" of Van Gogh: The brothers Gaston and René Secrétan; Vincent as they saw him).

In his conversations with Doiteau, René reminisced about the summer of 1890 when he and his friends amused themselves by teasing the artist, whom they regarded as *un fou*, a crazy man. The boys made fun of Vincent and pulled various pranks on him. They put salt in his coffee and pepper on the tip of a brush he liked to suck on; once they even put a snake in his paint box. René had a beat-up old revolver, which he either borrowed or bought from the innkeeper Ravoux, who ran the inn where Vincent was staying. That summer, René paraded around in a Buffalo Bill cowboy outfit and used the gun to shoot small game. Vincent tolerated the immature teenager only because he was friendly with René's older brother, Gaston, who was interested in art and who admired Vincent.

Naifeh and Smith hypothesize that behind these colorful anecdotes is a veiled confession by a man with a guilty conscience who was nearing the end of his life. Their conclusion is that, although he never admitted it, René Secrétan shot Vincent accidentally during some kind of horseplay. The shooting took place not in a wheat field, as previously thought, but near a haystack or dung heap in a farmer's yard. Yet Vincent said nothing of this—why? Naifeh and Smith speculate that because he welcomed death at this point in his life, Vincent accepted his fate and assumed the blame himself.

On the other hand, a verdict of suicide is consistent with everything we know about the troubled artist's life—his depression, fits (which may have been epileptic), previous self-mutilation and institutionalization, his loneliness, despair, lack of recognition, poverty, and complete dependence on his brother for financial support. Newly married, Theo was starting a family and thinking of striking out on his own as an art dealer, placing a new constraint on his ability to help his brother. That Vincent might try to kill himself at this stressful juncture came as no surprise to those who knew him.

What exactly happened on Sunday, July 27, 1890? This much is agreed upon by Van Gogh's several biographers. After lunch at the inn, Vincent packed up his painting gear and went out to resume his morning's painting, as was his habit. He usually stayed out all afternoon and returned for dinner. However, on this day he failed to return at dinnertime. Hours later, he staggered back to the inn clutching his stomach and climbed the stairs to his little room. He was heard moaning. Ravoux, the innkeeper, went up to see him and asked what was wrong. "I wounded myself," Vincent replied, and showed Ravoux a small hole under his ribs (Naifeh and Smith 850). Vincent was living in Auvers that summer so that he could be cared for by the local doctor, Paul Gachet, who had experience in the treatment of melancholy. Gachet was summoned along with another physician, a Dr. Mazery. The two doctors examined the wound but determined that nothing could be done. They sent for Theo, and Theo was at his brother's bedside when Vincent died from his wound two days later.

Where had Vincent been all afternoon? The dying man told those who had gathered at his bedside that he had shot himself and then passed out. By the time he regained consciousness, darkness had fallen. Though he searched for the gun to finish the job, he couldn't find it, so he made his way back to the inn (Naifeh and Smith 869).

Several witnesses at the inn who later gave accounts of what they remembered of that night were: Adeline Ravoux, the daughter of the innkeeper, who repeated several versions of her story more than sixty years later; Paul Gachet *fils* ("Jr."), the son of Dr. Gachet, who put together notes for a book about Vincent's stay in Auvers; and Anton Hirschig, a fellow Dutch artist who roomed at the inn and recorded his recollections twenty-one years later in a letter. Hirschig recalled that Vincent said, "I wounded myself in the fields, I shot myself with a revolver" (quoted in Rohan 104). Hirschig got the date wrong, though— he thought the shooting occurred in August—and he may have forgotten other details as well.

The earliest written mention of the shooting appeared in a letter by the painter Émile Bernard, who came to Auvers to attend Vincent's funeral. In his letter, written two days after the funeral, Bernard stated that the innkeeper Ravoux told him that Van Gogh "placed his easel against a haystack and went behind the château to shoot himself with a revolver" (quoted in Rohan 88). However, Ravoux left no firsthand account of his recollections.

The narrative accepted by previous biographers is based largely on several accounts provided by Ravoux's daughter, Adeline. In one version, she claimed that her father had loaned Vincent his pistol to ward off crows in the wheat field where he was painting, and it was there that the artist shot himself. However, as Naifeh and Smith argue, her tale contains inconsistencies, if not fabrications. It was popularly believed that Vincent's last painting was *Wheat Field with Crows*, and Adeline probably adjusted her recollection to fit the romantic myth. (It is now thought that Vincent painted that work several weeks earlier.) Adeline's accounts, many years after the fact, are based on her recollections of what her father told her and are thus hearsay. Each time she retold the story, she elaborated and added dialogue that she couldn't possibly have overheard.

One discrepancy in her account is the detail she related of Vincent searching in the dark for his pistol. Paul Gachet *fils* recalled that it was still light out at about 9:00 p.m., when his father was summoned to Vincent's bedside (Gachet 247). In France in midsummer, the days are long. If Vincent dropped the revolver after shooting himself, and it was still light out when he regained consciousness, why couldn't he find it?

Naifeh and Smith offer a dramatically different explanation of what happened that day. According to their reconstruction of events, the shooting occurred not in a wheat field but in a different part of town, in a farmyard just off the main thoroughfare leading to the hamlet of Chaponval, near a dunghill or haystack in a courtyard. Their conclusion is based on comments made by two townswomen, Madame Liberge and Madame Baize, although those accounts are based on hearsay as well. The first woman reported what her father had told her years before, and the second what her grandfather told her.

Naifeh and Smith argue that it would have been easier for a wounded Vincent to return to the inn from the farmyard location than from the wheat field, which presented more difficult terrain to traverse. But the chief import of the location is that it fits their reconstruction of an accidental shooting by teenage boys, because it puts Vincent on a road leading to the boys' favorite fishing hole and riverside tavern, where an encounter would have been likely.

In their biography, the authors do not mention that Paul Gachet *fils*, who was an amateur painter, later painted a view "from the Spot Where Vincent Committed Suicide" (reproduced in Distel and Stein 149; discussed in Rohan 58–59). Gachet's 1904 painting shows a road in town with a low wall marking a courtyard with haystacks on the viewer's left, a wall enclosing the grounds of the town's château on the viewer's right, and several houses with thatched roofs straight ahead. The site, while in town, is within sight of a wheat field and not far from the cemetery.

This location might well account for the conflicting rumors at the time: one mentioning a site in a farmer's yard, the other asserting a wheat field in the vicinity of the cemetery. Today the town of Auvers has a plaque on the wall near the road indicated in Gachet's painting marking the probable spot where Vincent shot himself.

The question, of course, is how Paul Gachet *fils* knew or thought he knew where the shooting took place. Was he a witness? Did Paul Gachet know René Secrétan? They were both the same age (sixteen), both had a connection to Vincent, and Auvers was a small town (population under three thousand in the 1890s). Yet Gachet states he never knew René Secrétan or his brother, Gaston: "As to the Secrétan brothers, we never saw them" (Gachet 192).

How important is the question of the site? After all, where the shooting took place doesn't tell us who did the shooting. However, a farmyard or field just a few steps from the main road does raise the question of why Vincent would have chosen such a public place to end his life. A lonely wheat field far from town would have been more isolated. The farmyard site makes it less likely that he intended to commit suicide that day. So does the fact that he carried his easel and painting equipment along with him. Why encumber himself if he planned to commit suicide? These various circumstances, in addition to the absence of a suicide note, suggest either an accident or an unpremeditated act, a spur of the moment decision. But do they suggest a murder?

The strongest evidence that others might have been involved is that the gun, the easel, and Vincent's painting equipment were never found, suggesting that someone "cleaned up" the scene afterward. The police who investigated the death searched for a discarded gun in the location indicated by Vincent but found nothing. In 2012 Alain Rohan published a short book claiming that an old revolver matching the description of the gun used by Vincent may have been the one found in the 1950s by a farmer in a field not far from the site painted by Gachet (*Vincent van Gogh: Aurait-on retrouvé l'arme du suicide?*). But there's no conclusive proof that this gun was the weapon in question. And suppose it were; what of Vincent's other gear? It may have been hard to find a pistol in a field blooming with vegetation, but an easel?

And what of Vincent's evasive statements at the time? Naifeh and Smith maintain that Vincent was vague about what happened. When he staggered back to the inn, he said, "I wounded myself." In reply to the question posed by a policeman, "Did you want to commit suicide?" he answered: "Yes, I believe so." He added: "Do not accuse anyone, it is I who wanted to kill myself." The police may have doubted whether he acted alone. Why else, the authors ask, would Vincent have made the comment? (Naifeh and Smith 850–51). However, the source for these quotations is the same Adeline Ravoux whom the authors dismiss elsewhere as unreliable. "She often added dialogue to enhance the drama of her stories, sometimes conjuring whole scenes" (879). If the police ever filed a report on the incident, it has long since disappeared (Rohan 106–11).

Therefore, the freight of the argument rests almost entirely on Naifeh and Smith's interpretation of René Secrétan's recollections. They believe René stepped forth when he did because he was burdened with guilt. They point out that the shot that killed Van Gogh was fired from René's gun (according to his own account), and they assume that he and his friends "cleaned up" the crime scene to remove any incriminating evidence. They argue that the surest sign of his guilt is that Secrétan's father, a wealthy Parisian who summered with his family in Auvers, "spirited" the brothers out of town right after the shooting. Such a move would certainly seem incriminating.

It is problematic that in their otherwise well-documented book (the authors amassed five thousand typewritten pages of notes, which they published separately on a website: www.vangoghbiography.com), Naifeh and Smith provide no footnote to support the claim that René was "spirited away with his brother Gaston after the shooting by their pharmacist father in the middle of the summer" (Naifeh and Smith 855). In fact, René told Doiteau that he and his family left Auvers *before* the shooting, not after it, "around the middle of July" (Doiteau 48). The shooting occurred on July 27. Such was the family's usual summer practice, he added. According to René, "during July, with my hunting and fishing gear, we used to fly off to Granville, where we had a villa" (Doiteau 47–49). Bastille Day is celebrated on July 14. Like the Fourth of July weekend in the United States, it marks the launch of many summer vacations in France. Therefore, there was nothing inherently suspicious about the family leaving town at that time, certainly nothing to support the insinuation that the father interrupted the boys' vacation and hastily sent them away to protect them.

Obviously, if René Secrétan had already left Auvers before the shooting, the case against him falls apart. Therefore, it becomes crucial for Naifeh and Smith to challenge his testimony on this all-important issue. To do so, they point to René's evasiveness in the interview as to his departure date. First, they question his explanation of how and when Vincent stole the revolver from him; and second, they argue that René seems vague on when he learned about the shooting. To discredit his claim that he left for Normandy in mid-July, the authors write that René "implied that Vincent had stolen the pistol from him on the very day of the shooting, placing himself still in Auvers at the time" (876).

However, there is no basis for that charge. Here are René's words, followed by our translation:

Nous laissons sur place tout notre barda de pêcheurs, musette, etc . . . , et même nos blouses. C'est dans ce barda que se trouvait cette vielle pétoire et c'est certainement là que Van Gogh l'a trouvée et l'a prise. Elle appartenait à Ravoux et je crois qu'il l'a mettait dans son tiroir. C'etait un vieux pistolet tirant le caliber 380 qui partait quand il avait le temps car il était démantibulé et le sort a voulu que le jour où Van Gogh s'en servit, il ait fonctionné. (Doiteau 46)

[We used to leave our fishing kit, socks, and even overalls there [on shore]. The old gun was in this kit, and that's certainly where Van Gogh found it and took it. It belonged to Ravoux and I believe he put it in his drawer. It was an old .038 caliber pistol [9mm] that went off when it felt like it because it was falling apart, but as fate would have it, on the day Van Gogh used it, it worked.]

René never implies that Vincent may have stolen the pistol from him "on the very day of the shooting." What he says is that on the day Vincent *used* the gun, it worked, not that it worked on the day he *took* it. He adds that he believes Vincent put the gun in his drawer, indicating that a period of time elapsed between its theft and its use. More to the point, nothing René says in his interview places him in Auvers on the day of the shooting, as any defense lawyer might argue.

What of René's vacillation on the question of when he first learned of Van Gogh's death? He told Doiteau that he may have learned about it when the family returned to Auvers at the end of their vacation, or he may have read about it before then in a Paris newspaper. Naifeh and Smith point out correctly that his memory seems sharp on all other points, which makes this lapse suspicious. Moreover, they claim there was no such story in any of the Paris newspapers. And yet an article on Van Gogh's death did appear in *La Petite Presse*, a Parisian newspaper, on August 18, 1890 (Rohan 90). That could have been the article René saw. Furthermore, if René had been implicated in the shooting, would his father have brought the family back to Auvers at the end of that summer? That seems unlikely. In any case, René's uncertainty as to when he learned of the shooting is a dubious platform on which to build an indictment for manslaughter.

The main thrust of the authors' argument—that René Secrétan was easing his conscience by offering a disguised confession when he spoke to Doiteau—is open to debate. There are moments in the interview when René's self-revelations appear self-satisfied and even smug. Secrétan looks back on his teenage years with amusement. He pokes fun at himself as a callow youth interested only in girls, guns, and fishing, and acknowledges that he was the "head dunce" in his *lycée* (Doiteau 39). He boasts about his amours. He jokes about Vincent's scruffy clothes and smirks about the time they caught him masturbating in the woods. For a confession, the tone is off.

It may not be necessary to look for a hidden motive to explain why Secrétan came forward in 1956 to reminisce about Van Gogh. That was the year the movie *Lust for Life* appeared, the film version of Irving Stone's biography of Van Gogh, with Kirk Douglas in the starring role. Secrétan said it was the movie that had stirred his memories and prompted him to set the record straight. In his conversation with Doiteau he complains about all the details the film got wrong. He takes issue with the physical appearance of the actor Kirk Douglas, the costumes, and other matters. Doiteau reveals that René Secrétan also knew Toulouse-Lautrec and had similar complaints to make about the accuracy of the 1952 film *Moulin Rouge*. He may not have cared much about art, but René was a fan of the movies.

At the end of his interview with Doiteau, René, who was eighty-three, sensing that the end of his life was near, offered the following summation: "In any case, I'll be able to say as I go out that I had the most beautiful life that a man of my generation could have wished for. All the friends of my youth are dead, and I'm the last ninepin to fall. Amen" (Doiteau 58). That doesn't sound like a man with a guilty conscience.

We might also question the notion that Vincent played the martyr by refusing to implicate René Secrétan in his death (Naifeh and Smith 875). Why would Van Gogh have protected an annoying teenager who tormented him? All his life Vincent was quick to attack others and to accuse them of harming his interests (even, on occasion, his loving brother and patron, Theo). How likely is it that he would lie to protect a boy who had done nothing all summer but make him miserable? He might have been willing to protect Gaston, René's brother and his one friend in Auvers, or some other boy who had been kind to him, but surely not René.

Van Gogh shared every intimate detail of his thoughts and feelings with Theo, and according to all accounts, the brothers had time to converse in Dutch for several hours before Vincent died. Vincent might have lied to the police about the shooting, but wouldn't he have told Theo the truth? Yet Theo never gave any indication that he thought his brother's death was anything other than a suicide. "Poor Fellow. . . . He was lonely, and sometimes it was more than he could bear," wrote Theo (Naifeh and Smith 857). Moreover, if several boys had been involved in the affair, wouldn't one have talked over the course of fifty years, after Vincent became famous?

The same holds true for the townspeople, if we are to believe there was a conspiracy of silence to protect the boys. Naifeh and Smith suggest that possibility. As evidence they cite remarks made by the respected art historian John Rewald, who interviewed surviving townspeople in the 1930s and reported hearing a rumor that some boys had shot Vincent accidentally and, fearing punishment, had never come forward. To protect them, Vincent played the martyr (Naifeh and Smith 856, 879). Rewald never expressed an opinion in print on the matter, perhaps because he had no way to confirm what he had heard.

Can forensic evidence resolve the question? What is known about the wound, the angle of the shot, and the distance from the body? Naifeh and Smith argue that the facts about the gunshot wound support an interpretation that the shot was fired from a distance. But Rohan cites medical analysis using Dr. Gachet's description of the wound, showing it as perfectly consistent with a small caliber gun fired from close range—perhaps two or three centimeters from the body, as in the case of suicide (Rohan 79). Two recent critics of Naifeh and Smith accept Rohan's opinion (Van Tilbrough and Meedendorp 459). Naifeh and Smith reply that their version of the ballistic evidence is supported by a leading expert on handguns, Dr. Vincent Di Miao, who doubts that the wound was self-inflicted based on the bullet's trajectory (Naifeh and Smith). These dueling interpretations rely not on new evidence but on what observers reported (or failed to report) at the time.

The most baffling question remains: what became of the easel, Vincent's painting gear, sketchbooks, and the canvas he took with him on the day of the shooting? During that summer he was working at a fevered pitch and often finished a painting in a single day. What happened to Vincent's last work, whether completed or uncompleted? For that matter, what became of the six paintings René says Vincent made for the boys earlier that summer? He even describes them by subject (indeed, a remarkable feat of memory). According to René, the subjects were:

1. "Road leading up from the station with a woman in the background wearing a red apron."
2. "Path and a bend in the riverbank next to *père* Martin's bar. (This bar would have been destroyed during the war of 1914–18.)"
3. "Myself, the terror of the smoked herrings, as Vincent called me, fishing but bearing no resemblance to me other than the color of my clothes, a red jacket and white trousers."
4. "Two fishermen in a boat seen from behind and from the opposite path."
5. "A green pathway going down to the river."
6. "A study of my nymph [girlfriend] at the time. I wasn't jealous." (Doiteau 42–43.)

Doiteau speculates that the brothers' father threw these paintings away because he didn't think much of Gaston's wish to become an artist. (As it turned out, Gaston became a cabaret singer.) In any case, no paintings matching these descriptions have survived.

Finally, who else besides Gaston was part of René's gang? He mentions one other boy by name who used to astonish Vincent with magic tricks. There are suggestions of a larger group of boys up from Paris on their summer vacation, and it would be interesting to know who they were and what they might have remembered about the events surrounding Vincent's death.

As we mulled over these conflicting arguments, we began to construct a backstory for our novel that would be consistent with the following facts:

1. In the months leading up to the shooting, Vincent was friendly with a group of boys who taunted him, one of whom, René Secrétan, had a gun.
2. The gun used in the shooting was probably the one René had been playing with all summer.
3. René claimed that he and his family had left Auvers before the shooting, and there is no reason to question his alibi.
4. The bullet was fired at close or fairly close range; there are disputes as to distance and trajectory.
5. After the shooting, someone—a person or persons unknown—collected Vincent's painting paraphernalia, including the painting he was working on, no trace of which has ever been found.

We used these facts as guidelines and relied on our imagination to fill in the gaps. As Naifeh and Smith have shown, there may be reason to suspect that someone other than Vincent was involved in the shooting. But we decided it would be wrong to repeat an unsubstantiated charge against an actual person. So we invented a fictional character to take the place of René Secrétan.

For many scholars—most perhaps—the conclusion that Vincent committed suicide remains unshakeable (Van Tilbrough and Meedendorp 462). Yet in the end, there is no way of knowing whether Vincent was alone at the time the gun was fired. Certainly there are enough questions surrounding the shooting to leave room for speculation.

For instance: suppose one of the boys Vincent befriended that summer was present, one for whom Vincent felt more sympathy than he did for René. And suppose that boy struggled with Vincent for the gun before it went off—struggled to prevent Vincent from shooting himself. Suppose it happened that way. If it did, a number of issues might be explained. Vincent's decision to take the blame for the shooting would make perfect sense, and his equivocal statements to the police would be understandable. At the time of the shooting, the boy might have been posing for Vincent. We know, according to René, that Vincent made several paintings using the boys as models. In that case, the boy would have disposed of the gun, easel, and painting to protect himself, which would explain their disappearance. Of course, that is all supposition.

But it could be the stuff of fiction.

References

Boulon, Jean-Marc. Vincent Van Gogh à Saint-Paul-de-Mausole. Saint-Rémy-de-Provence: Association Valetudo, 2005.

Distel, Ann, and Susan Alyson Stein. *Cézanne to Van Gogh: The Collection of Doctor Gachet.* New York: Metropolitan Museum of Art, 1999.

Doiteau, Victor. "Deux 'copains' de Van Gogh, inconnus: Les frères Gaston et René Secrétan; Vincent, tel qu'ils l'ont vu." *Aesculape* 40 (1957): 38–62.

Gachet, Paul. *Les 70 jours de van Gogh à Auvers.* 1959. Auvers-sur-Oise: Valhermeil, 1994. In their *Vanity Fair* article (see below), Naifeh and Smith disparage Gachet's reliability.

Naifeh, Steven, and Gregory White Smith. "NCIS: Provence: The Van Gogh Mystery." *Vanity Fair* Dec. 2014.

———. *Van Gogh: The Life.* New York: Random House, 2011.

Rohan, Alain. *Vincent van Gogh: Aurait-on retrouvé l'arme du suicide?* Paris: Fargeau, 2012.

Van Tilbrough, Louis, and Teo Meedendorp. "The Life and Death of Vincent van Gogh." *The Burlington Magazine* 155.1324 (2013): 456–62.

Acknowledgments

Thanks to Sebastian Testa, Maréchal des logis-chef of the National Gendarmerie of Vence, for information pertaining to criminal investigations in and around Saint-Paul-de-Vence; and to Heidi Marleau, associate director of the Ebling Library for the Health Sciences at the University of Wisconsin–Madison, for obtaining a copy of the Victor Doiteau article on Réne Secrétan, which we discuss in the afterword. Thanks again to our editor Raphael Kadushin for his encouragement and support and to all our friends at the University of Wisconsin Press who helped to produce this book, especially Sheila McMahon and Sheila Leary.

In addition to our debt to Steven Naifeh and Gregory White Smith, the authors of *Van Gogh: The Life*, we drew upon the following works: Irving Stone, ed., *Dear Theo: The Autobiography of Vincent van Gogh* (1937; New York: Plume, 1995); Serita Stevens and Anne Bannon, *How Dunit: A Book of Poisons* (Cincinnati: Writer's Digest Books, 2007); and David Edmonds, *Would You Kill the Fat Man: The Trolley Problem and What Your Answer Tells Us about Right and Wrong* (Princeton: Princeton University Press, 2014).

To our friends and family: We are grateful that you've stayed close in spite of our absences and failures to write, call, or visit when we were in the world of Nora and Toby. We thank you for your patience, and we look forward to every future moment we will share with you.

Books by Betsy Draine and Michael Hinden

A NORA BARNES AND TOBY SANDLER MYSTERY
Murder in Lascaux
The Body in Bodega Bay
Death on a Starry Night

A Castle in the Backyard: The Dream of a House in France
The Walnut Cookbook by Jean-Luc Toussaint (translators and editors)